The Devil Close Behind

MYSTERY FICTION BY JANET DAWSON

The Devil
Close Behind

A Jeri Howard Mystery

JANET DAWSON

2019
PERSEVERANCE PRESS / JOHN DANIEL & COMPANY
PALO ALTO / MCKINLEYVILLE, CALIFORNIA

A Perseverance Press Book
Published by John Daniel & Company
A division of Daniel & Daniel, Publishers, Inc.
Post Office Box 2790
McKinleyville, California 95519
www.danielpublishing.com/perseverance

Distributed by SCB Distributors (800) 729-6423

Book design by Eric Larson, Studio E Books, Santa Barbara, www.studio-e-books.com

Cover photo: DNY59/iStockphoto

10 9 8 7 6 5 4 3 2 1

LIBRARY OF CONGRESS CATALOGING-IN-PUBLICATION DATA
Names: Dawson, Janet, author.
Title: The devil close behind : a Jeri Howard mystery / by Janet Dawson.
Description: McKinleyville, California : John Daniel & Company, [2019] | Summary: "Jeri Howard's on vacation in the Big Easy, but a friend asks a favor and the vacation turns into a case. Laurette Mason has given up her job and apartment and disappeared with her mercurial musician boyfriend. Slade, as he calls himself, has a hard time with authority. His response to being thwarted is to strike out, sometimes in a deadly fashion. With the help of a local NOLA PI, Jeri's investigation takes her from the French Quarter and the clubs on Frenchmen Street to warehouses and apartments in workaday New Orleans. The road leads from Louisiana back to California, and an explosive end"— Provided by publisher.
Identifiers: LCCN 2019029472 | ISBN 9781564746061 (paperback) Subjects: LCSH: Missing persons—Investigation—Fiction. | GSAFD: Mystery fiction.
Classification: LCC PS3554.A949 D48 2019 | DDC 813/.54—dc23 LC record available at https://lccn.loc.gov/20190294723

To Daisy, a cat with opinions

I am grateful for the assistance of my fellow writers extraordinaire, Julie Smith and J. D. Knight. Thanks for the NOLA love.

The Devil Close Behind

◢Chapter One

IT STARTED WITH A PHONE CALL, as such things frequently do.

I was in my office on a quiet afternoon in April. The PI business had been slow. I'd finished up a couple of big cases and a handful of small ones. Now I was drinking my way through a fresh pot of coffee as I caught up on paperwork and filing.

When the phone rang, I peered over the rim of my coffee mug at the caller ID readout. A new client? Or an existing one?

No. My father was on the other end of the line. Now retired from teaching history he was as busy now as he ever had been. One of the activities that filled his time was birding. In fact, when we'd had lunch two days earlier, he had been excited about his upcoming birding trip to New Orleans with a friend, another retiree named Steve who lived near Dad in Castro Valley.

I set down my mug and reached for the phone. "Hi, Dad. What's up?"

"The birding trip." Dad sounded glum. "Steve can't go."

"You two have been planning this for ages. What happened?"

Dad sighed. "He was up on a ladder, cleaning out the gutters at his house. He's ten years older than I am. A man his age has no business climbing ladders."

"Aren't you the one who fell off a stool last year while changing a lightbulb?"

"Don't remind me," Dad said. "That was just a minor tumble. The only thing that got injured was my dignity, from falling on my butt. Steve's fall was major. He broke two ribs and his left ankle."

Since birding involves a lot of walking, that put a damper on things. "So, the trip is off?"

"It's still on," Dad said, his mood lightening. "You're going with me."

"Going with you?" I repeated, coffee mug arrested midway to my mouth.

"Sure. Why not? You said the other day business was slow. Take a week off and go traveling with your old man. I've already got the reservations for the hotel. And a local birder will take us to all the hot spots. Come on, Jeri. All you have to do is buy a plane ticket."

"Well…" I drew out the word, hesitating, thinking of all the reasons I couldn't get away. Or were they excuses? I was too busy. But I wasn't. I was between cases with nothing much to do but shuffle paper. I'd gotten a phone call an hour ago saying that the court case I was supposed to testify in had been settled, with no need to go to trial.

Dan Westbrook, my sort-of fiancé, was out of town. I'd dropped him off at Oakland Airport the day before. Dan is a travel-and-recreation writer and his latest project is a book about hiking in New Mexico. His return was open-ended, he said. He would stay away as long as it took him to research the book, which involved moving from place to place, hiking trails, taking photos and writing during the evening on his laptop. Dan suggested that I fly to New Mexico and join him at some point during the trip. But that would depend on my schedule. Besides, I knew how he was when he focused on a project. I didn't want to distract him.

As for the home front—my cats and my house on Chabot Road—I had a built-in caretaker. Madison Brady, the University of California grad student who rented my garage apartment, could feed the cats, take in the mail and keep an eye on things.

How long had it been since I'd had an actual vacation, something other than a quick weekend getaway? How long had it been since I'd visited New Orleans? In both cases, too long.

I made a decision. "Okay, I'll do it. Big Easy, here we come."

⚜

Dad and I had been in New Orleans for a week and we were having a great time. We went on birding excursions, toured historical sites, and spent hours in local museums. We also ate our way through several wonderful restaurants and listened to great music in the clubs.

Through the Internet and the local branch of the Audubon Society, Dad had connected with a local birder. Esther Landau, like Dad, was a retired professor. In Esther's case, she had taught English at Tulane University. She was also an avid birder. They exchanged emails and set up several outings. Our first began early in the morning, when Esther picked us up at our hotel and took us to Bayou Sauvage National Wildlife Refuge, in the northeastern part of the city. Bordered by Lake Pontchartrain on the northwest and Lake Borgne to the southeast, the refuge was one of her favorite places to bird.

The first wildlife we saw, however, wasn't avian. As we got out of the car and headed down a pier that extended over the water, a pair of eyes surfaced and a large scaly green beast swam toward us. It was the first alligator I'd seen in the wild, and I didn't like the looks of it any better than the ones I'd seen behind bars and barriers in zoos.

"There's a roseate spoonbill, Tim," Esther said, raising her binoculars.

Dad and I followed suit, checking out the gorgeous pink plumage of the bird. In short order, we saw other species we hadn't seen in our part of the country, such as the tricolored heron and the anhinga, which Esther told us was sometimes called the snakebird, because of its long neck. I was thrilled to see a cardinal perched in a tree, my first actual cardinal in the wild. Of course, I'd seen photos of them, but cardinals are rare in California.

We had lunch at a Vietnamese restaurant in New Orleans East, then headed back to the city. After brief naps at our hotel, we strolled through the French Quarter and ate bowls of gumbo for dinner, finally queuing up to get into Preservation Hall, on St. Peter Street near raunchy, raucous Bourbon Street.

The following day was devoted to history. Dad and I spent hours at the impressive World War II Museum in downtown New Orleans. When we bought our tickets, we were each given a simulated dog tag with the name of a man or woman who had served in some capacity during the war. At various times as we toured the exhibits, we used our dog tags to activate terminals that gave us information on what the person whose name was on the tag had been doing at the time.

For me, our tour of the exhibits dedicated to the European and Pacific theaters of operation brought memories of Dad's mother, my Grandma Jerusha, for whom I'm named. When she was still alive, she often talked of her Rosie the Riveter days as a welder at the Kaiser shipyards in Richmond, California. By contrast, my grandfather, Ted Howard, didn't talk much about his time in the Navy during the war. He'd served in the Pacific theater, fighting what the historians called the island war, as Allied forces drove relentlessly toward Japan. Grandpa had lost his older brother at Pearl Harbor, the young sailor entombed, with so many others, in the sunken wreckage of the battleship *Oklahoma*. That was why Grandpa had joined the Navy early in 1942. Before leaving, he married Grandma. She had been a bit player in Hollywood, sharing a house with other aspiring actresses, taking small parts in movies at MGM and other studios. Putting that behind her, she traded lights, camera and action for coveralls and a welding torch.

Not talking about war experiences was common, I gathered. One of my Doyle uncles came ashore at Omaha Beach on D-Day and earned a raft of medals, but he would never talk about what he saw and did. At least Grandpa Howard shared a few stories before he died, prompted by Dad, the historian, and his younger sister Caro, a writer of historical novels.

One morning, we rented a car and drove to the Whitney Plantation. It was located on the west bank of the Mississippi River in St.

John the Baptist Parish, on the River Road, where several other plantations were located and open for tours. Dad particularly wanted to visit this one. The plantation, which once grew sugar, was now a museum focused on slavery and its brutal legacy. Various buildings, such as the small church and the living quarters, were filled with haunting statues of enslaved children. Some distance from the church was a series of granite walls, engraved with the names of those people who were enslaved on the plantation.

Our next outing with Esther was in New Orleans itself, at City Park, its acres covered with stately live oaks, followed by lunch at a restaurant Esther liked, Katie's in Mid-City. Then she drove us through the Garden District, Uptown, Audubon Park and the Tulane campus where she'd taught. We wound up at the Creole Creamery on Prytania Street, not far from Esther's home. Since I'm always in the mood for ice cream, I was fine with this particular stop. The creamery had a wide selection, everything from buttermilk lemon pie to brown butter and on to chocolate, which had its own dedicated case filled with multiple varieties.

Today was our last day in New Orleans. Dad and I took a cruise on a paddlewheeler called the *Creole Queen*, heading downriver to Chalmette. Dad, ever the professor, informed me that what was known as the Battle of New Orleans, at the end of the War of 1812, was actually a series of clashes that took place from December 14, 1814 to January 18, 1815. The battle here at Chalmette took place on January 8, 1815.

"It's as important as some of the Revolutionary War battles," Dad told me as we left the steamboat and made our way along the levee to a staircase that led down to the battlefield, now covered with grass. "If the British had won..."

But they hadn't. Andrew Jackson and his troops, which included a contingent of pirates led by Jean Lafitte, fought off a much-larger British force intent on capturing New Orleans.

"It really makes a difference to walk the battlefield," Dad said as we reached the bottom of the stairs and set out across the expanse. "It helps me understand how the battle played out." He pointed.

"The British sailed into Lake Borgne and then they marched over-land. The Americans set up a line of defense here, along this ditch. It's called the Rodriguez Canal."

He set off, happily tramping along the canal, which ran perpen-dicular to the levee. I smiled as I quickened my pace to catch up with him. He was the same way when we went to Gettysburg, when my brother, Brian, and I were kids.

We walked for a while, then repaired to the visitors' center to check out the offerings in the gift shop. Dad bought a few books and then we headed back to the levee to catch the steamboat.

We walked from the waterfront back to the French Quarter, talking about which restaurants we liked best. Our splurge meal had been at Commander's Palace. I loved Bayona and Atchafalaya. Dad preferred Galatoire's and K-Paul's Louisiana Kitchen. As for musi-cal venues, Preservation Hall was at the top of the list, though we'd also been to several of the clubs along Frenchmen Street, as well as Tipitina's and the Maple Leaf.

Now, on this balmy Tuesday evening, we'd had an early din-ner at K-Paul's on Chartres Street and headed for a second visit to Preservation Hall.

When we left the hall later that evening, we strolled along the banquette—that's New Orleans talk for sidewalk. The tune of "Joe Avery," one of my favorites, still bounced around my head. I'd pur-chased a CD at the Hall, and now I was tapping my hand against it, using it to keep time. Dad laughed as I sashayed down St. Peter Street. Nobody else gave me a second glance.

"I like traditional jazz," Dad said.

"So do I, but I also like Rebirth Blues Band and Kermit Ruffins." We'd seen both during the week we'd been in New Orleans.

My phone rang. I pulled it from my pocket and looked at the screen. The call was from Davina Roka, a friend at home who was a New Orleans native.

Back in the day, Davina and I had both worked for Errol Seville, the private investigator who'd helmed the Seville Agency in Oak-land for many years. I considered Errol my mentor. He'd taught me everything I know. He'd died last fall and I felt his loss keenly. Davina's path and mine had diverged after Errol closed the agency and retired. I had opened my own shop, continuing as a private investigator.

Davina, who had an undergraduate degree in Planning and Urban Studies, had gone off to Europe for a few months, and when she returned, she went to work for a nonprofit that was working to build affordable housing. At one point she considered getting a master's degree in City Planning at UC Berkeley's College of Environmental Design. Then she veered off in a different direction, heading up the hill to the nearby School of Law, where she was in her third and final year, focusing on social justice and public interest law.

Before getting on the plane to New Orleans, I'd consulted with Davina about which restaurants, clubs and museums to visit while Dad and I were in NOLA. Perhaps she was checking in with me to see how the trip was going, or whether I was home yet.

I answered the call. "Hi, Davina."

"Jeri, are you still in New Orleans?"

Something was wrong.

◿Chapter Two

DAVINA'S VOICE WAS usually cheerful. She was one of those people who was steady, on an even keel, unperturbed. Nothing much fazed Davina. But right now, there was a worried note in her voice.

I stepped into the doorway of a now-closed shop. Dad moved away, then stopped to look at the touristy wares in the window of a store that was still open.

"Yes, I am," I said. "We're heading home tomorrow afternoon. What's up?"

"I need your help." Davina took a deep breath and released it in a sigh. "My sister, Laurette. She's missing."

Missing.

The word conjured up all sorts of feelings, most of them bad. Last year, in August, my brother had gone missing. I was the one who spent several tense days searching for him, talking with people, developing leads and following up on them. I had tamped down my own alarm and frustration, masking my fear, holding it together for my parents while I scoured Sonoma County for clues. I'd finally found him, but it had been a rough week. And Brian's marriage, rocky for a lot of reasons, might yet be a casualty.

What had Davina told me about her family? The basics. Davina's father, who had worked on the New Orleans docks, had died in a workplace accident when she was seven. A couple of years later, Davina's mother had remarried, another dockworker who'd been a friend of her first husband. She and her second husband had two

18

children, a girl and a boy. Davina was thirty-four now. Her siblings were in their twenties, I thought.

"Tell me what happened. And how can I help?"

Davina sighed. "Laurette's had a rough time."

She gave me a quick overview. Laurette was twenty-six years old. She'd married a man she met in college, Chris Mason, and they'd had a child, a daughter named Hannah. Chris had gone to school via the Navy Reserve Officers Training Corps, which meant he was on active service for a designated period of time. Three months after graduation, he was on his way to the Middle East, where he died in a shipboard accident.

"I'm sorry," I said. "I can see what you mean by Laurette having a rough time."

"Damn war," Davina said. "It gets worse, though."

What could be worse than losing a husband?

Davina told me. "Laurette was holding it together, after Chris was killed. She got some counseling through the VA there in New Orleans. She was working full-time and talking about taking some classes. Then, a year ago, Laurette was in a car accident. She had just picked up Hannah, her daughter, from the day care center and she was driving home. It was raining."

I shook my head, knowing what was coming.

The other driver was at fault, Davina told me, but that was cold comfort. He ran a stop sign and sent Laurette's car careening into a building. Laurette survived the crash and her injuries. Her daughter didn't. The little girl was pronounced dead not long after arriving at the emergency room.

The twin blows of losing her husband and child sent Laurette spiraling into depression. "She took a leave of absence from her job," Davina said. "She works at Entergy. That's the local power company in New Orleans. When she wasn't at home in bed, brooding, she was drinking a lot, hanging out at the music clubs all over town."

"The party girl," I said, thinking out loud. "Trying to numb the pain."

Davina agreed. "Yeah, that's what I thought. She was getting better, though. She came out to see me for a week, last year just before fall semester started. Then she went back to work. From what she said, I think she liked her job. Then a few months ago she met this guy, a musician. She really likes him. But my parents took an instant dislike to him. And they've been very protective of Laurette these past few years."

"Tell me about this guy. What's his name?"

"Eric Slade," Davina said. "Laurette tells me he prefers to call himself Slade. I only met him once, when I was home during the Christmas holidays. He plays guitar. That's how Laurette met him. She and a friend from work were at one of the clubs on Frenchmen Street. He asked Laurette for her phone number."

"You say your parents don't like him," I said. "How do you feel about him?"

"Ambivalent. He and Laurette came over for Christmas dinner. At the time I didn't have any feelings for him one way or the other. He's good-looking. I can see how Laurette would be attracted to him. Though he's nothing like Chris, her husband. Chris was blond and sunny. This guy's dark and brooding. I guess I was glad to see that Laurette was dating, after everything that's happened. Having someone in her life has been good for her. But—" Davina paused, as though gathering her thoughts. "He seemed domineering and Laurette deferred to him, a lot. That wasn't like the old Laurette, before she lost her husband and child. Laurette and Chris were so well-matched. The old Laurette wouldn't let a man boss her around. She certainly never acted like that with Chris. That may be why my folks don't like him. Anyway, when he was there at Christmas, he was living in an apartment in Treme. Then he moved in with Laurette at the end of February, I think. She had an apartment not far from where my folks live."

"But now she's missing? What happened?"

"Jeri, she's disappeared. She quit her job, gave up her apartment and it looks like she's left town with Slade. My parents are frantic."

"When did they realize she was gone?" I asked.

"This past weekend," Davina said. "My brother Henry's birthday was on Saturday. He works on an oil rig out in the Gulf. He came home for his birthday and Mom and Dad cooked up a party. It was a big deal, all of Henry's favorite foods, a cake. Mom took a few days off work and invited all the relatives. Laurette was supposed to come over for dinner. She didn't show. Mom called, several times, and the calls went straight to voice mail."

"And that's unusual behavior for Laurette?"

"It certainly is," Davina said. "Laurette has always been good about keeping in touch with my folks. She comes over for dinner every week or so. And calls every few days. On Sunday, Mom and Dad went over to Laurette's apartment. Jeri, they were gone. The manager said Laurette and Slade had moved out. They loaded up all their stuff and drove away. Mom got hold of one of Laurette's friends that same day and found out Laurette quit her job. She gave notice and left, on Thursday of last week. It's a crazy situation. My folks had no idea she was going to do this, and they're upset, especially because Laurette's not answering her cell phone or responding to the messages they've left."

I didn't say anything, processing what Davina had told me. How did all the pieces fit? Laurette was in her mid-twenties. She was certainly an adult. If she wanted to leave town with her boyfriend, that was her business. But quitting her job and leaving without saying a word to her family seemed precipitate. It made me wonder what else was going on.

"How can I help?" I asked.

"I'd hop on a plane right now, but I can't get away," she said.

"And I'm already here."

"Jeri, I know you've got clients and cases and obligations waiting for you back in Oakland. And you're supposed to fly home tomorrow. But if you could just give me a couple of days."

Clients and cases and obligations, I thought. I needed to consult my calendar. I had cleared time for the New Orleans trip, and at the time I'd scheduled it, business had been slow. But I did have a meeting with a client on Wednesday morning, a week from tomorrow. That meant I had to fly home on Tuesday at the latest.

"I can stay a few days longer. At least give it a start, go talk with your folks. I'll find an investigator to help. There's a guy I met a couple of years ago, at a convention. He worked for a firm here in New Orleans. I'll see if he's still in business — and available to do some digging around."

"That would be wonderful, Jeri. Thanks so much. I'll text my parents' address and phone number. I really appreciate your doing this. I worry about my sister. Ever since her daughter died, it's like Laurette is running from something. Her grief, her feelings. I guess she figures if she lives fast and hard, she'll outrun the devil, but it's not working."

Outrun the devil, I thought as I ended the call. Somehow the devil always catches up.

"Problem?" Dad said, joining me.

"Yes." I explained the situation. "It looks like I'll need to stay here in New Orleans a few days longer."

"Much as I would like to stay and help," he said, "I have to go home. I'm participating in that seminar at the university. I can't get out of it at this late date."

Even though Dad was retired after many years as a history professor at the California State University campus located in Hayward, he still had an active intellectual life and a busy schedule. The seminar in question was a two-day event, Thursday and Friday, on campus at the University of California in Berkeley. Dad was one of the speakers. We were booked on a flight that left New Orleans tomorrow afternoon.

"When we get back to the hotel," I said, "I'll see if I can extend my reservation for a few days. Then I'll change my flight."

"How long do you think you'll stay?" Dad asked as we continued along St. Peter Street.

"I have appointments next week. I'll have to go home Tuesday at the latest. That gives me a few days' leeway. My plan is to involve a local investigator. Two years ago, at the investigators' convention, I met a private eye from New Orleans. He seemed like a sharp guy. Now if I can just remember his name." We crossed Royal Street and I stopped on the other side. "The name of an old car."

"Hudson?" Dad asked. "DeSoto? Packard? Cord?"

I shook my head, then waved a finger at him. "Lasalle. That's it. He worked for a big firm. At least he did at the time I met him. As soon as we get back to the hotel, I need a computer."

We quickened our pace. When we reached Chartres Street, we turned left, walking through Jackson Square, site of St. Louis Cathedral. I glanced across the square, where Café du Monde was. Dad and I had stopped frequently for *café au lait* and *beignets*.

Our hotel was two blocks away, on Dumaine Street. The converted townhouse, once a private residence, had been owned by a cotton broker, according to the information we'd been given when we checked in. It had been in the same family until the end of World War II, then it changed hands, eventually turning into a hostelry. The rooms overlooked the street and an inner courtyard with tables and a fountain. When I had agreed to come to New Orleans with him, Dad had upgraded his reservation to a small suite, which gave both of us some privacy. We were located near the back of the hotel, and our balcony looked down on the courtyard. The location was great, was walking distance to the Quarter's myriad attractions, as well as those in the nearby Faubourg Marigny district.

When we entered the lobby, Dad headed upstairs to our suite. I walked over to the hotel's business center, a big name for a small room off the main lobby, where guests could use computers and a printer. A swipe of my room key on the pad opened the locked door. I sat down at one of the computers and logged onto my business account, looking at my email and calendar.

Clients and cases and obligations, Davina had said. That was certainly true. I had been away from my office for a week. Although I was on vacation, I'd been checking my email and office voice mail daily, responding to messages and returning calls as needed. Judging from the messages I'd received in the past forty-eight hours, business was picking up. A client with whom I had a long and financially lucrative relationship had a case for me and wanted to schedule a face-to-face meeting soon. I had two email queries from prospective clients wanting to consult with me about cases. My voice mail included, among other messages, one from Gary Manville, the head

of a security firm in downtown Oakland. I'd met Gary last fall while
working on a case involving the death of a mutual friend. Earlier
today, he'd left a terse message saying he had something he needed
to discuss with me. By now it was after ten in New Orleans and after
eight in Oakland. I'd call him back tomorrow.

I looked at the calendar screen. Here was the client meeting
scheduled for next Wednesday morning. I had another meeting that
afternoon, as well as one on Thursday. I responded to the emails, setting up tentative appointment dates on my calendar, explaining that
I was out of town and would be back in the office by Wednesday.

Could I stay longer in New Orleans? I wanted to help Davina find her sister. After all, I'd been in that scary place when my
brother was missing. Yes, I could stay a few days longer, but not
indefinitely. All the more reason to find a local investigator to steer
Davina's way.

I pictured the investigator I'd met at the convention two years
ago. He was a tall, slender man in his mid-thirties, about my age, and
we'd hit it off. "Next time you're in New Orleans," he said, "call me,
I'll show you around. I know all the best places to eat—and drink."
We'd traded business cards. His was in a desk drawer in my office
back in Oakland. Since I was with Dad this trip and we had a full
schedule of birding, museums and other activities, I hadn't dug out
the card before my travels. I remembered the man's face and his first
name, Antoine. As for his last name, I was reasonably sure it was
Lasalle. I wasn't sure of the name of the firm he worked for. Garden,
I thought. That was it. The name of the firm? Or was it located in
the Garden District?

As it happened, neither was true. My Internet search turned
up a firm called Gerdine Investigations, located on Tchoupitoulas
Street, in the neighborhood known as the Irish Channel. I jotted
down the phone number and business hours, intending to call first
thing in the morning.

I logged off my account and shut down the browser. When I
went back out to the lobby, I headed for the registration desk, to
ask if I could extend my stay in the room. "I can do it for three more

nights," the clerk said, her eyes on the computer screen as her fingers played over the keys. "After that, we're booked up solid, unless we get a cancellation."

"I'll take the three nights." I stifled a yawn. That would give me the next three days to make some progress looking for Davina's sister. After that, I'd have to figure out something else.

For now, though, I needed sleep.

When I woke up the next morning, I checked my phone for messages and saw that Davina had emailed three photographs. She'd also sent a text message with the address and phone number of her mother and stepfather, the Tedescos, adding that they were expecting my call. I opened the first attachment. The picture showed Laurette alone. As I looked at the image displayed on my smart phone, I saw a young woman with shoulder-length dark hair and a sad expression on her pale face. There were dark circles around her eyes. Davina's accompanying note told me the picture had been taken a few months after the car accident that killed Laurette's daughter. The second photo had been snapped a year or so before, showing Laurette in happier times. She sat on a green sofa with a younger man who resembled her, presumably her brother, Henry. On Laurette's lap was a little girl of about three, with a head of blond curls. This was Hannah, Laurette's daughter. The third picture had been taken last Christmas, when Laurette and her boyfriend, Slade, came to dinner. They were seated together on the same green sofa, Laurette leaning into his shoulder, a smile on her face. She looked a lot happier than she did in the first photo, dressed for the holiday season in a sparkly red-and-gold blouse and a black skirt.

The man sitting next to her had one arm draped over her shoulder. He looked funereal in gray slacks and a black knit shirt, enlivened with a tiny sprig of holly pinned above his breast pocket. My fingers moved across the phone screen, enlarging the man's face. Dark and brooding, Davina called him. He was certainly that, with a long narrow face, a hawklike nose and an olive complexion. His eyes were blue, so pale as to be colorless, and the smile that curved his thin lips didn't seem to extend to his eyes. It was as though he was trying to be pleasant and not quite succeeding.

Who knows why one person is attracted to another? I'd been attracted to the dark-and-brooding guys a time or two in my past. Something about him must have filled one of Laurette's needs. She was vulnerable, I thought. She'd lost her husband and child in a short period of time and must have been vulnerable to the first man who'd come along. On the other hand, maybe Slade himself was what she needed right now. I didn't know anything for sure. It was up to me to find out.

I heard Dad stirring and he called to me, asking if it was all right if he took the first shower. "Sure," I said, as I got out of bed. "I'll start the coffee."

A short time later, showered and dressed, Dad and I headed downstairs. The hotel had a complimentary breakfast for guests, featuring cold and hot dishes. The meal was served in a light, airy dining room on the first floor. It opened onto the courtyard, where tables were set up near the fountain. Dad and I helped ourselves to coffee and moved to the tables that held platters of fruit and pastries, as well as chafing dishes full of scrambled eggs, grits, bacon and sausages. We filled our plates, then carried them outside, claiming a table.

Dad sprinkled hot sauce on his scrambled eggs. "I should call Esther."

Esther had volunteered to drive us to the airport and proposed lunch beforehand, since the flight back to Oakland left in the late afternoon. Now my schedule was uncertain. I planned to call the Tedescos to set up a meeting with them, which might very well impinge on lunch plans. I was going to rent a car.

"Yes, call her. After we eat, I'll call the Tedescos." I ate a slice of bacon with a forkful of eggs, then spooned up some berries and eyed the little chocolate croissant I'd liberated from the pastry tray. When we'd finished breakfast, I left Dad sipping coffee and eating his second croissant. I headed into the lobby and the concierge's desk, where I arranged a rental car. That done, I found a quiet corner and called Davina's parents. We agreed to meet at eleven o'clock. I looked at my watch. It was a quarter to nine. Plenty of time to do everything on my list and get over to the Tedescos.

I pulled a slip of paper from my pocket and consulted it before punching in the number of Gerdine Investigations on the keypad of my phone. "I'm an investigator from California," I said, when a woman answered the phone. "I'm looking for someone I met a couple of years ago. I think he works for your firm. His last name is Lasalle."

"That would be Antoine Lasalle. But he doesn't work here anymore. Would you like to speak to one of our other associates?"

"No, I'd like to speak with him. I told him I'd look him up if I was in town. Where is he working now?"

"He set up his own shop," she told me. "AL Investigations. I've got his contact information right here."

"Just a minute. Let me grab a pen." I stepped over to the concierge's desk and got a pen and some paper. I jotted down the information as she read it off, thanked her and ended the call. Then I logged into the browser on my smart phone and searched for the address. It was on North Villere Street, just this side of Esplanade Avenue, and not far from the hotel. I called the number and got a message inviting me to leave one of my own, so I did.

I went back out to the courtyard, but I didn't see Dad. He'd left the table where we'd eaten breakfast and was seated on the wall surrounding the fountain, talking on his phone. I guessed he was talking with Esther Landau. I waited until he ended the call and slipped the phone into his pocket before joining him.

"Esther's going to pick me up and we'll go on to lunch," he said. "Then she'll take me to the airport. So I'll say good-bye before you leave for your meeting."

⚐ Chapter Three

I DROVE UP IBERVILLE STREET, in the New Orleans neighborhood known as Mid-City. I realized I'd been in this area before. Katie's, the restaurant where Dad and I had lunch with Esther, was in this neighborhood. The Tedescos lived in the middle of the block. I parked at the curb and got out, looking at the two-story house. It was painted white, with olive green trim, and the yard looked well-tended. A wide gallery stretched in front, furnished with two comfortable-looking chairs with faded green cushions.

Silencing my phone, I headed up the front steps and rang the doorbell. A moment later, George Tedesco opened the door. He ushered me into the living room, where I sat on the same olive green sofa I'd seen in the photos Davina had sent to me. The Tedescos offered coffee. I took a sip, tasting a strong dark roast with a hint of chicory. Then I looked around me at the living room, furnished with oak furniture that looked like family heirlooms, well-kept and burnished to a shine. An old quilt was draped across the back of a wingback chair and a set of double doors led back through a dining room to the kitchen. Nearby shelves held books and framed family photos.

George Tedesco was a sturdy man in his early sixties, his thinning brown hair going gray. I saw echoes of Davina in her mother's face. Sabine Tedesco had the same vibrant red hair as her elder daughter, though it was streaked with silver and worn shorter than Davina's wild mane. She was about the same age as her husband. Davina had told me that her mother managed a restaurant here in

Mid-City, while her stepfather still worked at the busy New Orleans port, in an administrative job now, though he'd started out on the docks, loading and unloading freight.

In our phone conversation last night, Davina had already given me an overview of the events leading up to the current situation. I went over this in more detail with the Tedescos.

Laurette had graduated from a local high school and gone on to college at the University of New Orleans, which was part of the state university system. She had declared a major in English, planning to take some education classes, with the intention of becoming a teacher. Early in her sophomore year, Laurette met Chris Mason, who was a junior. He was from Covington, in St. Tammany Parish on the north side of Lake Pontchartrain. A few years older than Laurette, Chris was in the Reserve Officers Training Corps at the university. That meant the Navy was paying for his education, with the caveat that when he graduated, he was commissioned as an officer on active duty. Laurette and Chris had married the summer before Chris started his senior year. That was Laurette's junior year. In the middle of the fall semester, she discovered she was pregnant. She didn't finish the term. Instead, she dropped out of school.

"Her morning sickness was just awful," Sabine said now. "She could barely sit through class without having to rush to the bathroom. Mine was the same, with all three of my children."

Sabine sat next to me on the sofa, with a photo album in her lap. Arrayed on the coffee table in front of us were more photos. Laurette and Chris at their wedding, with Laurette in a lacy white dress, her dark hair swept up and covered with a white veil. Chris, tall with broad shoulders and blond hair, had worn his uniform. Davina had been her sister's maid of honor, in a pale green dress that set off her red hair. A group shot showed the Tedescos arrayed next to Laurette, with the Mason family clustering around the groom. More photos showed Chris on his graduation, the day he was commissioned as an ensign in the Navy. And Laurette, next to him, beamed in a flowered maternity dress over her pregnant belly. Their daughter, Hannah, had been born a few weeks later, in June. Photos of the new parents showed the baby, nearly bald except for a few wisps of hair, looking chubby and sweet in a frilly pink dress, the kind that babies outgrow in an instant.

"Chris went to school for several months over at Pensacola," George said, mentioning the West Florida city about two hundred miles east. "They have a lot of Navy stuff over there. He and Laurette rented an apartment there in town. Then he got his orders. He was going to a ship in the Middle East. Once he went overseas, Laurette and the baby came back here and got an apartment here in Mid-City, about a mile away. Then we got the news. There was a fire aboard the ship. Chris and two other guys were killed."

We sat for a moment in silence, while a series of emotions played across the faces of Laurette's parents. Then Sabine took up the story. "Hannah was just a year old when her daddy died. Laurette was devastated, of course. There was a counseling group for military wives offered through the VA. She went to that and it helped. At the time, I suggested that she go back to school and get her degree, but she said she wasn't ready to do that. She got a job instead, at Entergy, the power company. They have a big office downtown. She worked as an admin assistant. She seemed to like it. A good job, with benefits. That's what she called it."

Sabine picked up one of the framed photos. "This is Hannah, on her third birthday. That was nearly two years ago. She would have been five this year."

I nodded, acknowledging the sadness in her voice as I glanced at the little girl, blond like her father, smiling in a blue-and-yellow polka-dot dress. "The accident happened last year?"

She nodded. "A year ago, in January. Laurette had just picked up Hannah from day care. That car ran a stop sign and crashed into Laurette's car. Pushed it into a building. Hannah was in a car seat in the back, of course. But...she died in the emergency room. Laurette was badly hurt. She was in the hospital for nearly two weeks. And then..." Sabine's voice trailed off.

"She took some time off work," George said. "Had to. The physical injuries healed, but she was so low."

"I'm sure it was devastating, for all of you."

"It was terrible." Tears threatened to spill from Sabine's eyes as she set the photograph of her granddaughter back on the coffee table.

George put his hand on her shoulder. Then he looked at me. "Laurette got some counseling after Hannah died, like she did when she lost Chris. After a time, she went back to work. I asked if it was too soon and she said she couldn't stand being at home all day. I thought things were getting better, or at least going along as well as could be expected. Then she met this guy. And believe me, he's the wrong guy."

Worry shadowed both parents' faces. Sabine grimaced. "Laurette says his first name is Eric but he prefers to go by his last name, which is Slade. I don't even know for sure if that is his real name. It sounds made up. As far as I'm concerned, everything about him is phony."

It did sound like an alias, I thought. A nickname, perhaps, among musicians. As to whether everything about Slade was phony, I'd have to find out more about him before I could make that call. At one end of the coffee table was a folder containing printouts of digital photos taken on Christmas Day, when Laurette had brought Slade to her parents' home for dinner. Most of the photos showed the Tedescos—the parents, plus Davina and her siblings. Very few of the shots showed Slade. It made me wonder if he didn't like having his picture taken. There could be plenty of reasons for that. I looked at the few photos there were. He was good-looking, with dark brown hair that fell over his ears and the collar of his shirt and flopped over to obscure his forehead.

"How did they meet?" I asked. "And when?"

"She first mentioned him last fall," Sabine said. "It was before Thanksgiving, I think. She could have been going out with him before that. We used to talk more, but since the accident, well, Laurette's had a hard time. I understand that. Recovering from the loss, even though we're here for her, she's been keeping us at arm's length, and that upsets me, and her father." She glanced at her husband. "She hasn't been forthcoming about what she's doing, or who she's with. When I ask, she acts like I'm prying. And I don't mean to, really, I don't." She sighed. "As for where she met Slade, she was out with some people from work, going to clubs on Frenchmen Street."

I nodded. Frenchmen Street in the Faubourg Marigny district was famed for its music venues, bars and restaurants, a place where locals went to hear the music, rather than the crazy, touristy and sometimes raunchy scene on Bourbon Street in the French Quarter.

"He was playing guitar at one of the clubs," Sabine continued. "He asked for her phone number and later he called her. They started going out. She really seemed to like him. And it was good to see her smile again. But when she brought him over for Christmas dinner, I just didn't like him."

"Neither did I," George said.

Why did they dislike Slade so much? I really needed to find out. "Why? Is it because he's a musician?"

"It's not that," Sabine protested. "I really don't have anything against musicians. I've got a couple of cousins who are musicians. But I do have some concerns about the lifestyle some of those musicians have. Playing gigs, night after night in the clubs can lead to a lot of drinking and a lot of drugs. I know, firsthand. My cousin Alfie, the one who plays trumpet, he had problems with drugs for years. He's clean now, thank goodness."

"And I don't like Slade because there's something about him that's slippery," George added. "I can't describe it any better than that. You know that feeling you get when something's off? That's the feeling I get when Slade's in the room."

I knew the feeling very well. It had steered me right through many years of doing investigative work. For now, Slade was slippery to me as well. I didn't have enough information to get a clear picture of the man. But I would get there.

"He bosses her around a lot," Sabine added. "And she lets him. That bothers me. Her husband, Chris, he wasn't like that. They had a good marriage, a marriage of equals, and if they got into it, Laurette could give as good as she got. But when she's with Slade, it seems like she goes out of her way to defer to him. It's as though she's afraid of him. And I certainly don't like that."

I nodded. Davina had said much the same thing during our phone conversation last night.

Slade had moved into Laurette's apartment at the end of February, much to her parents' dismay. They didn't understand what Laurette saw in this man. Besides, she hadn't known him all that long, just a few months. Pressed for a reason why the musician was now living with her, Laurette told her mother that Slade had to move out of his Treme apartment because the owner wanted the apartment for a relative.

"I'm not sure I believed that story," Sabine added.

Her husband scowled. "I certainly don't. This fellow had a job when Laurette met him. Working in a warehouse somewhere, according to Laurette. When I asked him about it at Christmas, he said he was going to quit that job. So he could focus on his music, that's the way he put it. I have to wonder if he moved in with Laurette because he couldn't afford his own place."

"That's a possibility. I'll check it out. Now, tell me what happened this weekend."

"Henry, that's our son, had four days off from his job on the oil rig," Sabine said. "His birthday was on Saturday. We planned a big party that afternoon, with a lot of relatives and a bunch of Henry's friends. Laurette was supposed to be there. I'd mentioned it to her the week before. I called her cell phone several times. She's one of those people who gave up having a land line, so she just used her cell. She didn't answer the phone and she didn't call me back. I left several voice mails."

"I drove over to her place that night," George said. "But her car was gone and nobody answered the door. It was late, and I figured she'd gone out, but I was upset that she hadn't called us back. Sunday morning, we still hadn't heard from her. Sabine and I drove over to the apartment. They've got a resident manager, name of Bert. He told us Laurette had given up the apartment. She and Slade packed up everything into a big SUV on Friday, he said, and left. You could have knocked me over with a feather."

Tears spilled down Sabine's cheeks. "I had a phone number for someone she worked with. A woman named Brenda. I called and left a message and later Sunday night, Brenda called me back. She told me Laurette gave notice and quit her job at Entergy. And Brenda said she had no idea where Laurette was. Gone. Just like that. Without a word to any of us."

There was something odd about Laurette's actions, I thought. Maybe I could get some answers, or at least a lead as to where Laurette had gone. But I couldn't make her come home if she didn't want to return.

"I'd like to talk with Brenda, and Laurette's other friends," I said. Davina had already steered me to Laurette's Facebook page, which was of little help. There were lots of posts and photos of Laurette and her husband, from a few years back, the photos of Laurette and her daughter—up until a year ago, when Hannah died in the car accident. Since then, the page had been neglected. Laurette lost interest in sharing her life on the Internet.

Sabine reached for a notepad on the coffee table, tore off a sheet and handed it to me. "I made a list. Brenda Kohl is the woman who worked with Laurette at Entergy. Grace Boudreaux is a friend she met at the university. They stayed in touch and they get together now and then. And Mary Abbott, that third name, she and Laurette were in that counseling group for military wives."

It was a short list, I thought, examining the names and phone numbers. It appeared that Laurette didn't have that many friends. I could understand how that could happen. When she was married, her focus had been on her husband and child. As a widow, the focus had narrowed to her child. With the death of her daughter, Laurette had been floundering, according to her sister, Davina, trying to make sense of her world.

More tears swam in Sabine's eyes. "How could she just leave like that, without letting us know? And with that man. Laurette wouldn't talk about him much, not to us, not to Davina. She knew we didn't approve of him. So she was very closed-mouth about him. We had an argument about it, after he moved in with her. She told me I was suffocating her." As she said this, her eyes filled with tears again. "I don't mean to do that. She's a grown woman, of course. But I just have a bad feeling about this. Call it mother's instinct, call it what you will. I wish my little girl would come back. Not just from wherever she's gone right now. But the way she was, before her husband and baby died."

I knew what Sabine Tedesco was saying and I thought I understood her sense of loss. Laurette wasn't a little girl anymore. She was a woman who'd had a husband and child—and lost both. The old Laurette wasn't coming back. It would never be the same. The Tedescos would have to come to terms with that, to get used to the new Laurette and accept her choices.

As for me, I was only doing this as a favor to Davina, my friend. Though right now I wondered if this was a wild goose chase.

◢ Chapter Four

THE TEDESCOS DIDN'T KNOW what had happened to Laurette's car. She drove a green Honda Civic, purchased after her other car had been destroyed in the car accident that killed Hannah. The resident manager at Laurette's building had told her parents that Laurette and Slade had loaded their belongings into an SUV. I was guessing that Laurette had sold the Honda and used the money to purchase the vehicle. I copied down the information on the Civic and hoped that Antoine Lasalle, if he called me back, could help me trace it.

I said good-bye to Laurette's parents and left the house. The car I'd rented was a Nissan sedan, metallic green, and I sat in the driver's seat for a moment, taking a sip from the water bottle I'd left on the console. It was warm on this sunny day in April, but not unpleasantly so. During my week-long visit to the Big Easy, the temperatures had been in the high 70s, with the nights in the high 60s, and we'd had a few rain showers. I'd been told the mild spring weather was quite different from the heat and humidity of the summer and the early fall. It was also very different from the climate back home in the Bay Area, where microclimates vary by town and neighborhood. This spring in Oakland had been a season of contrasts. A couple of weeks ago, we'd had a hot spell, then it had given way to several days of wind, rain and chilly temperatures.

After another sip of water, I took out my cell phone and turned up the ringer. I saw three missed calls and one voice mail. Two calls were from the Bay Area and the third showed a New Orleans area code.

The voice mail was from Antoine Lasalle. His message said he had an appointment in the Sixth Ward this morning and was planning to have lunch around noon. "If you're in town, you have to try Willie Mae's Scotch House. Meet me for lunch at noon," he added, and rattled off the address. "Text me at this number to confirm."

I sent a text telling him I'd meet him there, then I started the car and took off, heading out of Mid-City into the Sixth Ward. Dad and I had eaten at Willie Mae's twice during our week in New Orleans. The restaurant served what many customers viewed as the best fried chicken on the planet. It was located on the corner of St. Ann and North Tonti streets. As had been the case on my previous visits, customers were queued up outside the white building. I joined them. A young woman came out of the restaurant and went down the line, asking how many people were in each party. I told her there would be two of us. Then I sent another text to Antoine, telling him I was at the restaurant. Soon after, my phone pinged with a response—"ETA 15."

About ten minutes later, I was admitted to the inner sanctum and seated at one of the tables. The interior walls were caramel-colored, decorated with framed art and copies of the restaurant's various awards. In 2005, owner Willie Mae Seaton received the James Beard Award denoting her eatery as "America's Classic Restaurant for the Southern Region." The restaurant had been badly damaged later that year, when Hurricane Katrina wrought destruction all over the city. Willie Mae's had reopened in 2007, to more accolades from the Food Network and the Travel Channel.

I'd just gotten my glass of unsweetened iced tea when the door opened and Antoine walked in. He looked much as I remembered him, tall and lean, with a *café au lait* complexion and his hair cropped close to his head. I knew from our earlier meeting at the convention a couple of years ago that he was a native of the Big Easy. He was also an Army veteran who had served in Iraq and other duty stations, in a criminal investigation capacity. When he returned to New Orleans after mustering out of the service, he'd gone to work for a local investigative firm, the one he'd left to start his own business.

Today he wore gray slacks and a lightweight jacket over a blue shirt, open at the neck. He spotted me and crossed the dining room to join me. "Jeri, good to see you. What are you doing in town? Vacation?"

"That's how it started. It's gotten complicated. It's a case, and I hope you can help me."

Interest sparked in his dark brown eyes. He pulled out a chair. "Sure thing. Let's order first, though." He signaled to a server, who greeted him by name. "Bring me some of that iced tea. You know I like it sweet."

"You must be a regular," I said, glancing up from the menu.

Antoine grinned. "Of course. Best fried chicken in town— except for my mother's fried chicken."

"I know I'm going to have the chicken. I mean, why come to Willie Mae's for anything else? It's just a matter of which side dishes."

"I'm partial to fried okra," Antoine said. "I really like the mac-and-cheese, too. Hey, everything's good here."

When the server brought Antoine's tea, we both ordered fried chicken. It came with three pieces of the delectable chicken and with one side per order, but we got several more—okra and mac-and-cheese, of course, along with green beans and that New Orleans staple, red beans and rice. We also got a green salad, just because.

"So you left the other firm and opened your own shop," I said.

Antoine nodded. "Yeah, that's what I wanted to do all along. I learned a lot working for the criminal investigation command when I was in the Army, and working for the big investigative firm here in town got me the PI's license. But I always wanted to be my own boss. I bought a little house on Villere Street a few years ago and remodeled it myself. I live in the back and my office is in the front. Low overhead."

"I know about overhead." I'd recently left the office I'd had for several years because the rent had gone up so much. Now I had office space in another building owned by a friend's law firm. Personally, I didn't care for the idea of having my office and my home in the same place, but to each his own. Or *chacun à son goût*, since we were in New Orleans.

The server returned, delivering our fried chicken and side dishes. For a moment there was no conversation as we communed with our food. It was that good. Then I set down the remains of my first piece of chicken and wiped my greasy hands on a napkin as I told Antoine the initial reason for our trip. "Birding and history. I'm here with my dad, though he's going home today. He's retired now, but he was a history professor at Cal State. Since he stopped teaching, he's gotten into birding."

"I like history. Took several classes when I went to the University of New Orleans, before I joined the Army." Antoine speared okra with his fork. "If you're into history, you're in the right place. History we've got. Have you done one of the plantation tours? Or gone out to Chalmette?"

"We went to the Whitney Plantation earlier in the week. And Chalmette, yesterday. We took that paddlewheeler, the *Creole Queen*, from the foot of Canal Street. And Dad connected with a local birder. She took us to City Park and Bayou Sauvage."

"You've covered a lot of territory." Antoine scooped up another serving of mac-and-cheese. "My grandma was interested in birds. She had a backyard feeder, was always pointing out the different kinds. I hope you saw some good ones. Now, what's the story with this case that's cropped up?"

"I got a call last night from my friend Davina, who lives in the Bay Area. She was born and raised here. She's concerned about her sister, a woman named Laurette Mason who's had a rocky time the past few years. Both her husband and daughter died recently." I helped myself to red beans and rice and gave Antoine more details. "Sometime last fall, Laurette started dating a musician named Slade. Her parents, George and Sabine Tedesco, don't like him. Slade moved in with Laurette in February. This weekend, the Tedescos discovered that Laurette quit her job at Entergy, gave up her apartment and car and left with Slade. I don't know if she left town or just moved somewhere else here in New Orleans. Her parents are worried. I went to see them this morning." I gave him an overview of my conversation with the Tedescos. "There could be all sorts of reasons Laurette didn't tell her folks what she was up to," I added. "She'd called her mother on being overprotective, from the sound of it."

"Yeah, they do sound overprotective. I mean, this lady's old enough to know her own mind, right? You having second thoughts?" Antoine asked. "About agreeing to do this?"

"Maybe. However, I said I'd do it, so I'm gonna do it."

"Okay." Antoine picked up another piece of chicken. "I'll do whatever I can to help."

"I'm wondering about Laurette's car. It's a green Honda and her dad gave me the license plate number."

"Easy as pie," he said. "I've got a connection at the Office of Motor Vehicles. I'll see what I can find out about that car. I'm betting she sold it."

"That's my best guess. And if that's the case, there's a transfer of title somewhere in the public records."

"This guy Slade's a musician? I can definitely help you on that. My sister Daisy is a singer. She's got her own band and she knows a lot of people in town. I'll ask her if she's ever heard of this guy. In fact—" He wiped his hands on a napkin and pulled out his phone, moving his fingers over the screen. Then he looked up. "Daisy's band has a gig tonight at the Spotted Cat on Frenchmen Street. How about we go over there and ask her?"

"Good idea," I said. "I know where the Spotted Cat is. Dad and I were there a few nights ago." I paused for another sip of iced tea. "Once we're done with lunch, I suggest going over to the apartment where Laurette and Slade lived. It's in Mid-City."

Antoine nodded. "I'll go with you to the apartment. Then I have another appointment this afternoon, across the river in Algiers. Daisy's first set is at six o'clock. I'll pick you up at your hotel around five-thirty and we can head on over to the Spotted Cat. You said your dad's going home later today. How long are you going to stay in town? And where?"

"I can stay a few more days, but I have to be back in Oakland by Tuesday, for some meetings on Wednesday. As for where I'm staying, I extended my reservation a few days." I gave him the name and address of the hotel.

"I know where it is." Antoine finished his last piece of chicken. "Now, they do have some fine bread pudding here."

I looked at the chicken bones on my plate and shook my head. "I couldn't eat another bite. As it is, we're going to have to get some boxes for the rest of these side dishes. You want to take them home?"

"I absolutely do," Antoine said. "And I'm gonna have some bread pudding."

◣Chapter Five

THE APARTMENT Laurette and Slade had vacated was on Palmyra Street, a mile or so from her parents' house. The two-story red brick building looked old, but well-kept. A sign in front advertised an apartment for rent. I parked the rental car at the curb, behind Antoine's silver Toyota RAV4. We headed for the front of the building. There were eight units, four on each floor, each door painted bright yellow and opening onto an exterior walkway. A parking lot with numbered spaces ran from the street to the alley. A smaller, one-story building stood separate from the apartments at the back of the lot. The door had been propped open and I saw a woman with a laundry basket, putting clothing into a front-load washing machine.

Antoine and I walked to the bank of mailboxes at the front, near the black metal stairs that led up to the second floor. The mailbox for apartment A had a sign reading MANAGER. I rang the bell for that apartment. There was no answer, but I saw a smaller, hand-printed sign on the door, reading IF NO ANSWER, PLEASE CALL THE NUMBER BELOW. I pulled out my phone, called the number, and heard it ring, both on my phone and somewhere toward the rear of the building.

A man answered, "This is Bert."

"I'm at your front door," I said. "I'd like to talk with you about a tenant."

"Sure thing. Come down to apartment D, first floor at the back."

A man came out of a door at the rear of the building, holding his phone to his ear. He waved.

We headed back to where the man stood. He looked to be in his fifties, with receding brown hair above a flushed face. He wore an orange T-shirt over faded jeans, both stained with paint. "How can I help you folks?"

We introduced ourselves. "We'd like to ask some questions about Laurette Mason."

"She moved out. I was sorry to see her go. She was a good tenant, most of the time." He gestured at the open door. "This was her apartment. I'm doing some repairs, so I can get it rented again."

"I know she left. We're friends of the family. They're worried about her."

The manager was nodding as I spoke. "Yeah, I figured. Her folks came over on Sunday. They hadn't seen her or heard from her and she wasn't answering her cell phone. Like I told them, on Friday Laurette and that guy that was living with her packed up a bunch of stuff into a big SUV and took off."

"We're looking for information," Antoine said. "Did Laurette or the guy say where they were going?"

"Nope." Bert pulled a handkerchief from his back pocket and mopped the sweat that glistened on his skin. "Come on in."

We followed him into the apartment, which had a standard layout, the beige carpet worn and stained in places. The paint on the walls was cream-colored, in need of touch-ups here and there. A wheeled cart stood in front of the living room window, holding a can of paint, a plastic bin with supplies, and a toolbox. A stepladder was open in the corner. Bert reached into the bin and pulled out a bottle of water, unscrewing the top. He took a drink.

"You said she was a good tenant, most of the time. What did you mean?" I asked.

"It wasn't her. I guess I should have said that different. She was always a good tenant. It was that guy." Bert shook his head, a sour twist to his mouth. "He called himself Slade. Things went downhill after he moved in, toward the end of February, I guess it was. He was a musician. Played the electric guitar at all hours. I had complaints from the other tenants about noise, especially from the lady that lives next door and the man upstairs. And there was the parking. Slade had run-ins with other tenants about parking in their spaces. All the parking slots are assigned, one space per unit. And I was getting grief from the other tenants when they couldn't park in their spaces because Slade's Ford was taking up a slot."

"What was he driving?" I asked.

"A beat-up hatchback, gray with lots of rust spots. Anyway, he was always parking that piece of junk in the lot instead of on the street. I was glad to see him leave. But Laurette? I hope she knows what she's doing, going off with that guy. With the guitar and the parking, he was two for two on my bad-tenant scale."

I steered Bert back to the vehicles. "But that's not the car Laurette and Slade were loading up on Friday."

Bert shook his head. "Nope. They wouldn't have been able to get all their stuff in his junker, or her little Honda Civic. The car they loaded up was one of those SUVs, looked like a box on wheels. Red, it was."

"What make and model?" Antoine asked.

"Hell, I don't know. Let me see—" Bert scratched his chin, eyes narrowed as he attempted to recall what he'd seen. "Ford. I'm pretty sure it was a Ford."

"Any chance you remember the license number?" I asked.

"Louisiana plates, for sure," Bert said. "Don't remember the letters or numbers. Wait. I do remember double fours. Two fours right next to each other. I'm sorry, that's all I remember."

"Every little bit helps," I said.

While Bert talked, Antoine had been walking around the living room. Now he stopped and motioned to me. "Jeri, look at this."

I joined him and peered at the spot he indicated, on the back wall of the living room. Someone had slammed a fist into the wall, hard enough to dent the Sheetrock and crack the paint. "This looks like—"

"Looks like what it is," Bert finished. "Somebody punched the wall and I'm here to tell you it wasn't Laurette."

Antoine and I traded looks. The fist-sized hole in the living room wall bothered me. It looked larger than a woman's hand. It spoke to violence, a temper. That, coupled with the Tedescos' description of Slade as the wrong guy, was troubling.

Bert was still talking. "I thought Laurette had more sense than to take up with a guy like him. But there's no accounting for taste."

"I know Laurette's family doesn't like him. What else can you tell me about Laurette and Slade?"

Bert swallowed more water. "I was real surprised that Laurette was leaving. It was sudden, you know. She'd lived here about three years. Her and her little girl. You knew she had a little girl that died in a car accident?" I nodded, and he went on. "It was really sad. She took it hard. Who wouldn't?" Bert took another drink of water. "It seemed like she was dealing with it. She went back to work. Things going along just like normal. Then she took up with Slade, he moved in and things went to hell in a handbasket. She didn't give me hardly any notice. Told me a couple of days before that she was moving out. I told her I couldn't return the security deposit because of that and she said not to worry about it."

"What did she do with her furniture?" Antoine asked. "I'm assuming you rent these places unfurnished."

"Yeah, we do. She sold a bunch of her furniture and stored a lot of stuff," Bert said. "That's what her neighbor said. Mrs. Santini, lives right there in apartment C. She told me Friday morning a truck from a secondhand furniture place pulled up and two guys loaded up the furniture and took off."

"I'd like to talk with Mrs. Santini," I said.

"She's not here right now. I saw her leave an hour ago. She had her cart with her, so I guess she went to make groceries," he added, using the local term for grocery shopping.

I looked around the stripped-bare living room. Why would Laurette suddenly sell her belongings, store the rest and leave town with Slade? It was possible that, after the deaths of her husband

and daughter, she was ready for a change. Maybe New Orleans held too many memories. Maybe Slade had promised her a new life in a new town.

Bert was anxious to get back to work and didn't have much else to tell us. He followed us to the door as we left the apartment, then stopped and pointed toward the front of the building. "There's Mrs. Santini now. She can probably tell you more about Laurette, seeing as they were next-door neighbors." He waved. "Hey, Norma."

The woman who was coming our way appeared to be in her seventies, a bit shorter than I was, with a head of curly gray hair. She wore a pair of faded jeans and a red-and-white checked shirt, her feet laced into comfortable-looking sneakers. She was pulling a wheeled shopping cart made of bright blue fabric. Bert made the introductions.

"Just let me get my groceries put away," Norma Santini said. "Then I'll be happy to talk with you."

She unlocked her front door as Bert went back to his repairs. Antoine pulled Mrs. Santini's cart into her unit, which had the same sort of layout as Laurette's apartment. In the kitchen, she unloaded the cart, putting her perishables in the refrigerator. She left the rest of her purchases sitting on the counter.

"Can I get y'all something to drink?" she asked.

"Nothing for me, ma'am," Antoine said.

I shook my head as well. "Thank you, Mrs. Santini. I'm fine."

"Call me Norma," she said in a tart voice. "Being called ma'am or missus makes me feel twenty years older than I am. Go ahead, have a seat." She took a bottle of Abita root beer from the refrigerator and popped off the cap, taking a drink before she joined us in the living room. "Now, what is it y'all want to know?"

"We're private investigators," I said. "I'm from Oakland, California, and Antoine is local. Laurette's sister is a friend of mine. She knew I was here on vacation and she asked me to help. Laurette's family is worried. They can't get hold of her and they were upset to find out she'd left her apartment."

"Well, I guess she wanted a change," Norma said. "That young man who moved in, well, he was real different from her husband, from what she said. I guess that was part of the attraction. I know Bert didn't like him. That business about the loud music and the parking spaces. But you can't take Bert's word on everything." She smiled. "Bert's a grouchy old guy. He doesn't like anybody." She paused for another sip of root beer. "Laurette is a nice young woman. I remember when she moved in, about three years ago, with her little girl, Hannah. Such a sweet little girl." Sadness shadowed Norma's face. "Laurette was devastated when Hannah was killed in the car wreck. She was just a lost soul after that baby died. I don't know how she survived. First her husband and then the baby. It was just horrible. I know she needed somebody in her life. If Slade is the one, well, I think her parents should let things run their course."

There was something to be said for that viewpoint, I thought. Though it didn't jibe with what looked like a fist slammed against the wall hard enough to damage it. "Did they seem comfortable together?"

"Oh, yes," Norma said. "Laurette likes to cook and she'd fix dinner and sometimes they'd invite me over. Laughing, drinking wine, having a good time. I remember once Laurette was trying to make divinity candy and it wouldn't set. So she made a cake and used the divinity to frost it." She chuckled. "She gave me a piece and it was really good."

"Anything else you can tell us?" Antoine asked.

Norma thought about it for a moment as she took another swallow of root beer. "Well, there was this other woman. I wonder if it was an old girlfriend of Slade's that tracked him down here. It was a couple of weeks ago. This woman showed up and she got in Slade's face. It was quite a confrontation."

Now that sounded interesting. "What did she look like?"

"Tall, blond and skinny," Norma said. "She had really short hair, like a boy's. Except these days, boys have long hair. Anyway, I saw the whole thing because I was walking home from the library branch over on Canal Street. It was the middle of the afternoon. Laurette wasn't home from work yet. Slade had parked that old hatchback in Laurette's parking spot. This woman was waiting for him on the sidewalk. As soon as he got out of his car, she practically jumped out at him, shouting at him. I wasn't close enough to hear what she was saying, but there was a lot of hostility between them."

Antoine voiced what I was thinking. "And a week or two later, Slade and Laurette pack up and move."

"Any idea who this woman was?" I asked.

Norma shook her head. "Never seen her before, or since. I hope you find Laurette, if only to set her parents at ease. But I'm sure she's fine. She'll get in touch with them soon enough. They need to give her some room."

Chapter Six

ANTOINE AND I LEFT Norma Santini's apartment and walked out to the street. "I have a list of Laurette's friends to contact. That should keep me busy the rest of the afternoon."

He used the fob on his key ring to unlock his RAV4. "Cool. You do that while I head on over to Algiers to meet that client. I'll pick you up at your hotel around five-thirty. If I'm running late, I'll text you. We can get some dinner later, somewhere on Frenchmen Street, after we talk with my sister."

"After lunch at Willie Mae's, I don't know that I'll need dinner," I said.

"This is New Orleans. Eating, that's how we do." He waved and slid into the driver's seat.

After he drove off, I sat in my rental car, with the window down, sipping water as I got out the list Laurette's mother had given me. I called each of the women whose names and numbers were written on the sheet. In all three cases, the calls rolled over to voice mail, so I left messages. That done, I checked my list of recent calls. One was from Gary Manville, who'd left a voice mail as well. His message was terse, asking me to call him as soon as possible. I hit the call-back button on the phone. When the receptionist at Manville Security answered, I identified myself and she put me through to Gary.

"Jeri, thanks for calling me back," he said when he came on the line. "I've been trying to reach you for a couple of days. Any chance you can drop by my office today?"

"I'm out of town right now. But I'll be home in a few days, by next Tuesday at the latest. Can it wait?"

He hesitated. Then he said, "Yeah. It'll keep till you get back."

"All right. I'll call as soon as I get back to town."

Wonder what that's all about? I thought. Gary sounded as though he was worried about something. He ran his own firm, providing security to a number of businesses in the East Bay. If he was calling on my investigative services, it must be something he couldn't handle on his own. But as he'd said, it would have to wait until I got back to Oakland.

A moment after I'd ended the call, my phone rang. I answered and heard a woman's voice. "This is Grace Boudreaux. I'm returning your call."

"Thanks for getting back to me." I gave her a quick overview of why I wanted to talk with her.

"I don't know if I'll be of much help," she said, sounding as though she was convinced she wouldn't. "But sure, I'll talk with you. I'm at the university and I have some time right now. Can you come over here?"

"I'm in Mid-City, at Laurette's apartment building."

"Okay, you should be able to get here in half an hour," she said. "There's a coffee shop at University Center. I'll meet you there."

The University of New Orleans campus was located at the north end of Elysian Fields Avenue, the street Stella and Stanley lived on in Tennessee Williams's play *A Streetcar Named Desire*. The campus hugged a section of the Lake Pontchartrain shoreline. The lake, actually an estuary, connected to the Gulf of Mexico by several straits and passes. One of the guidebooks I'd read told me the lake was about forty miles from east to west and roughly twenty-four miles north to south, bridged by a long causeway that went from Metairie on the south to Mandeville on the north side of the lake. Farther to the east was Bayou Sauvage, where Dad and I had gone birding, its narrow strip of watery islands and channels separating Lake Pontchartrain from Lake Borgne to the southeast. A body of water as large as Lake Pontchartrain has lighthouses and one of these, now part of the university campus, was the Milneburg Lighthouse.

I parked on a street near campus and walked to the University Center, which I'd located on a map. Students of all varieties crowded the walkways, going in and out of buildings. Outside the University Center was a long green lawn, with UNO excised into the grass. The building itself had white pillars stretching two stories high. I went inside. Grace Boudreaux had told me she had brown hair and glasses, and she'd be carrying a gray nylon bag. I had no trouble spotting her, standing near the coffee counter, her light brown hair brushing the shoulders of her blue cotton blouse and a pair of wire-rims perched on her nose. Slung over one shoulder was the gray nylon bag, large enough to hold a laptop, I guessed. It had a blue-and-white UNO logo on the side.

"Grace? I'm Jeri. Thanks for meeting me. How about some coffee?"

"What really appeals to me is that strawberry smoothie." She pointed at the menu.

"Coming right up." I ordered my usual latte and a few minutes later carried our drinks over to where Grace stood. I looked around for an empty table in the center's main hall, but they were all occupied by students.

"Let's go outside," she said. "It's such a pretty day, and I've been in the library most of the day."

We found a place to sit near the building. Grace took a sip of her smoothie, a thick pink concoction that didn't look appetizing to me. She explained that she was a graduate student now. "When I met Laurette, we were both freshmen, studying English. I got my bachelor's degree and now I'm working on a Master's of Education in Curriculum Instruction. I hope to be finished later this year."

"So you've known her for several years. What about Chris, her husband?"

Grace nodded. "I knew him, too. She introduced us not long after they met. Which was in the fall of sophomore year. At Swampball."

"What in the world is Swampball?"

She laughed. "It's a mud volleyball tournament, with the proceeds going to a scholarship fund. The people who put it together dig two pits on the library quad and fill them with water. People put together teams and they play. There's music and food. It's one of the big campus events in the fall."

"I can just imagine." I was trying to, anyway, picturing college students playing volleyball in the mud. It didn't sound like fun to me, but I'm getting old and curmudgeonly.

"Laurette and Chris were on the same Swampball team that year, that's how they met. They started going out and in the spring he asked her to marry him. I was at their wedding. Chris was such a nice guy. It's such a shame he was killed in the Mideast. That damn war." Grace sighed.

That damn war, indeed, I thought.

"I think Laurette would have stayed in school," she continued. "Except she got pregnant. And oh, the morning sickness. She was miserable, throwing up all the time. Seeing what she went through was enough to make me think twice about having kids. People say the morning sickness doesn't last. Anyway, she was so sick she couldn't focus on school, so she dropped out. And then, with a brand-new baby, well, it's hard to think about anything but diapers and feedings, let alone getting a degree. I think she would have come back to school eventually, but when Chris died, she was in a bad place. Then her little girl, Hannah, died in that car accident. How much heartache can one person take?"

I didn't have an answer for that.

Grace took another sip of her smoothie. "I thought things were getting better for her. Now you tell me she's left town with Slade? That really surprises me."

"It surprised her parents, too. I'm trying to get a sense of what has been going on with Laurette, which is why I wanted to talk with you. I gather you've stayed in touch with her all these years. When was the last time you saw her?"

"January," Grace said. "We got together for dinner one night, in the middle of January. But we talked on the phone more often, every month or so."

I sipped my latte. "And your most recent phone conversation? How long ago was that?"

She thought about it for a moment, one finger toying with a strand of her hair. "It was after Mardi Gras."

"That's how you folks keep time down here?"

Grace laughed. "Yeah, you're right about that. Anyway, it was March, after Slade moved in with her."

"What do you know about Slade?"

"He's a musician, plays guitar. I suppose some people would think of him as good-looking. I know Laurette did. Though I must say, he wouldn't be my cup of tea. Laurette met him in November, when she was out with some people she knows from work. She said they were working their way through the clubs in Frenchmen Street and Slade was playing at one of them. He asked if he could call her and she gave him her number. To hear her tell it, they hit it off right away. Laurette seemed happy in the relationship. I was glad for her. She needed someone in her life. But..." She hesitated. "It must have heated up pretty fast. She only met him a few months before and then he moved into her apartment at the end of February."

"What did you talk about, the last time you spoke?"

"Oh, the usual. My studies, her plans."

"Plans with Slade?" Had Laurette told Grace she was thinking of leaving? Perhaps Laurette had voiced something vague and unformed, something Grace dismissed as idle talk.

But now Grace was shaking her head. "No, nothing like that. She was thinking about changing jobs and maybe going back to school. When Laurette and I met for dinner in January, she said she was bored with her job at Entergy. She was working as an admin assistant. It wasn't very challenging, she said. Same old, same old, day in and day out. She was ready for a change. She said she wanted to do something else, to reinvent herself. The trouble was, she didn't know what she wanted to do or who she wanted to be. I encouraged her to sign up for some classes, either here at the university or at one of the community colleges. Find a class that engages you, I told her. Something you always wanted to study, just for the heck of it. Take art history or a pottery class, just something new. I thought that would be a good way for her to figure out what she wanted to do. She said she'd think about it. In fact, she thought art history sounded interesting. But when I talked with her in March, she hadn't done anything. I guess she was all wrapped up in her relationship with Slade."

"Did she ever say anything about wanting to leave New Orleans?"

Grace took another sip of her smoothie before answering. "Yes, she did. More than once. It was after Hannah, her little girl, died in the car accident. Laurette was getting some counseling and I talked to her more often, giving her what support I could. A couple of times, she told me she wanted to get away. The memories of Chris and Hannah were too much."

"Did she say where she might be interested in going?"

"She talked about Florida," Grace said. "She has a cousin who lives in Pensacola, in the Panhandle. That's about two hundred miles from here, so it's not that far away. It would have been a change of scenery, though. But her family's here. She's close to her parents. And there are all sorts of relatives in New Orleans. So I wasn't surprised that she didn't do anything about going to Florida. Maybe she has now."

"Something to check out." I needed to call Davina to ask for contact information on the Pensacola cousin. It was possible, then, that Laurette and Slade had gone east, to the Sunshine State.

Grace didn't have anything more to add and, checking her watch, she told me she had an appointment. After she'd gone, carrying her smoothie, I went back inside the University Center, tossed my coffee cup into a trash receptacle and located a restroom.

I walked back across campus to the street where I'd parked the rental car. When I checked my phone, I had a message from Mary Abbott, who said she'd be happy to talk with me. I called her back and she gave me the address of the shop she owned in the Lakeview District, saying that she'd be there all afternoon. "I'll come over now,"

I told her. When I ended the call, I looked up the address and started the car.

I drove north through the campus, past the lighthouse, and headed west on Lakeshore Drive, crossing the London Avenue Canal and then Bayou St. John. I pulled over in a parking lot and got out of the car, looking out at the lake, vast and roiled with blue-green water. Whitecaps dotted the surface, and waves crashed against the shore. I'd seen the maps of New Orleans after Hurricane Katrina devastated the city in 2005. The neighborhoods along the lakefront, Lakeview, Gentilly and New Orleans East, had been inundated, like the Lower Ninth Ward to the southeast, with standing water eight to ten feet deep, and more. It had been more than ten years since the hurricane, but during this visit to the city, the signs of the devastation were still visible, with abandoned and derelict houses, or vacant lots where houses had once stood.

I started the car and continued west along Lakeshore, then took a left on Canal Boulevard, heading south into the Lakeview District, the area west of City Park. Mary Abbott, the woman Laurette met in a counseling group for military spouses, owned a quilt shop on Harrison Avenue. I found the address in a small retail district with a bank, shops and several restaurants. I parked and walked to the shop, a storefront with a window decorated with quilts, patterns and bolts of fabric, all of them in bright-colored florals for spring. I went inside and threaded my way past more fabric displays to the counter, where a woman worked the cash register, ringing up a sale for a customer. I stepped to the end of the counter and examined a flier about classes offered at the shop, then I looked at a small bookshelf that held books about quilting. I pulled out a volume about the quilts made by the African American women of Gee's Bend in Alabama. A few years ago, I'd seen an exhibit featuring those quilts at San Francisco's de Young Museum.

The woman at the cash register finished the transaction and I put the book back on the shelf.

"Are you Mary Abbott?"

"No, I'm Alice," the woman said with a smile. "Mary's in the back room." She waved toward the rear of the building, where shelves filled with bolts of fabric served as a partition.

"Thanks." I walked past the wall of fabric and found myself in a work room with tables, several of which held sewing machines. In the middle of the room was a long, waist-high table used for cutting fabric. A short, sturdy woman in her forties leaned over the table, wielding a rotary cutter over a length of purple fabric spread out on a dark green cutting mat. She looked up as I entered. Comfortable and down-to-earth were the impressions I got when I saw her laugh lines and pleasant hazel eyes.

"Hi, I'm Jeri Howard. We spoke on the phone a little while ago. Thanks for agreeing to talk with me."

"It's nice to meet you, Jeri." She pushed a button on the rotary cutter to keep the round blade from moving and set it on the table. "I wish the circumstances were different, given what you said in your message about Laurette. I'm happy to do whatever I can to help."

I'd had enough coffee for the time being, but talking over a cup of java is one of the best ways I get information. When I suggested finding a coffee shop, Mary shook her head. "Thanks, but I don't drink coffee in the afternoon or evening. Can't take the caffeine." Her smile turned impish. "However, there's a branch of the Creole Creamery just around the corner on Vicksburg Street. Are you up for some ice cream?"

"Oh, yes. I am always up for ice cream."

We left the shop in the hands of Mary's assistant and headed out to the street. Having been to the ice cream shop's Prytania Street outlet in Uptown, I was happy to give the place another try. The creamery was crowded on this warm afternoon, which didn't surprise me. I strolled along in front of the glass-topped counters, filled with enticing cartons of frozen delights, and sampled a few flavors. Mary decided on a waffle cone with two scoops, Buttermilk Lemon Pie and Bananas Foster. I went for the waffle cone, too. For me, there's chocolate and everything else, so I selected something called I Scream Fudge to go with the Triple Chocolate Brownie Brittle. We settled in at a small table near the back and enjoyed our ice cream for a few minutes, trading pleasantries.

Then I got down to the reason I was here, giving Mary more details than I'd provided in my earlier phone message. "I'm talking with Laurette's friends. I understand the two of you met several years ago in a counseling group."

Mary took her time answering, using a napkin to wipe ice cream from her lips. "Yes, we did. My husband was a master sergeant in the Army. He died about the same time as Laurette's husband died. The Veterans Administration here in New Orleans has a counseling group for people whose spouses have been killed in action. I'm about twenty years older than Laurette and my husband was career Army. Sam and I had been married for twenty-one years and we had three kids. My oldest two are in college and the youngest is still in high school. But we did have something in common, in that we're both New Orleans natives and we both lost our husbands like that. So we got to know each other. Talking about the loss helps us get past it. I think both of us benefited from the group. Then we went our separate ways. I opened this shop and she got that job at Entergy. But we stayed in touch."

"How often did you talk?" I asked.

"Every couple of months. Saw each other now and then. But not that often," Mary said. "Then after the car accident, I got a call from her. She was distraught. Who wouldn't be? She needed to talk with someone who wasn't her mother or sister or another relative. So we talked on the phone every few days. I would meet her, every couple of weeks. I urged her to get some grief counseling. In fact, I steered her to another group I'd heard about, for people dealing with the loss of a child. She did go to the group and told me that it helped. Groups usually do, if you give them a chance. I even tried to get her interested in quilting," she added with a smile. "Just so she'd have something to do with her time. But that didn't take. She said she wasn't interested in anything crafty. As the months passed, she seemed to be handling the loss. She talked about going back to school, and I encouraged her to do that."

"Then she met Slade." I reached for a napkin, since the waffle cone had leaked. My fingers were sticky with melted ice cream.

Mary smiled at me over her cone. "Yes, she met Slade. She was quite smitten. I never met him, but I certainly heard all about him and she sent me a picture. I thought he looked a little too brooding and enigmatic for my taste. But what do I know? I'm a middle-aged lady in my forties and I've been on exactly two dates since my husband died."

Her description of Slade made me smile. "Enigmatic? That's certainly a good description. No one seems to know much about him."

"That's part of the attraction, I'm sure. He plays the guitar, like a thousand other guys in this town, living by night at those clubs on Frenchmen Street and Bourbon Street. He's something different from the kind of guy her husband was, the kind of guy a nice young woman from Mid-City goes out with. Except...he moved in after a short time, and Laurette told me her parents were upset about that. They don't like him." Mary paused, a thoughtful look on her face. "You know how some women, they meet a guy and everything—and everyone—else goes out the window?"

I nodded. "Yes, I do. Suddenly the woman has no time for her friends. That's happened to me. I had a friendship go by the wayside because of it."

"I was afraid that might be happening with Laurette, because of Slade. It seemed like she was throwing everything away, including the possibility of going back to school and looking for a better job, just so she could be at Slade's beck and call. And now," Mary added, "you tell me Laurette has gone off with him, somewhere, but nobody knows where and she hasn't been in touch with her family. I can understand why they are worried. I would be, if one of my kids did that."

"Had she ever talked about leaving town?"

Mary nodded. "She mentioned Florida, last year after Hannah died. A cousin lives in Pensacola, I think. But I didn't think she was serious about it. Maybe she changed her mind."

"Someone else suggested Pensacola," I said. "It's worth following up. But I wouldn't think there would be that much in Pensacola to attract a musician. Not like New Orleans, with all those clubs you mentioned."

"True enough." Mary looked thoughtful. "Maybe they've just moved to a different place in New Orleans."

It was possible, I thought. But something about buying the SUV and loading it up made me think they'd left town.

"Or another town with a big music scene," I said. New York City? Los Angeles? But Austin was closer. "When was the last time you talked with her?"

"I called her a couple of weeks ago," Mary said. "Just to see how she was doing. She sounded good, happy. I didn't have a clue that anything was going on. If Laurette was giving off signs of doing something like this, I certainly didn't pick up on them."

⚑Chapter Seven

DAISY LASALLE WAS CHANNELING Billie Holiday, singing "Fine and Mellow" in a rich contralto. She had a white gardenia tucked into her curly dark hair and her sleeveless white silk dress set off her tawny skin. Backing her was a combo that included horns—trombone, saxophone and trumpet—plus drums, guitar, bass and a guy in a lemon-yellow shirt, playing the upright piano that was against the wall between the bar and the stage. Daisy and the rest of her band were up on the stage. The saxophonist and the bass player were women, and the rest of the musicians were male.

The Spotted Cat Music Club was on Frenchmen Street, in the New Orleans neighborhood known as the Faubourg Marigny. On this mild evening in April, it was a popular destination, the street clogged with traffic and people. The club itself occupied a weathered, two-story building with windows on either side of its recessed entrance. Inside, a railing separated the doorway from the raised stage at the front. A long bar took up most of one wall. Small tables, chairs and benches filled the space opposite the bar. In front of the stage was a small dance floor, where a few couples swayed to the music. The club's familiar logo, painted on the wall between the piano and the front window, was a cat with spots, wearing a hat and playing the saxophone.

The set had just started when we walked into the Spotted Cat. Daisy saw her brother and gave him a wave and a smile, then focused on making music. We claimed a table on the wall opposite the bar.

"I'm buying," I said. "What are you drinking?"

"Abita Amber," Antoine said.

I crossed over to the bar and waited my turn. Abita was the local brew, its brewery located in Covington, on the other side of Lake Pontchartrain. Amber was popular, but I'd acquired a taste for the rich dark version called Turbodog. I paid the bartender and carried the bottles over to the table where Antoine sat.

Daisy segued into a smoky-voiced rendition of "You Don't Know What Love Is." She looked to be a few years younger than Antoine, late twenties, I guessed. As she sang her way through the first set, she plumbed the Great American Songbook, switching from jazz to blues to the popular songs of the forties and fifties, equally at home with all of them. She finished the set with a playful version of "Up a Lazy River."

As the audience applauded, Daisy said, "Thank you. We're going to take a little break now, but don't go away, we'll be back."

The band dispersed as customers dropped bills into the tip jar in front of the stage. Several musicians made a beeline for the bar. Others went outside. The piano player stuck a cigarette in his mouth as he walked out the front door and joined a group of smokers on the banquette, some with cigarettes and others with vaping devices. As a Californian, I was used to the Bay Area's strict smoking regulations, but New Orleans was different.

Daisy stepped off the stage and wound her way through a cluster of customers to join us at our table. Antoine stood up and brother and sister enveloped each other in hugs. Then she stepped back and tilted her head to one side. "Hey, there, big brother. What brings you to my turf?"

"This and that. Baby sister, I'd like you to meet my friend Jeri Howard, from Oakland, California. Then I'll buy you a drink."

"Why, thank you. Jack on the rocks, just a little one."

"Coming right up." Antoine headed for the bar, which was three-deep in people.

Daisy turned to me with a smile. "So, Jeri Howard from Oakland, how do you know Antoine?"

"I'm a private investigator. I met your brother a few years back at an investigators' convention."

"Are you in town on business, or pleasure?"

"It started out as a vacation," I said. "My father and I were here birding and seeing the sights."

"I have a friend who's into birdwatching," Daisy said. "She goes out to Bayou Sauvage a lot."

"We were just there a few days ago," I said. "Beautiful place. We saw lots of birds. And an alligator."

Daisy laughed. "It's not unusual to see an alligator out in the bayous. I guess if you haven't seen one before..."

"I haven't, except in zoos," I confessed. "This particular critter swam toward us as we walked out on the dock to look at birds."

"What got you interested in birdwatching?" Daisy asked. "Me, I don't pay that much attention to them, except to think that they're pretty. And I love to hear them sing."

"I got interested in birds about the same time my father did," I said. "He was curious about the birds showing up on his patio and I had a lot of birds in my yard. I wanted to identify them, and the birds I saw on my walks, so I bought a book about birds of the Bay Area. My father took a birding class and joined the Audubon Society, started going on field trips. A friend of his was supposed to come with him to New Orleans but at the last minute he couldn't go. So Dad talked me into coming with him. The past week has been a lot of fun. It's always good to have an excuse to visit the Big Easy."

Daisy raised her hands. "Who says you need an excuse? Just come on down when the spirit moves you. We've got the best music, and the best food."

"I certainly have enjoyed the food," I told her. "Dad developed a taste for K-Paul's, and I love Bayona. And there's great music everywhere. We've been to Preservation Hall twice. Tennessee Williams supposedly said, 'America has only three cities: New York, San Francisco, and New Orleans. Everywhere else is Cleveland.' Of course, I don't know if he actually said that, but it's a great quote. At least I saw it on a T-shirt in one of the shops in the French Quarter."

"Well, I agree wholeheartedly," Daisy declared. "Whether Tennessee Williams said it or not. Where's your father now? Did he stay at the hotel?"

"He left for home today. The vacation is over. It's now a case."

"I see." Daisy glanced up as Antoine returned with her drink. She took a sip, set the glass on the table and fixed her brother with a look. "Jeri tells me she's working on a case. Now, did you come to hear me sing? Or is there something else on your mind?"

He laughed. "You know me too well. As a matter of fact, we're looking for information on a guy."

"I figured." Daisy nodded, pulling her face down in a mock grimace. "You only come to see me when you want information."

"That is not true." Antoine defended himself, spreading his hands wide. "I like to hear you sing. Ever since you were doing it in the shower when you were just a little girl. Besides, I took you out to brunch on your birthday."

"Well, I'll let you have points for that." Daisy sipped her Jack Daniel's. "Tell me about this guy."

"He's a musician, plays the guitar."

She laughed. "Yeah, we got a few of those in this town."

"I'm thinking you or the folks in your band might have heard of him," Antoine said.

"What's this guy's name?" Daisy asked.

"He goes by Slade," I told her.

"Slade, hmmm?" Daisy thought for a moment. "That tickles my memory. Somebody said something about him. Now who was it?" She swirled her glass and the ice cubes tinkled. Then she beckoned to the woman who played saxophone. The sax player was short and stocky, her hair in cornrows. "Zina," Daisy said, "this is my brother, Antoine, and his friend from California, Jeri."

"Hey." Zina raised one hand. The other held a bottle of Abita Amber. "How y'all doing?"

We returned her greeting and Daisy told her why we were there. "You ever hear of this guy Slade? Plays guitar."

"I heard of him, indeed." Zina nodded. "He plays here and there, round the way. Last I heard he was gigging on Bourbon Street." Zina waved in the direction of the front door. "You want to talk to Rick, the piano player. He knows Slade, might have played with him a time or two. That's Rick in the yellow shirt, out there with all the other nicotine fiends."

Rick's lemon-yellow shirt made him easy to spot among the smokers clustered outside the music club. Antoine and I left Daisy at the table and headed out to the street, where we were enveloped in the cloud of cigarette smoke. Rick was tall and skinny with a white-blond buzz cut. He looked us up and down through a pair of narrowed blue eyes. "You're Daisy's brother, right? The private eye?"

"Right," Antoine said. "And this is Jeri Howard. She's also a private eye."

Rick took a puff of his cigarette and dropped it to the pavement, grinding out the butt with his boot. "To what do I owe the honor? Am I in trouble?"

"Looking for a guitar player named Slade," I said. "Zina says you know him."

Rick frowned. "Wouldn't say I know him. Played a few gigs with him. But it's not like we're friends or anything."

"What can you tell us about him?" Antoine asked.

The piano player shook his head. "Not a whole lot. Keeps himself to himself, you know what I mean? I got a buddy who can probably tell you more about him. His name's Troy. Another guitar player. In fact, come to think of it, he crashed in Slade's apartment for a couple of weeks. That was sometime last year."

I backed away from another smoker and coughed. "Where can we find Troy?"

Rick pointed to the other side of Frenchmen Street. "He's playing a gig over at Café Negril. I saw him earlier, hauling his gear inside."

"Thanks for the info," I said.

We went back inside. "We gotta go," Antoine told his sister. "Rick gave us the name of someone who knows Slade, and this guy is playing over at Café Negril."

Daisy downed the rest of her drink and stood up. "That's cool. I've got to start the next set. It was nice to meet you, Jeri. As for you, big brother, I'll see you Monday night at Auntie Lola's."

Antoine looked confused. "Monday night?"

"Monday night at seven, and you'd better show up." Daisy put her hands on her hips. "It's Auntie's eightieth birthday. The whole family is coming. Mama is making that carrot cake you like so much."

"Auntie Lola, carrot cake. I'll be there, I'll be there." Antoine raised his hands in supplication, then pulled his phone from his pocket. "I'm putting it on my calendar right now. Wait, it's already there. Guess I'd better set myself a reminder."

"Or two. Or three," his sister said, shaking her head. "I don't know about you. I have to remind you about everything. And while I'm at it, don't forget that the band is playing at Jazz Fest in a couple of weeks." She gave him a quick hug and headed back to the stage, where the band had assembled. With a flourish, they swung into "Mambo Italiano," that old Rosemary Clooney stalwart.

We carried our beer bottles with us as we left the Spotted Cat. Café Negril was on the other side of Frenchmen Street, but there was music coming from the nearby intersection of Frenchmen and Chartres, drawing us toward that instead. A large crowd had gathered around a group of kids who looked like they were in middle school. With trombone, trumpet, sax and snare drum, the kids were giving the bands inside the clubs a run for their money, playing a lively version of "Roll With Me, Knock With Me." They were passing the hat, in this case a cardboard box, which was now loaded with coins and greenbacks. We stopped to listen and I found myself moving. Like the other people around me, I was unable to resist dancing to the infectious music.

As the kids started their next number, we headed across the street to Café Negril. I'd finished my beer, so I pitched the bottle into a receptacle. The sign outside the venue declared that the club had live music 365 nights a year. Inside, a huge Bob Marley mural loomed large on the wall behind the stage. Opposite that was a counter where patrons ordered food. The floor space on the right was crowded with tables. On stage a band was playing straight-up rhythm and blues. They finished "Rockin' Pneumonia" and drove right into the old Chuck Berry song, "Nadine." We asked around and determined that Troy was the lead guitarist. He had a head of dirty blond curls and wore a black New Orleans Saints T-shirt over baggy black jeans. He appeared to be in his mid-thirties, deep into his music zone, concentrating as he worked the strings on his electric guitar.

"They just started the set," Antoine said. "Let's get drinks and wait for the break."

We found a table, ordering drinks. Since I'd already had a beer this evening I switched to sparkling water. I wanted to keep my wits about me.

The music was great. After songs by the three R&B Kings—Albert, Earl and Freddie—the band swung into Fats Domino's "Blue Monday." Antoine asked me to dance and we went out onto the floor. "You're a pretty good dancer," he said into my ear.

"It's been a while. I should do this more often."

"You're in New Orleans now. It's all about the music. And the food."

We stayed on the floor for the next song, which had also been recorded by the great Fats, "I Hear You Knocking." When the song finished, the band took a break. Troy positioned his red Fender on a guitar stand and stepped off the stage, heading for the bar. Antoine and I intercepted him, introduced ourselves and offered to buy him a drink.

The guitar player looked wary as he examined us. "Why?"

"We need information on a guitar player who calls himself Slade," I said. "Rick down at the Spotted Cat suggested we talk with you."

Troy still looked suspicious. "How do you know Rick?"

"We don't, actually," Antoine said. "I'm Daisy Lasalle's brother and Rick plays piano in her band."

Troy's face relaxed. "Okay. Daisy's cool. I'll take that drink. Rum and Coke."

Antoine moved to the bar. When he returned, I let Troy take a swallow before I spoke. "Rick says you used to live with Slade."

The guitarist shrugged. "I wouldn't call it living with him. Crashed on his sofa for a couple of weeks, that's all. I was in a bind and I stayed there until I could get a place of my own." He took another sip of his drink and grimaced. "I'm glad I got out of there when I did."

"Why is that?" Antoine asked.

"Slade's kind of a weird dude," Troy said. "Not the easiest guy in the world to live with."

"How so?" I asked.

Troy sipped his rum and Coke. "It's all about him. Everyone else is playing second fiddle. You know what I mean?"

"I do."

"On the other hand," he added, "I've been told I'm not the best roommate either. I'm messy. And I snore. Big time." He took another swallow of his drink. "Anyway, he doesn't live in that apartment anymore. He moved in with his girlfriend. Laurette, a nice-looking lady."

"You've met her?" I asked.

"Yeah, same night he did. I was playing here that night, and so was Slade. He was subbing with the band on guitar. It was a fix-up deal, you know."

"No, we don't know," Antoine said. "Tell us what you mean."

"This lady I know, she told me she was going to be here at Café Negril that night, with some friends from work. She wanted to introduce one of her girlfriends to Slade. She thought they'd hit it off, you know, be cool together."

"What's this lady's name?" I asked. "And how does she know Slade?"

"Her name's Brenda."

I nodded, a couple of puzzle pieces falling into place.

"We used to go out together, last year," Troy continued. "Stayed friends. And she met Slade when he and I were playing together at a club down on Bourbon Street. She knew Slade had been gigging with us, so she called me a couple of days before to make sure he'd be here that night. Said she was going to fix him up with this lady named Laurette."

"Was Slade in on this fix-up?" Antoine asked, glancing at me. "Did he know Brenda was going to introduce him to Laurette?"

"Don't know," Troy said. "Could be, since Brenda knows him. I guess it worked out. Slade and Laurette hit it off and they started dating. Then sometime after Mardi Gras, Slade told me he was giving up his apartment and moving in with Laurette. She had a nice place in Mid-City. It was bigger. The place where Slade was living in Treme was really small and kinda funky." He stopped talking long enough to take a swallow of his rum and Coke.

"Is there anything else you can tell us about Slade?" I asked. "Where is he from?"

"That I don't know," the guitarist said. "He's not from NOLA, though. From somewhere out of town."

I wondered if Slade, with Laurette in tow, was headed back to wherever he came from. "Did he have an accent? Was he a southerner, or from back east?" I'd already asked Laurette's parents that question, but I wanted to hear what Troy had to say.

He was shaking his head. "No accent that I can remember. I mean, if it was a deep south drawl or one of those easterners from 'Noo Yawk,' I would have noticed. I'm thinking he was from somewhere out west. I didn't see anything in his apartment that struck me as being souvenirs from home, either. Sorry, that's all I can remember." He downed the rest of his drink, then he added, almost as an afterthought, "Good thing Slade moved out of that place in Treme when he did. There was a fire. That apartment got totally trashed."

That could be a reason for Slade to change his living arrangements. But Troy had just said the fire happened after Slade moved in with Laurette. "Any idea how it started?"

"Not really." The look on Troy's face told me he didn't think the fire had anything to do with Slade. "I guess it was an accident, probably some electrical problem. Wouldn't surprise me. It was an old building and the wiring in that place was kinda funky. I noticed that when I was crashing at Slade's place. Plug in too many things and the fuse would go. That's rough when you're trying to practice with an electric guitar, I can tell you."

"Where was the apartment?" Antoine asked. "What address?"

"Marais Street, off Esplanade." Troy rattled off the street address.

Antoine looked thoughtful. "Who owns the building? Was it Doucette Properties?"

Troy shrugged. "I don't know. The apartment was in Slade's name. Like I said, I only crashed there a couple of weeks. I gave him some cash to cover it. Don't know who the landlord was." Another member of the band gave Troy a tap on the shoulder. "I gotta go." Troy headed back to the stage and picked up his guitar.

"Something about the name Brenda?" Antoine asked. "You got a look on your face when Troy mentioned the name."

"And here I thought I had such a good poker face," I said.

"It is good. Only another private eye would have picked up on it. So what's the story with Brenda?"

"That's one of the names on the list Laurette's mother gave me. If it's the same woman, and I'm guessing it was, since Troy said Brenda was at the club with some people she worked with. Laurette worked at Entergy with someone named Brenda Kohl."

"Did you talk with her today?"

I shook my head. "She never called me back. I'll track her down tomorrow, if I have to go to Entergy headquarters to do it. So Brenda introduced them. I'd like more details on how she knows Slade and why she decided to introduce him to Laurette. And you're interested in that fire."

"I sure am. Doucette Properties is Patrice Doucette, and I know her. We grew up together in the Treme. Pat lives on Marais Street, which is just around the way from where I live on Villere. She owns a bunch of apartment buildings all over that neighborhood. Plus I remember that fire. It was in March, so it was definitely after Slade moved in with Laurette. The fire was just a couple of blocks from my house. I heard the engines and went outside. It was late at night, but I could see the smoke and the flames. I heard later it was one of Pat's places. But I didn't hear anything about how it started. Like the guitar player said, those are old buildings. Could have been an accident."

"Or not. We need to check it out."

He nodded. "Agreed. I know a guy at the fire department. I'll see what I can find out. Go see Pat tomorrow. I'll text you her address. I'd go with you, but I've got a meeting with a client tomorrow morning."

We left Café Negril and headed back to the French Quarter to a restaurant Antoine wanted to try. After dinner, he dropped me at my hotel. I headed upstairs, where I called Dan before going to bed.

⫞Chapter Eight

THE FOLLOWING MORNING, I had breakfast at the buffet in the hotel courtyard, then headed for the business center off the lobby. I checked my office email and responded to messages. My plan was to visit Doucette Properties this morning, to get some information on the apartment that Slade had rented before he moved in with Laurette. At some point I needed to update Davina and the Tedescos on the progress of the investigation, but it was early yet. I didn't have much information for them. They had agreed to pay for Antoine's time, though. I was doing this as a favor to Davina, though she'd promised to kick in some funds when I got back to the Bay Area.

As for talking with Laurette's friends, I'd met with Grace and Mary yesterday. But Brenda Kohl, Laurette's coworker at Entergy, had never returned my call. Time for a reminder. I looked at my phone screen and found the list of calls I'd made the day before, calling Brenda's work and home numbers. The calls went straight to voice mail, so I left messages. Then I called her cell number. These days, with caller ID, it was easy to ignore a ringing phone if one didn't recognize the number. It was possible that was how Brenda was playing it. After several rings I was sure the call would bounce over to voice mail. Then I heard a voice say, "Hi, this is Brenda."

"Jeri Howard. I called you yesterday." I launched into my explanation for why I wanted to talk with her, the same message I'd left on her voice mail earlier. When I was finished, she didn't say anything, and I wondered if she'd ended the call.

Then she said, "Yeah, I got your message yesterday. A private eye, huh? I don't know how I can help you. I have a few minutes now, so ask your questions."

"I'd rather talk with you in person." I always prefer a face-to-face meeting. It lets me observe a person's body language, facial expressions and mannerisms, which are sometimes more telling than a person's words. "I'm in the French Quarter right now. I can come to where you are, if you can take a break at some point during the day. Are you at work?"

I heard a sigh on the other end. Her reluctance to talk with me was clear. But maybe she realized that I wasn't planning on taking no for an answer.

"I'm not at work," she said. "I took the day off. Look, I'm out running errands and then I've got an appointment. I guess I could meet you at ten. There's a coffeehouse on North Carrollton, the Bean Gallery. Look for the green awning over the front door."

"How will I recognize you?"

"I'm wearing khakis and a tropical print shirt."

I was about to tell her how to recognize me, but she ended the call before I could get the words out of my mouth.

The clock on my phone said it was a quarter after nine. That gave me plenty of time to get there. I looked up the coffeehouse on the computer in front of me, with the map giving me an idea of how best to get there. I went upstairs to get my bag and the keys to the rental car. I left the French Quarter and drove to my destination, parking on a side street.

It was a few minutes before ten when I entered the Bean Gallery. I looked around but didn't see a woman in a tropical print shirt. She said she was running errands, so I'd give her the benefit of the doubt. I ordered a latte, then carried my cup to a small table on the wall opposite the counter, taking the chair that gave me a view of the door. Five minutes stretched into ten and still no Brenda Kohl. The benefit of the doubt was giving way to wondering if she was going to keep the appointment.

It was nearly twenty minutes past the hour when the door

opened, and a woman walked in, wearing a shirt with a pattern of bright red and yellow flowers splashed across a pale green background. I'm five eight, and she was taller, perhaps five ten. As I looked at Brenda Kohl, I recalled Norma Santini's description of the woman who'd had words with Slade on the sidewalk in front of Laurette's building. Tall, blond and skinny, Norma had said, adding that the woman had short blond hair, like a boy's haircut.

Was this the same woman? It could be. Descriptions were notoriously subjective. Brenda Kohl wasn't what I'd call skinny. She had plenty of curves filling out her khaki cropped pants and her hair, while short, was longer than a boy's, with curls clustered on her temples and the back of her neck.

I stood up and waved to her. As I introduced myself, I noticed the small red parrot tattooed on her forearm. It went with the enameled earrings dangling from her lobes that were also parrots. She appeared to be a few years younger than me, maybe thirty.

"Sorry I'm late," Brenda Kohl said, a slight smile curving her lips. "Errands. Always takes longer than you think."

"Can I get you a coffee?"

"Sure. A mocha would be great. I like chocolate and whipped cream with my coffee."

I stepped up to the counter and ordered. When the drink was ready, I carried it to the table and sat down.

Brenda took a sip of her mocha. "Ah, just right. So what's this all about?"

I told her the situation.

Brenda laughed, a throaty sound. I don't know what I was expecting, but it wasn't that. "I know. They called me on Sunday evening when they didn't find her at the apartment. I told them she'd quit her job. Y'know, the Tedescos really need to let go. They've had Laurette wrapped in cotton for years. She's an adult, for God's sake. Hiring a private eye to find her is really overkill."

I took a sip of my latte. "I'm a friend of the family and I happen to be in town. And I'm certainly interested in your perspective. Did you know what Laurette was going to do?"

Brenda crossed one long leg over the other, jiggling her foot, which was encased in a sandal that showed off a bright red pedicure. "Laurette told me she was thinking about it. Throwing the dice to do something different, maybe heading out of town. I didn't really think she'd do it, but now that she has, more power to her. It's not like it was all that sudden. She gave the company two weeks' notice that she was leaving the job."

Which was more than she'd given her parents, who knew nothing about her plans, and Bert, the manager of the apartment building. That made me wonder about Laurette's relationship with her family. Brenda thought the Tedescos were overreacting, and overprotective. That could very well be the case.

"She didn't tell her parents she was leaving," I said. "And she missed her brother's birthday party."

Brenda shrugged. "I can't say that I blame her for taking off. She's a grown-up, for God's sake. She's twenty-six years old, been married and had a kid. That means she gets to make her own choices." She paused for another sip of her mocha and licked a bit of whipped cream from her lips. "Laurette is not as fragile as her parents seem to think. Yes, it was really hard on her, losing her husband, and then her little girl in that horrible car wreck. But life goes on. It has to. She feels smothered by her family, everyone tip-toeing around her and treating her like she's made of glass. But she's ready to move on. If she's made the choice to do that with Slade, I'm all for it. I think the two of them living together is natural and wonderful and healthy. Laurette is getting on with her life."

Maybe she was, I thought. But I wished she'd let her family know she was okay. "Do you have any idea where she's gone?"

"Not a clue," Brenda said. "But hey, it's a big wide world and I hope she's gone to look at some of it. That girl has lived in New Orleans her whole life, born and raised. I'll bet she hasn't been more than a couple of hundred miles from this town, ever."

I noticed that she didn't mention Pensacola, as Mary and Grace had, or Laurette's visit to her sister in California.

Brenda continued, running her hands through her hair. "Me, I'm a transplant. I came here after Katrina, liked the place and found a job. I don't know if I'll stay. If I get bored, I'll move on. I'm from the east, so I might check out California. Or Denver. Or New Mexico. I hear Santa Fe is wonderful. Maybe Laurette feels the same way I do. While you're young, you've got to get out and see the world. It could be she's on a road trip with Slade. Or she's decided to relocate. Don't worry, Laurette will get in touch with her family. She's having an adventure somewhere. Good for her. If she's on the road, maybe she's having cell phone trouble."

I sipped my coffee. "My impression is that the Tedescos don't like Slade."

She rolled her eyes. "I don't think they'd like anyone who came between them and their daughter. Hell, I've met them a time or two and I don't think they like me."

"I see. Tell me about Slade. I know he's a musician."

"Good-looking." Brenda grinned. "And a very talented musician."

"Does he do anything else? I know a lot of musicians can't support themselves just playing gigs. Does he have a day job?"

"Don't know." She shrugged. "Well, come to think of it, Laurette said something about Slade working in some warehouse. But he quit that job because they wanted him to work overtime and it was interfering with his gigs. At least that's what she told me."

It sounded like Brenda knew a lot about Slade. I thought again about the blond woman who'd supposedly confronted him outside the apartment building. "Did you know Slade? Before he met Laurette?"

She shook her head. "Know Slade? No. I'd seen him before, playing at clubs around town. But no, not to speak to."

First lie, I thought. But who was telling it? Last night at Café Negril, Troy had told Antoine and me that Brenda had engineered the meeting between Laurette and Slade, because, in her words, they'd be a good match. But now Brenda was telling me she didn't know him.

Was Brenda lying? Or was Troy? Deliberately? Or was one of them having a memory lapse?

My money was on Brenda. There was something in the way she tensed when I asked the question, the way her eyes skewed around the room before she answered me. Maybe it was the way she'd denied it, twice. I decided to give her a bit more rope and see what happened.

"How did Laurette meet Slade?"

Brenda relaxed. "We were out, listening to music."

"Who's we? You and Laurette? Or were you with a group of people?"

"With a group." Brenda looked a bit annoyed at my interruption. "Some people from work. Just a casual get-together. Someone suggested that we have dinner and listen to music. So that's what we did, headed over to Frenchmen Street after work and had a bite to eat. Then we went from place to place. Some people split off. A few of us ended up at Café Negril, listening to this band. Slade was playing guitar with them. He kept looking at Laurette during the set. I just knew he was going to ask for her phone number. When the band took a break, he came up and introduced himself. And he did ask for her number. She hesitated about giving it to him, and I said, Go on, what have you got to lose. You might go out on a date and have fun. And what could be the harm in that? So she did go out with him, and she had a blast."

"Who were the other people you were with?"

Now the woman on the other side of the table looked irritated. "I don't see why you need to know their names. They're just people from work."

"I'm just trying to get a sense of how Laurette and Slade met."

"They'll tell you what I just told you." Her lips compressed in a tight line. "There was a guy named Frank from accounting. I don't even know his last name. And a woman named Abby." Slowly, reluctantly, she gave me a few names. I jotted them in my notebook.

"This was last fall?"

"Yeah. Right before Thanksgiving. So Laurette started going out with Slade. And I was happy for her. It's like she got a new lease on life. He's good for her, he really is. They're good together. Wait, I'll show you what I mean. I took this video a month ago, when we were hanging out down in the Quarter."

Brenda reached into her pocket and pulled out her phone. Her fingers played over the screen as she searched through the photos and videos she'd taken. She scrolled down, found what she was looking for and started the video, handing the phone to me.

The image showed Laurette and Slade sitting side by side, his arm around her shoulders. I recognized the place, Café Envie, near the French Market. The video wasn't very long, but long enough to show Slade with a smile on his narrow face as he turned and kissed Laurette on the cheek. She laughed, her face a contrast from the more reserved look I'd seen in the photo Davina had sent to me, the one taken on Christmas Day at the Tedescos' house. In that one Slade had been taciturn, his face a mask. I could understand his wanting to be formal and on his best behavior, since the occasion was Christmas dinner with Laurette's family. Slade had to know that the Tedescos didn't approve of his relationship with Laurette. Maybe he didn't want to give them any excuse to dislike him even more. This Slade was a lot like the one Laurette's neighbor had described.

Still, I thought, Brenda's pretty pictures didn't tell the whole story of Laurette's relationship with Slade, any more than Davina's photo did. Or was I being cynical?

I handed the phone back to Brenda. "What else can you tell me about Slade? Where is he from?"

"How would I know?" she shot back, irritated. "Why do you ask?"

"I just want to find out more about him."

"So you can find Laurette and force her to come home to Mother?"

"I'm not going to force Laurette to do anything. I just want to know that she's all right. That's all her parents want."

Brenda took a sip of her coffee. From the look on her face, I guessed she was deciding whether to throw me a crumb. "I don't have any idea where Slade is from. Passing through, like a lot of musicians in this town. Some of them stay, some of them move on."

It was time to call Brenda on her bullshit. "Do you know a guitar player named Troy?"

She shrugged. "I know a few guitar players."

"He knows you, or says he does. In fact, he says the two of you used to date. Last night he told me you cooked up the meeting between Slade and Laurette. That makes me think you knew Slade before. Which version is true?"

Brenda set the coffee cup on the table and narrowed her eyes at me. "I don't know what you're talking about. I may have met this guy Troy at some club or another, but the name doesn't ring a bell."

"Funny, I don't believe you. I think you knew Slade before you introduced him to Laurette. And I think you know where they are."

She pushed back her chair and stood up. "I don't have to listen to this. Besides, I'm going to be late for my appointment. Thanks for the coffee," she added, with a mild tone that didn't match the poisonous look in her eyes.

I watched her go. She knew more than she was saying, I was sure of it. Again, I wondered if she was the woman who'd argued with Slade outside the apartment building.

I got up from the table and put the two coffee cups into a bin near the counter. Leaving the Bean Gallery, I walked half a block to the street where I'd left my rental car. As I slid into the driver's seat, my phone rang. It was Antoine.

"Where are you?" he asked.

"Near a coffeehouse called the Bean Gallery. I just had a meeting with Brenda Kohl and it left me with a lot of questions. I'll tell you about it when I see you."

"Can you come over to my office right now?" Antoine's voice sounded subdued. "I had a conversation this morning with my fire department buddy. That apartment fire is more complicated than we thought. Somebody died."

◤Chapter Nine

THE SHOTGUN HOUSE supposedly got its name because one could fire a shotgun through the front door of such a house and bird shot would fly out the back door without hitting any walls. I don't know the veracity of that story, but the long narrow houses were common all over New Orleans.

Antoine's house was one of them. It was located on North Villere Street, just a couple of blocks off Esplanade Avenue. The exterior had been painted a sunny yellow with white trim. Like many of the shotguns I'd seen in the city, the house and its small front stoop jutted all the way to the edge of the sidewalk. Antoine sat on the stoop next to a pot of red geraniums, a mug of coffee in his hand.

He stood up to greet me. "Come on in. I just made a fresh pot."

The classic shotgun single, like the one Antoine owned, was one room wide. What had been the living room was now Antoine's office. The bedroom in the middle of the house now served as living and sleeping space, with a bed tucked into one corner and opposite this, a comfortable-looking recliner angled in front of a wide-screen TV on a stand. Through an open door I glimpsed the bathroom. Another door, closed, presumably led to a closet. Antoine led the way through the middle room to the kitchen at the back of the house, near a door that led out to a small backyard. Antoine took a mug from a hook on the wall and filled it with coffee. He handed it to me and I took a sip. Good and strong. He motioned to the kitchen table. With its retro yellow Formica top, I wondered if he'd found it in a vintage store, or more likely in a relative's storage shed. We sat down on the yellow vinyl-covered chairs that went with the table.

"Tell me about the fire in Slade's apartment—and the fatality."

Antoine nodded. "My friend at the fire department says when the firefighters put out the fire, they found a body. A man, later identified as Ray Brixton. The autopsy says smoke inhalation probably got him first."

I gave an involuntary shudder. Death by fire is an awful way to go. "Was the fire an accident? Or deliberately set?"

"They haven't made that call yet," Antoine said. "Or they're not saying. The building was old, a double shotgun house that had been carved up into four units. Could be some problem with the electrical wiring, just like Troy said last night. Although Pat Doucette, the woman who owns the building, told the investigators that everything was up to code. I've known her for years, so I'm inclined to believe her. The place was empty and she was doing some touch-ups and repairs before renting it again. There were cans of paint and paint thinner in the place."

"Those things are highly flammable." I took another sip of coffee. "Say it was something with the wiring. A spark from the wiring ignites the paint? Or say it's arson. The paint could have been used as an accelerant. Who was the victim? Do we have any more information other than the name?"

"Ray Brixton was another musician," Antoine said. "We do have a lot of those in this town. At first the investigators thought he might be squatting in the apartment, since it was empty at the time of the fire. But when they identified the body, they found out Brixton had a place of his own in the Marigny. I tracked down the obit in the *Times-Pic*. And a picture."

He handed me a couple of printouts. Ray Brixton was twenty-five years old and a guitarist, according to the obit. The photo Antoine had found showed that he had blond hair to go with a wispy mustache and a goatee. In the picture, he was playing at a club on Bourbon Street, the establishment's name on the wall above the bandstand.

"What was Brixton doing in Slade's old apartment? How did he get in? Did he force the lock, come through a window?"

"Good questions. Nobody knows." Antoine got up and poured himself another mugful of coffee. He rejoined me at the table. "He could have broken in. They couldn't tell if the door had been forced or a window broken, because the fire took care of that. But why would this guy be there?"

"Unless he's the one who set the fire," I said. "And got caught before he could get out."

"It's possible. But why would he do that? And here's a completely different theory. Brixton's got a sister named Cindy. She's been telling anyone who will listen that her brother was murdered. By Slade."

I stared at him. "That puts a different spin on things. We know Laurette's parents don't like Slade. Neither does Bert, the apartment manager. But Laurette's neighbor Norma and her friend Brenda both seem to think Slade is a nice guy. Last night Troy said he was self-centered and hard to live with. But murder? If Cindy Brixton is accusing Slade of killing her brother, that could be the reason Slade and Laurette suddenly decided to leave town."

"I'm with you there. It's suspicious."

"We need to talk with Cindy. I wonder what she looks like. Remember, Norma Santini said Slade had been confronted by a tall skinny woman with blond hair. It looks like Ray was blond. Maybe the mystery woman is his sister. However, Brenda Kohl is tall and has blond hair."

"Skinny?" Antoine asked.

"I wouldn't call her that."

"Could be either of them. I got a phone number for Cindy Brixton from my fire department pal, but she's not answering calls or responding to my message. I located an address for her. We'll just have go over to where she lives, to see if we can catch her at home. I can't do that till later today. Tell me what you found out from Brenda Kohl."

I gave him an overview of my conversation with Laurette's coworker. "I'd like to find out where Slade is from originally or even just before he came to New Orleans. It's possible he's gone back to wherever that is, and taken Laurette with him."

"Agreed." Antoine nodded. "Most musicians in this town have other gigs. Daisy works in an admin job over at Tulane and sings at night. So in order to rent that apartment from Pat Doucette—"

"He had to fill out an application," I finished. "I'll go over and talk with her when we're done here."

"Which is right about now." He looked at his watch. "I've got some things I need to do on a case. I'll text you later."

⩍ Chapter Ten

MARAIS STREET WAS NARROW and potholed, with cars parked at the curbs on both sides. Shotgun singles and doubles crowded the lots, sitting close together, along with a scattering of two-story houses, some of them looking as though they'd been converted to apartment buildings.

I located Doucette Properties in a storefront office near an intersection. The plate glass window was decorated with pasteboard signs and photographs showing apartments and houses available for rent. A woman was seated behind a desk, gesturing as she talked on the phone. When she saw me, she waved, as though to let me know she would be with me soon. A moment later, she ended the call and stood up, stepping from the desk through the doorway. She was tall and shapely, her hair in long cornrows decorated with colorful beads. Her fingernails were a vibrant purple, and a lavender scarf set off her beige knit top. She smiled, assuming I was a prospective renter.

"Are you Patrice Doucette?" I asked.

"Yes, I am. Are you looking for a place to live? We have a number of apartments available."

"It's about the fire in one of your units here on Marais Street, back in March."

Now her brown eyes flashed. "Are you from the insurance company? Because if you are, I have been going round and round with you people. And I'm tired of it."

I shook my head. "No, I'm not from the insurance company." I handed her one of my business cards.

She examined the card and looked up. "Oakland, California? Girl, you are way off your home turf."

"I'm doing a favor for a friend."

She still looked skeptical. "Even so, why should I talk to you?"

"Because Antoine Lasalle is helping me with my investigation."

Her face relaxed. "Oh, Antoine. We grew up together, right here in the Treme. We may even be cousins, somewhere down the line."

"I get the impression New Orleans is a small town, no matter what the population figures say."

"You got that right. How do you know Antoine?"

"We met a few years ago at a convention."

"Now, who knew private investigators had conventions." She laughed. "Call me Pat. My mother's the only one calls me Patrice. How can I help you?"

"I'm looking for information on a guy who calls himself Slade. I understand he rented the apartment from you and moved out some time before the fire."

Pat's cheerful expression turned into a thundercloud of fury. "That son of a bitch. Moved out indeed. I evicted his sorry ass. He wasn't paying the rent. Owed me two months before I had him served with the five-day notice, which he ignored. So I took him to court. It took weeks and cost me a bunch of money. By then he was four months in arrears. And I never got any money from him, that's for damn sure."

That put the lie to what Slade had told Laurette. His story was that he'd been forced to move because the property owner wanted the unit for a relative. All the better to persuade her to let him move into her apartment. "He stiffs you for the rent. And then the fire."

"I wouldn't be surprised if he torched the place to get back at me," Pat said.

The possibility of arson had been hovering in my mind ever since I'd heard about the fire. "You're sure it was Slade?"

She gave me a look. "Who else would it be? The place went up in smoke less than two weeks after he left. What do you think?"

"You've got a point," I conceded. "I can see his torching the apartment as retaliation for you evicting him. But where does Ray Brixton, the dead guy, fit in?"

"Beats the hell out of me. I understand he was a musician. Maybe he came along to help torch the apartment."

It was a plausible theory, I thought. If it weren't for the claims made by the dead man's sister. "I understand that the victim's sister says her brother was murdered. By Slade."

Pat frowned and fingered a strand of her beaded hair. "Good Lord, I didn't know that. I just know they found that man's body in that apartment after they put out the fire. The investigators haven't told me anything other than that. Murder? I wouldn't put it past Slade."

The phone rang in her office. Pat beckoned to me to follow as she moved through the doorway to her desk. She answered the phone and sat down in her desk chair. I took a seat in a chair in front of the desk, listening as Pat fielded questions about a two-bedroom rental she was offering on North Rocheblave Street. She set up an afternoon appointment to show the unit to the prospective renters, then she hung up the phone and pointed to a coffee mug on the desk. "I have a pot of coffee in the back room. You want some?"

"No, thanks. I'm coffee'd out for now. Tell me about Slade."

Pat sighed and leaned back in her chair. "Where do I start?"

"The beginning. When you rented him the apartment. How long ago was that?"

"Last fall, October. I had a bad feeling about him, from the start. I should have gone with my gut. My gut steers me right every time. But the apartment had been empty for a while, and he was interested in renting it, so I went ahead. Then I wound up with this mess on my hands."

"Why did you have a bad feeling?"

She thought about it for a moment. "His attitude. He's one of those people who acts like the world owes him something. Oh, he hit all the check marks on his application. He had a job, a work history, a bank account. On paper, he looked like a good bet."

"May I see the application?"

"Oh, sure." She swiveled in her chair and pulled out a draw-er in one of the filing cabinets. She leafed through the tabs on the manila folders. Then she pulled out one, turning back toward me. She handed over the file folder and I opened it, examining the rental application. Here, finally, was Slade's full name—Eric Charles Slade. Calling himself Slade wasn't far off the mark. For identification, he'd provided a Texas driver's license, with a date of birth that told me he was twenty-seven years old, and an address in Austin.

At the time he'd filled out the form, Slade had been employed as a stocker at a warehouse here in New Orleans. Pat assured me she'd verified his employment status and his salary, which wasn't much. Evidently he'd been supplementing his income by playing gigs. Or, as was more likely for a musician, the day job was something he took so he could supplement what he really wanted to do, which was playing guitar. His previous job, in Austin, was similar, working in another warehouse. According to the form, he'd held that position for five months. Before that, he'd spent two years working as a car-pet installer for a flooring warehouse in Concord, California. Was he from California?

Austin. The Texas capital was a music hub, just like New Orleans. There was nothing unusual about a guitarist leaving the Lone Star State to try his luck in the Big Easy. But Brenda Kohl, Laurette's coworker, and Troy, the fellow guitarist who'd lived brief-ly with Slade, had both said that Slade didn't have an accent that readily identified his origins. Troy theorized that Slade was from somewhere out west. Austin was certainly west of New Orleans, but if Slade was from Texas, I would have expected a hint of a Texas twang in the way he talked. Was Austin just another way station on Slade's journey? And had he decided to go back, taking Laurette with him?

"He told me he was new in town," Pat said. "And I didn't think anything about that. At least not at the time. His income wasn't that great, but he told me he was making money playing gigs. I try to be fair with musicians. They're all over New Orleans, and they're in and out. I rent to a lot of them in this part of town, because it's close to the Quarter and Frenchmen Street. We lost plenty of housing during and after Katrina, and rents went up. I keep my rents reasonable, and I try to give people the benefit of the doubt. Sometimes that backfires on me, like it did with Slade."

She paused, then went on. "About that job, when he stopped paying rent and I called that place, they told me he'd quit his job. I wonder if he got fired."

"I'll check it out. The bank, too." Slade had listed an account at a local bank. If he'd left town for good, he'd probably cleaned it out.

At the bottom of the application form was an entry asking for an emergency contact. The name Slade had given was Millicent Patchett, with a phone number in the 925 area code. That was in California, the East Bay, and it encompassed most of Contra Costa County as well as the eastern part of Alameda County. Concord, where Slade had worked before moving to Austin, was in Contra Costa County. It appeared Slade was from California, or at least he'd lived there for a while. Did that mean he was on his way back to the Golden State, with Laurette in tow?

The other papers in the folder were related to the eviction proceedings. There was a copy of the five-day notice and the court filings. I glanced at them, but it was the information on the application that was most useful to me. I could follow up with the employer, and the former address and employer in Austin would be helpful as well. "May I have a copy of this form?"

"Sure." Pat took the form from me and stood up, crossing the office to a small copier on a table in the corner. She made the copy and handed it to me, then put the original application back in the folder. "I hope that helps. I hadn't really thought much about that man who died. I honestly thought he could have been the one who set the fire. I have been focused on my battles with the insurance company and dealing with all that property damage."

"Sounds like it was a major hassle," I said.

"Oh, Lord, it's been nothing but a mess." She threw her hands in the air. "Almost as much of a mess as what I went through after Katrina. The unit that burned is part of a fourplex, at the back. The other apartments had some fire and smoke damage and the guy next to the unit that burned already gave notice and moved out. And the people in the front units, they're talking about leaving, too. It has been such a hassle. Like I said earlier, I've been fighting with those insurance people. They act like I torched the place myself. Believe me, I would not have done that. That was a good rental property, four units, and now I've got all that fixing up to do. Filling out paperwork and dealing with the police and the fire department. Then to have somebody die in the fire. It's just too much."

⬥Chapter Eleven

ACCORDING TO THE rental application Pat Doucette gave me, Slade had been employed at Melancon Supply. The company was located in a warehouse on Tchoupitoulas Street, in an industrial district not far from the Mississippi River. I parked near a funky-looking corner bar called Shorty's and walked to the address, an L-shaped building surrounded by a tall chain-link fence. Across the driveway was a wide gate on wheels, accessed electronically, judging from the square black metal box on one side. It was open now, during business hours. Beyond the gate was a paved lot, with cars and trucks parked in slots on the left side. Directly in front of me were side-by-side metal roll-up doors. Both were open and led into the warehouse itself. I glimpsed tall shelves loaded with supplies, with aisles in between, and heard a beeping sound as a forklift lumbered into view. A tan pickup truck had pulled up near one of the doors and two men were loading cartons into the bed.

The short end of the L pointed toward the street and it looked like a business office. I walked through the gate and turned right, heading for the door that led into the office. It was utilitarian, with concrete floors and off-white walls, bisected by a counter. The woman seated at the desk looked to be in her forties, with strawberry blond hair and a pale, washed-out complexion. She was on the phone. While I waited, I studied one of the brochures arrayed atop the counter, learning that Melancon supplied paper and janitorial products, selling everything from office supplies like cartons of paper, to paper plates and cups, cleaning products, supplies and equipment.

The woman ended the phone call and looked up at me as she put an invoice back in its file folder and set it aside. "Can I help you?"

"I'd like to get some information on a former employee."

She looked doubtful. "There's not a whole lot I can tell you. Privacy rules and so forth. I can just confirm whether the person was employed here. What's the name?"

"Eric Slade."

When she heard the name, she narrowed her blue eyes and looked me up and down. "What is this about?"

Pay dirt, I thought, noting her expression. That was a sign she knew plenty. Now to get her to talk.

I flashed my best friendly, non-threatening smile. "Hey, it's not official or anything like that. I'm just doing a favor for a friend, trying to find out more about the guy. He's dating her sister and my friend doesn't like him." Which was true enough.

The woman was nodding, a sympathetic look on her face. "I get that. I really do. I'd like to help, but I don't want to get in bad with the boss, you know."

"I do know. And I understand." I decided to lay out a plausible story. "It's just that Slade told my friend that he worked here for a while and then he quit. Because it was interfering with his gigs. Because he's a musician, plays the guitar. My friend is not sure whether to believe him."

She pursed her lips and gave a derisive snort. "Quit? Is that what he said? Oh, honey, they fired him."

"Oh, yeah? Given what I've heard about him, that doesn't surprise me." I leaned forward, elbows on the counter, as though getting settled for a long chat. "So, why did they let him go?"

She hedged again, having second thoughts about dishing up some dirt. "I don't know if I should tell you."

"I don't want you to do anything that would get you in trouble. Can you put me in touch with his supervisor?"

She thought about it and happily passed the buck. "Yeah, better you should talk to him. Stan Hollis, that's his name. He's the ware-house manager." She glanced at the clock on the wall, which showed the time as nearly noon. "He should be going to lunch about now. Let me see if he's in the building."

She picked up the handset and punched a couple of buttons. I heard her voice echoing over an intercom, somewhere deep in the warehouse. "Stan, line three. Pick up line three." A few seconds later, she said, "Hey, it's Ella. Glad I caught you before you went to lunch. Say, I got a lady here in the office. I think you need to talk to her." She hung up the phone. "He'll be up in a minute."

A short time later, a big man came out of the warehouse and walked briskly across the lot, opening the office door. Stan Hollis was over six feet tall and he had broad shoulders and a muscular frame. There was a lot of gray in his black hair, and his coffee-colored face was round and friendly, with laugh lines. "Hey, Ella. What's up?"

Ella pointed at me. "This lady here has some questions about Slade."

All vestiges of friendliness vanished from the man's face. I had a feeling that if I could get him to talk, I'd hear plenty. "Why?" he asked me.

"My name's Jeri," I told him. I launched into the same story I'd given Ella, that I was tracking down information on Slade for a friend. "Ella seems to think you might have something to tell me."

"Oh, yeah," he said. "I can tell you plenty. Your friend is right to be concerned. I sure as hell wouldn't like it if Slade was involved with any woman I know."

"Great. Can I buy you a cup of coffee?" That was my go-to for collecting information. Surely the corner bar I'd seen had coffee.

"No place around here to buy coffee except Shorty's," he said. "And their coffee tastes like sludge. But it's my lunch hour and I'd sure take a beer with my burger."

"Lead the way." I turned to Ella. "Thanks for your help. Bring you something?"

"Why, thank you," she said with a smile. "I'd take a nice cold root beer."

Stan and I walked down to Shorty's. It looked the way I expected, like every dive bar I'd ever been in, with red vinyl booths and a
scuffed black-and-white checkerboard linoleum floor. There was a
TV attached to the wall over the bar, with the sound thankfully lowered and replaced by captions, showing some news program. On the
jukebox, Irma Thomas was singing "I Wish Someone Would Care."
The place was doing a brisk lunch-hour trade. The air was redolent
with the smell of grilled meat, onions and grease.

Stan and I slid into a vacant booth near the front. "Don't let the
funky looks fool you," he said. "They make great burgers here."

"Sounds good to me." It had been a while since breakfast and
I was hungry. I reached for the plastic-covered menu propped up
between bottles of ketchup, mustard and the inevitable Louisiana
Tabasco sauce, and consulted the short list of offerings.

A woman wearing jeans and a red T-shirt came over to our
booth. Her long dangling earrings jingled as she moved. "Hey, Stan.
Your usual?"

"Absolutely. Cheeseburger with grilled onions, medium rare,
with fries. And bring me an Abita Turbodog."

"Make that two Turbodogs," I said. "Bacon cheeseburger, with
cheddar, cooked medium. I'll try those sweet potato fries. And I'll
take an ice-cold Abita root beer to go later, on my way out the door."

"You got it," she said and headed for the kitchen.

It was the kind of place where you drink your beer out of a bottle
rather than a glass, I thought, and I was proved right when the server
delivered our Turbodogs. I raised the bottle to my lips and drank. It
went down easy and now the odors coming from the kitchen were
enticing.

Stan took a long pull from his own bottle and set it on the table.
"Hits the spot. So, Jeri, is this on the level?"

"It is." I took two business cards from my bag, mine and
Antoine's. I laid them on the table. "I'm a private eye, but I'm not
local. I'm in town on vacation and one of my friends from the Bay
Area calls me, tells me her sister disappeared with her boyfriend, a
guy named Slade. The sister quit her job, gave up her apartment, the

whole nine yards. She and Slade loaded all their stuff into an SUV and vanished. She hasn't gotten in touch with her family. My friend is worried and so are her parents. I contacted another private eye here in town. That's his card. He'll vouch for me if you want to call him."

Stan examined the cards, then he looked up at me. "No, I'm good. I believe you."

"Great. And thanks." I stopped as the server placed our lunches on the table. Melted cheddar oozed from beneath the bun. After doctoring the burger with condiments, I took a bite. Stan was right, the burgers were terrific. "So, you were Slade's supervisor. Ella says you let him go."

"I fired his ass." Stan set his burger on the plate and pulled paper napkins from a dispenser on the table. He wiped his hands and mouth, then reached for the fries, popping a handful into his mouth. "That guy Slade, he was a slacker. He never showed up on time, took off early, sometimes he just wouldn't show up at all. And he was mouthy. Always had something to say. Better at running his mouth than he was at doing his job."

"Which was?"

"Stocker," he said, picking up his burger again. "He was supposed to keep the shelves stocked after we got deliveries, keep on top of inventory, that sort of thing. But Slade didn't do a lick of work unless I dogged him. And I had to dog him all the time. I don't think he ever held a full-time job in his life. I bet you dollars to doughnuts all that stuff on his job application was a work of fiction."

"I don't suppose you could let me have a look at that application," I said, a hopeful note in my voice.

He shook his head. "I don't suppose I could. Who I talk to on my lunch hour is my business, but letting you have a peek at company paperwork wouldn't go down too well."

"I understand. But it was worth a try." I took another bite of my burger.

"So yeah," Stan continued, "I fired him. January, right after Christmas. He'd worked here since October. During that time, I gave him a couple of warnings, telling him that number three would be termination. Came the time he messed up again, I fired him. The boss backed me up. We told him to clear out his locker and get off the premises. He was pissed."

I considered this, setting down my burger in favor of the sweet potato fries. "Is he the type to get even?"

"Oh, yeah. He did. He started a fire."

Fire? That got my attention. I leaned toward Stan. "Are you sure it was Slade?"

"If you mean, did I see him do it, no. But it was him. Had to be." He took a swig of beer. "A fire in a place like that, all the paper and chemicals we've got in that warehouse. Somebody could have been hurt. Hell, somebody could have been killed."

I thought about the fire at the apartment Slade had rented. Somebody was killed there. Slade had a whiff of smoke about him and that was disturbing.

"Tell me what happened."

"It was two days after I told Slade he was fired. We work eight to five, sometimes later. The place empties out by evening and this part of town is deserted. Shorty's closes by midnight. So it was about one in the morning when I got the call. Got here in time to watch the fire department put out the fire. It caused a lot of damage. Not so much from the fire itself, but the sprinklers. Everything in that part of the warehouse was soaked. I don't have a dollar figure, but I know Mr. Melancon was upset, big time. The fire department guys said it was arson. Slade got in and piled up a bunch of stuff, doused it with some kind of liquid, they said, and set it off."

"How would Slade get into the place? I assume you terminated his access when you fired him."

"We certainly did. The employees get access by swiping a card on a key pad."

"So he came over the fence," I said. "It looks like it's eight feet tall."

"Yeah, I think it is. I couldn't climb it, but it would be easy enough for a young guy like Slade to climb over. There's no razor wire on top."

"How did he get into the building itself? Did he break a window? Would that have triggered an alarm?"

Stan shook his head, his burger in midair. "He didn't break a window. There's one door on the back side of the warehouse that opens with a key. I figure Slade must have swiped that key and had a duplicate made. It's got DO NOT DUPLICATE stamped on it, but locksmiths have been known to ignore that. At least that's my theory. I sure as hell can't prove it. And at that time of night, it should have triggered an alarm. But the damn thing had been jimmied. He planned it. He got that key made and disabled the alarm, then he went inside and started that fire. The son of a bitch." Stan frowned and went back to work on his burger.

"Security cameras?" I asked.

"Yeah, we got them. I heard they picked up a blurry image of a guy wearing a hoodie. Not much help."

When we'd finished our lunch, the server delivered the check, along with the root beer, the bottle icy cold to the touch. I grabbed the check. "This is on me, Stan. You've been very helpful."

I covered the check with bills and slid out of the booth, picking up the root beer. Ella was delighted when I delivered it to her in the office. Stan headed back to the warehouse and I walked to my rental car.

I checked my phone for messages. Antoine had called, twice. I called him back. "I have plenty to tell you," I said.

"Same here," he said. "Let's meet at my office and compare notes."

⚐ Chapter Twelve

"FIRE AND BRIMSTONE," I said. "It can't be a coincidence. Slade gets fired from his job at Melancon Supply in January. Two days later, there's a fire in the warehouse. Slade gets evicted from Pat Doucette's apartment building in February. Two weeks later, that particular unit goes up in smoke."

"With Ray Brixton inside," Antoine said.

We were at his kitchen table and he was eating an oyster po' boy, the ubiquitous New Orleans sandwich served on French bread. After my burger and fries at Shorty's, I wasn't even tempted to snatch a bite, although the sandwich was bursting with fried oysters.

"It's looking more and more like Slade set those fires, first at the warehouse, then at the apartment, to get back at Pat for evicting him. But why was Brixton there?" I was thinking out loud. "Was he an accomplice? Did he come along to help Slade set the fire? Or is something else going on? Something we're not seeing yet? We have to talk with Cindy Brixton."

Antoine nodded in agreement. He set his sandwich on the array of paper towels that served as a plate, then wiped his mouth with another towel. "She's not returning my calls. My contact at the fire department says she travels for work, so I'm thinking she's out of town. I say we go over to where she lives. I've got her address. In the meantime, we've got two leads to check out, the car dealership and the other musician."

Between bites of his po' boy, he had told me that his sister, Daisy, had called him earlier in the day. She'd been asking around and had come up with the name and phone number of another guitar player who knew Slade. The guy had a day job, like many of the local musicians. We'd called and left a message, hoping that he'd return the call.

"What about Laurette's car?" I asked. "You found out something?"

Antoine got up from the table, wrapped up the rest of his sandwich and stashed it in the refrigerator. As he washed his hands at the sink, he said, "Yeah. My buddy at the Office of Motor Vehicles came through. We help each other out now and then."

"A little *quid pro quo* never hurts. What did you find out?"

"Laurette went back to the same dealership where she bought the Civic. Which makes sense. That's what I'd do if I was going to trade in my car."

"Great. Let's take a ride over there."

He jingled his key ring. "I'll drive."

The Honda dealership was in Metairie, in Jefferson Parish, on the other side of the Seventeenth Street Canal. We located the salesman who'd handled the deal. He was a round-faced man in his forties, wearing a lightweight gray suit and a name tag that said his name was Ron. At first, he didn't want to give us any information, citing privacy concerns. We told him why we were there and offered to give him the Tedescos' phone numbers, so he could verify our story.

He shook his head and pointed us toward his office, a glass-enclosed space looking out on the showroom. "I'm sorry to hear that Ms. Mason is missing. I can't show you the paperwork or anything like that. But ask your questions and I'll answer them if I can."

"I just want to make sure we're talking about the same person," Antoine said. "She traded in a green Honda Civic." He consulted a slip of paper and rattled off the license plate number.

Ron took a seat at the desk and his fingers played over the keyboard. He squinted at the computer screen, then nodded. "That's right. That's the plate number on the Honda she traded in. She and the young man with her picked out a Ford Escape, red, with a gray interior."

"What's the plate number on that Ford?" Antoine asked.

Ron grabbed a slip of paper and a pen, jotting down the number. He handed it to Antoine, who showed it to me. Bert, the manager at Laurette's apartment, had been right about the double fours in the license number.

"What can you tell us about the man she was with?" I asked.

"I didn't talk with him," Ron said. "I did the transaction with her. She had the trade-in and the cash. The Civic was in her name. I assumed he was a friend of hers, along for the ride, so to speak, to help her pick out another vehicle. He went on the test drive with her and it came down to a choice between the Ford and another Honda. They talked it over. I heard a bit of that conversation. He was pushing for the Ford, because it was bigger." The salesman leaned back in his chair. "The guy was talking on a cell phone most of the time. In fact, at one point he got so loud one of the other dealers asked him to step outside. He acted as though he was going to get belligerent about that, but Ms. Mason talked with him. Eventually he did go outside."

"Did you overhear any of his end of the phone conversation?"

Ron thought about it for a moment. "Not much. But I did hear him say something about Kerrville. That's a town in the Texas hill country."

"What about Ms. Mason?" Antoine asked. "Did she say anything about plans to go somewhere?"

"She said she wanted to get a larger vehicle because they were going on a road trip," Ron said. "I don't recall that she said where they were going, just that she would be seeing a part of the country she hadn't seen before."

That could be a big section of the country, I thought. Laurette had spent almost her whole life living in New Orleans. Most of her family was here, except for that cousin in Florida. But the Texas hill country could be a clue, along with Slade's former address in Austin. Could be, she and Slade were headed west.

We headed back to Antoine's RAV4. We drove through New Orleans, into the Treme neighborhood. Then traffic came to a standstill and Antoine pulled over to the curb. "It's a parade," he said. "You've been in New Orleans a week. Have you seen a second line?"

"No, I haven't. I was hoping to."

We got out of the RAV4 and walked up the block, just in time to see a brass band playing "I Feel Like Funkin' It Up." People danced along the pavement, some of them wearing elaborate and colorful costumes made of satin, decorated with sequins and feathers. They carried banners proclaiming the name of their social club. Following in their wake were other people walking and dancing, some of them twirling parasols. Others waved handkerchiefs and bandannas in time to the music.

"This is the first line," Antoine said. "Sometimes they call it the main line. The band, and those people in the club that hold the parade permit. Those people following, that's the second line."

"Cool. And this is different from a jazz funeral, right?"

"Right. No casket, obviously. Going to the cemetery, the music is usually slow and solemn. Then maybe on the way back after the interment, the band plays something lively."

The brass band drew near. Antoine and I joined the second line and I laughed as he showed me the steps. We second-lined with the parade for several blocks, enjoying the music and the festive atmosphere.

"I think I'm getting the hang of this," I said. The parade reached an intersection and slowly turned to the right.

At that moment, Antoine's phone rang and he took the call. He gave a thumbs-up signal and from his end of the conversation I knew the musician had returned his call. "Be there in fifteen minutes," he said, then ended the call. He looked up at me. "We're in luck. The guy just got off work and he'll talk with us."

Luis Ortega worked for a local delivery firm with an office on South Galvez, a block or so off Canal Street. When we caught up with him, he was outside the building, stashing a backpack in the trunk of his blue Subaru hatchback. He was in his early thirties, with wide-set brown eyes and dark hair curling around his face.

He definitely had the Texas twang. "So you're Daisy Lasalle's brother," he said, when Antoine made the introductions. "I've met Daisy a time or two. She's really a great singer."

Antoine smiled. "Yeah, she's pretty good, even if she is my kid sister."

"How can I help you folks?" Ortega asked, looking from Antoine to me.

"We're looking for information on a guitar player named Slade," I said, watching as Ortega frowned. "You know him?"

"Well, I wouldn't say I know him. Not well, anyway. He's not a friend, you understand. Just musicians, you know. We both play guitar. I play bass and slide."

"That's cool," Antoine said with a shrug. "Just tell us what you know."

"I know him from back in Texas," Ortega said. "That's where I'm from, down around San Antonio. Before I made the move to New Orleans, I was playing gigs in Austin."

"When did you meet Slade?" I asked. "And how?"

Ortega leaned against the rear bumper of his Subaru. "It was last year. My band was playing at Kerrville. That's about an hour west of Austin. They got a big music festival there, the Kerrville Folk Festival. It runs late May to early June. Slade was in a band that was playing there. He was subbing for a regular band member. That was a stroke of luck, for him to get a gig with a band that was playing there. Because when I was talking with him, I got the impression he hadn't been in Texas that long. He said he'd been in a band that broke up, so he decided to try his luck in Austin. I figured that gig at the festival made him think getting gigs in Austin would be easy from then on. But the music business is up and down. Every musician knows that, or ought to." Ortega laughed and pointed at the building where he worked. "Me, I'm here delivering packages. We've all got day jobs, just to survive, so we can gig at night."

"True that," Antoine said, using a New Orleans expression I'd heard many times since I'd been here.

"Later," Ortega continued, "I'd see Slade in Austin from time to time. It's like that. You see the same people over and over. Sometimes Slade would be subbing in the band I was playing with. Same here in New Orleans. I moved here last fall. The band I was in back in Austin split up and I decided to try my luck in the Big Easy. There's a great music scene here. It's different from Austin, though."

"So you get to New Orleans and run into Slade again," Antoine prompted.

Ortega nodded. "Yeah. January, after Christmas, it was. I was playing with a band at a Bourbon Street club. Slade was with the group that was the opening act. We got together after the show, had a beer and talked. He wasn't in a regular band, he was just subbing that particular gig. We talked about gigs and music and New Orleans." Ortega shrugged. "I got the impression he was not feeling the NOLA love like I am."

"What does that mean?" I asked.

"I think he was expecting to do better here. Like he thought New Orleans is the Holy Grail for the music scene. Of course, when he was in Texas, he was talking like Austin was the place to be. Anyway, when I saw him on Bourbon Street, he talked like he was having a hard time getting gigs in New Orleans. As far as I could tell, he had only been here a few months. I said, Look, man, you need to give it more time. But he was talking about going back to Austin. Said he'd been working steady there. I don't know if that's true or not. Maybe it was just him talking."

I considered this. It was possible, given what I was hearing, that Slade decided that New Orleans wasn't all it was cracked up to be. If he wasn't working as much as he had back in Texas, that would make sense. And he could have persuaded Laurette, who by some accounts was ready for a change, to go with him. But still... There was something that didn't sit right with me. One look at Antoine told me he was thinking the same thing. It was the fires, at the apartment, at the warehouse.

"I guess it would make sense to go back to Austin," Antoine said. "If he figured he'd get more gigs."

"Maybe that was it. Me, ever since I got to New Orleans, I'm playing steady all the time." Ortega laughed. "Of course, I'm easier to get along with than Slade is."

I nodded. "Give me an example."

He thought about it for a moment. "He gets touchy, you know. If things aren't going his way."

Antoine and I traded looks. "I heard that. Can you give me an example? Did he ever get into a disagreement or argument with someone here in New Orleans? Or in Austin?"

Ortega took his time answering. "Well, I heard something, but I don't know if it's true. It's like thirdhand news. Don't they call that hearsay?"

"They do," I said. "But tell me what you heard. We might check it out."

"Well, I heard he got into some sort of a pissing contest with a guy, back in Austin. They played a few gigs together and they were best buddies. And then they weren't. I remember it because this other guy had a new car, he'd just bought it, and one night somebody torched it."

Fire and brimstone, I thought again. It looked like Slade's favored method of getting even was to strike a match. I didn't like it, not at all.

"The guy whose car was torched, do you recall his name?" I asked.

Ortega rubbed his chin, as he thought about it, then he shook his head. "Sorry. I don't."

"Do you know a guy named Ray Brixton?" Antoine asked.

Ortega looked perplexed, then his face cleared. "The name's familiar. Like maybe I met him once or twice. Plays guitar. Pretty good, as a matter of fact. Yeah, I did meet him. At a club on Frenchmen Street. He and Slade were playing in the same band at that particular gig. I heard later there was some bad blood between the two of them."

"Any idea why?"

He shook his head. "Not really. It's just something I heard." He paused, then looked thoughtful. "Seems to me it could have been about money. But I'm not sure. You could ask Brixton, but you know, I haven't seen him in a while. I'm wondering if he left town."

Brixton was gone, all right. He was dead.

I had another question for Ortega. "When Slade was talking about that band he was in that broke up, did he say anything about where he was from? Or the name of the band?"

"Not really," he said. "He mentioned California, but nothing specific about where in California. Big state, you know. As for the name of the band—" He shook his head again. "If he said the name, I don't remember." Then he stopped and cocked his head to one side. "Wait a minute. He said the band broke up because one of the players decided to come to Austin. And Slade decided to do that, too. It was—" He snapped his fingers, once, twice, then he grinned. "The Flames. That's what he said. The Flames."

Chapter Thirteen

"SLADE IS FROM CALIFORNIA," I said. "Or at least he lived in California before he moved to Austin. The rental application says he worked for a flooring company in Concord, in Contra Costa County. And the person he listed as his emergency contact has an area code from the Bay Area, which could be either Contra Costa or Alameda County."

"Let's see what the reverse directory has to say." Antoine's fingers moved across his computer keyboard.

After talking with Ortega, we'd gone back to Antoine's shotgun house in the Treme. He was in his office chair and I'd brought a chair in from the kitchen. We were looking at his computer monitor, where he'd opened an Internet browser. Now he typed in the ten-digit phone number for Millicent Patchett, the emergency contact on Slade's apartment rental application. We got an address in Lafayette, California.

I made a guess as I jotted down the address. "His mother. I'd bet money on it. Let's see what we can find out about that band he was in, the Flames."

We didn't find much on the band, or its gigs. These days, with the Internet, bands make videos and post them on YouTube or a website, but we couldn't find either for the Flames. Antoine kept searching, typing in keywords and clicking links. Finally he said, "Here's something."

I looked at the screen. It was a small article, no more than two paragraphs, listing the lineup for a concert at a festival in Brent-wood, in the eastern part of Contra Costa County. And it listed the Flames, saying the group featured Eric Slade on lead guitar, Cam Gardner on bass and slide guitars, and Marsh Spencer on drums. The accompanying photograph was black-and-white and grainy. Antoine enlarged it. Slade and Spencer looked about the same age, while Gardner appeared to be a few years older.

Antoine typed in Marsh Spencer's name. "Nothing else on Spen-cer, at least nothing relating to music. Maybe he's given it up. Let's see if we have better luck with Cam Gardner."

We did. Gardner looked like a serious musician, one determined to build his career. He had his own website, with links to a calendar and a Facebook page. He was based in Austin now and it looked as though he was working steadily, playing gigs all over town, and farther afield in Texas. According to the Facebook page, he was working as a studio musician on several recordings.

His website led us to a list of links for videos, mostly of Gard-ner playing with various bands. But at the bottom of the list, we found two early videos of the Flames. In the first, the group was performing at a club in Concord. The second was from a club in Oakland.

Antoine and I watched both of them. At the Concord gig, the Flames were performing "Light My Fire," which had been a huge hit for the Doors back in the 1960s. Slade was singing, attempting to channel Jim Morrison, but not quite succeeding. I was no judge of his guitar playing, or that of Gardner. The drummer, Spencer, was high-energy, bouncing on his stool and flailing away at the drums and cymbals. It seemed like he couldn't sit still. Between numbers he moved restlessly, tugging at his earlobe.

In the second video, the one from the Oakland club, the group sounded more polished as they worked their way through a fairly decent cover of the Subdudes' "All the Time in the World."

When the video ended, I said, "They're not bad. Just not that good either. Of course, I don't know anything about guitar playing or drumming. Slade's voice isn't that remarkable."

"Sometimes you don't have to be that good," Antoine said. "There are a lot of singers out there with voices that don't have much polish, but they make it work. They hustle and they stick with it."

"Point taken. It looks like Austin was a good move for Gardner. Maybe that's why Slade relocated to Texas, following in Gardner's footsteps. But he didn't stay long. He showed up in New Orleans in October. That's when he got the job at Melancon Supply and the apartment on Marais Street. So he spent barely six months in Austin."

Antoine nodded. "Impatience. That's what my sister says. A lot of musicians show up in New Orleans, or Austin, thinking they're God's gift to the music world. Then reality bites them in the butt. There are a lot of musicians in this town, as thick as flies on honey. The competition for gigs is fierce. That's why so many of them are playing on street corners, like the kids we saw on Frenchmen Street, for whatever cash people toss into the hat. It's not a matter of catching breaks. Like I said, you have to hustle to get those gigs and stay working. Got to keep with it, no matter how many times you get turned down. That's why Daisy's doing gigs at the Spotted Cat and Slade isn't. Daisy's been singing since she was in middle school and hustling for gigs about that long, too."

"What about luck? That must be a factor, too. Being in the right place at the right time."

"Daisy would say that behind every lucky break is someone who's been working at it for years," Antoine said.

"I would imagine that where you live is also important." I was thinking out loud here. "It would be hard to be a working musician in some small town at the back of beyond, though I'm sure some people are. It seems that every kid who has a guitar winds up with a band, even if it's playing gigs at the local high school. But if Slade does come from the Bay Area, the business about small towns and limited opportunity doesn't really apply here."

"Unless it's limited talent," Antoine said. "And that impatience I'm talking about."

"So Slade's impatient," I said. "He's not willing to do the hard work. He wasn't an instantaneous success in Austin, so he moved to New Orleans. Same story here. He's getting gigs, but it's hard to pay the bills, so he has to get the job at the warehouse. He gets fired from that. He gets evicted from his apartment and uses that as an excuse to move in with Laurette, so he's not paying rent. Now what? It looks like he's impatient with New Orleans, too. So he's leaving town, with Laurette. Somehow I don't think it's because he's madly in love with her."

"He's driving an old, beat-up car," Antoine said.

"But not anymore. He sells that car for whatever cash he can get. Then he persuades Laurette to trade in her Honda and buy a newer Ford. So now, in addition to Laurette, he's got the keys to a much better car. But where are they going? Where is there a better music scene than the two places he's already been—Austin and New Orleans?"

Antoine looked speculative. "New York City? Too expensive, is my guess. We got Memphis and Nashville. Maybe Chicago. Going west, Los Angeles. Or maybe up to Seattle."

"I think he's headed back to the Bay Area. Millicent Patchett must be his mother. So he's got family there." I paused. "We've got to follow up on what Ortega said about the car fire in Austin. A case of Slade getting even again?"

Antoine rubbed his chin. "I know a guy in Austin. I'll call him. In the meantime, we ought to contact Cam Gardner and see what he has to say about his former guitar-playing buddy."

The only contact information we could find for Cam Gardner was a "Contact Me" form on his website. Antoine filled out the form and sent it on its way. With luck, Gardner would get back to us.

Antoine called his friend in Austin, got voice mail and left a message. No sooner had he hung up the phone than it rang again. "That number," he said. "It's Cindy Brixton."

He answered the phone and put it on speaker. "Ms. Brixton? This is Antoine Lasalle. Thank you for returning my call."

The woman on the other end had a sharp, suspicious voice. "You keep calling me and leaving messages saying you want to talk about my brother. What is this about? You say you're an investigator. For who? Are you working for some insurance company? I've talked with the cops and the fire department people. What's your angle?"

I leaned toward the speaker. "This is Jeri Howard, Ms. Brixton. I'm working with Mr. Lasalle. We're private investigators, looking for information on a man named Eric Slade."

"That's right," Antoine added. "My contact at the fire department tells me you might have some things to say about him."

There was silence on the other end of the phone. As it stretched out I wondered if Cindy Brixton had ended the call. Then she spoke, her voice sounding subdued.

"I have plenty to say about Slade. I'm at home. Come on over." She rattled off the address.

⚜

Cindy Brixton had to be the woman who'd confronted Slade at Laurette's apartment.

She was tall, nearly six feet, and slender, with a body that seemed to be all angles. Her blond hair was short and sculpted around her head. She wore khaki cropped pants and a lime-green cotton shirt, her feet bare. I pegged her age as early thirties. Her manner was brisk and businesslike as she greeted us at her front door. She lived in a two-story double-gallery house on Terpsichore Street in the Lower Garden District. It was just off St. Charles Avenue, close enough that I could hear the streetcars going by. The house had been converted into condos and she had one of the upstairs units.

She ushered us into the living room furnished with sleek, modern furniture and waved us toward the sofa. "Can I get you something to drink? I've got iced tea and beer. In fact, I've already started." She indicated the end table, where a bottle of Abita Amber sat on a coaster.

"A beer would be great," I said. Antoine agreed.

Cindy headed for the kitchen and came back with two more bottles of Abita. I took a swallow of beer, enjoying the cold brew. Cindy sat cross-legged in a chair covered with a green-and-yellow geometric print. She picked up her beer bottle from the end table and took a sip, then cradled it in her hand. "Why are you looking for information on Slade?"

"He seems to have disappeared," I said.

"And we'd like to find out why," Antoine added. "And get a line on where he went."

"Disappeared?" She gave a short derisive snort. "That doesn't surprise me. That son of a bitch killed my brother. He knew I wasn't going to let go of that, no matter what the cops or fire department did—or didn't do. He's probably running for cover. I don't have any idea where, but I sure as hell hope the past catches up with him."

She leaned over and picked up a small framed photograph. I recognized the young man in the picture. This was the same photo that had appeared in Ray Brixton's obituary.

"Was it you?" I asked. "Waylaying Slade outside the apartment building a couple of weeks ago?"

"Yes, that was me. I'll bet that's why he left town."

"We don't know for sure that he left town," Antoine said. "We think so, but we don't have any confirmation of that. Right now, we're trying to find out everything that went down and make some sense of it all."

Cindy looked at Ray's photo. "It's been seven weeks. The police rang my doorbell and told me my brother was dead. My baby brother. Damn it."

Her voice broke and a crack appeared in her armor. She brushed away a tear, then set the photo on the table. The wound of her brother's death was still fresh. Not surprising. That kind of hurt doesn't go away.

"Why do you think Slade killed your brother?" I asked.

She took a sip of beer. Then her mouth settled into a firm, nononsense line. "Slade owed my brother money. That's what started it. Ray never should have loaned money to that bastard. But my brother was too damn soft-hearted. He was an easy touch. All he had to hear was that a fellow musician was having troubles. He would take out his wallet, or give the guy the shirt off his back, that sort of thing."

"I hear that," Antoine said. "Did Ray say why Slade needed money?"

"According to Ray," Cindy said, "Slade was having car troubles. He needed cash to get his piece-of-junk car fixed so he could take his equipment from gig to gig. I guess he was hitting up a bunch of musicians and he found my brother. Who unfortunately was an easy mark for Slade's scams. After a while, Ray was having some money troubles of his own. I offered to loan him some cash, but he said no, said this guy owed him money and he'd get it from him. So my brother wanted to get paid back and this creep Slade kept putting him off. Finally Ray told me he was going to meet Slade and get the money. He said Slade told him to meet him at his apartment. Turns out it wasn't his apartment anymore, he'd been evicted. He must have kept a key, because that's where my brother went to meet him. Next thing I know, I've got a couple of cops on my doorstep, telling me Ray's dead."

She grimaced and stopped talking, fighting down the emotions that made her voice shake. I gave her a moment to compose herself, then asked, "What do you think happened?"

"I think my brother went to that apartment to meet Slade and Slade killed him. Then he torched the place to cover it up. I can't understand why the cops haven't arrested that bastard and charged him with my brother's murder." Her hand tightened on the beer bottle. "Now you tell me Slade is missing. He must have known they were coming up on his ass and he left town. That son of a bitch. If I ever catch up with him, I'll…"

Later, as we left Cindy's condo, I said, "It could be the reason. She's pressuring the authorities, convinced Ray was murdered. Then she tracks Slade down to Laurette's apartment, confronts him. So he decides to leave."

"And persuades Laurette to go with him?" Antoine nodded. "Possible. I wonder what happened, there at Slade's apartment."

"We may never know. But what Cindy told us might fit. Slade and Ray meet at the apartment. Ray thinks he's going to get his money. They get into some sort of altercation, Ray's hurt, or dead. Slade sets a fire to cover his tracks."

Now that we were outside, I pulled out my cell phone. I'd silenced it before we went to Cindy's condo. I leaned against Antoine's RAV4 and looked at the screen. I had two voice mails. The first was from Davina and the second from her mother.

I listened to Davina's message first. Her voice sounded excited. "Jeri, we've heard from Laurette. Call me as soon as you get this."

◿ Chapter Fourteen

SABINE TEDESCO'S MESSAGE said much the same, asking me to come over to the Tedescos' house as soon as possible. I relayed the message to Antoine and we headed for Mid-City. As he drove, I returned Davina's call. It went to voice mail and I left a message, saying we were heading for her folks' house.

When we arrived, I introduced Antoine to George and Sabine.

"Laurette called," Sabine said, excited. "She said she and Slade are on a road trip and that she's sorry she didn't check in sooner, but she lost her phone. I'm so relieved to hear from her. I guess I was overreacting. I'm sorry about that. You had to stay in town looking for clues. But it's all right now. Thank goodness."

Overreacting? I didn't think so. Not with all I'd learned about Slade in the past few days. But I kept my opinion to myself, for the time being.

"She sent a video," George added. "Would you like to see it?"

"Yes, I would."

Sabine picked up her smart phone and accessed the video. It was about twenty seconds long. Laurette was outside, her long brown hair ruffled by a breeze, and she was laughing as she talked. "Hi, Mom and Dad. I just want to let you know that I'm all right. Lost my phone, got a new one now. Slade and I are on a road trip. We've been to San Antonio and Austin and some other cool places. I love seeing all these places I haven't been before. Now that I have a phone I'll be in touch more often. Love you. Bye!"

"When you talked with her on the phone, before she sent the video, did she say where they were right now?" Antoine asked.

Sabine looked confused. "She said San Antonio and Austin, on the video."

I shook my head. "They're in Santa Fe. At least they were there when the video was shot."

Antoine shot me a look. "How do you know that?"

"Play the video again. I'll show you." Sabine started the video, then handed the phone to me. About midway through, I touched the screen and paused the playback. I pointed at a building behind Laurette, long and made of adobe, with thick wooden pillars. "That's the Palace of the Governors, on the Plaza in Santa Fe. I'm sure of it."

Sure of it, I thought, because that's where Dan was, in Santa Fe, New Mexico, working on his travel book. He'd sent me a photo of the Santa Fe Plaza just two days ago, showing the native American vendors selling pottery and jewelry at the Palace of the Governors.

"They have adobe buildings in Austin, too," George pointed out.

"True enough, but I've been to Santa Fe and this looks like the Palace."

"Texas or New Mexico, they're still out of town and a long way from New Orleans," Antoine said.

When I found out Slade had lived in Austin before coming to New Orleans, I'd entertained the notion that he'd decided to move back to Texas. Admittedly, that theory was fueled by Luis Ortega's comment that Slade was finding it difficult to break into the NOLA music scene and was thinking about returning to Austin, or heading for another city to try working the music scene there.

Now Laurette said they were on a road trip. That implied that eventually, they'd come back to New Orleans.

But I wasn't so sure.

After leaving the Tedescos' house, Antoine drove back to his place in Treme, so I could pick up the rental car I'd left parked there. I then turned in the car, since I was heading home the next day. At the hotel's business center, I used one of the computers to book a seat on a nonstop flight home to Oakland.

When Antoine arrived, we walked over to Bayona, on Dauphine Street. Antoine ordered the pork chop with dirty rice and smothered greens. My plate held sautéed redfish with spinach and fingerling potatoes. It was delicious, just like the earlier meals I'd had at this restaurant.

Now, as we talked, I made patterns with my fork in the sauce on the plate. "This may be over as far as Laurette's family is concerned, but I don't think so."

Antoine cut a slice from his grilled pork chop. "You're preaching to the choir. I agree with you, a hundred percent. The Tedescos seem to be satisfied that Laurette is safe, but I'm not."

I nodded as I speared a potato. "First of all, I don't like this business of Laurette not calling her family because she lost her phone. She could have used Slade's phone to call them. I am assuming he has one. Almost everyone these days does."

"I'm with you there. I'm not buying it. Sounds like they wanted to be off the grid for a while." Antoine raised a forkful of rice to his mouth.

"We've found out too much about Slade, too much that's disturbing. It bears following up. I can give it some *pro bono* time."

"Same here." He paused and reached for his wineglass. "I'll work the Austin angle, when my buddy there calls me back."

"And I'll head back to California and check out Millicent Patchett." I ate some redfish and sighed. "I've been gone for over a week. I'm sure I've got plenty of work waiting for me. It will take a while to dig myself out."

We talked of other things as we finished our meal and the bottle of wine we shared. When the server brought the dessert menu, we decided on coffee and one shared dessert, the peanut butter banana pie, which had toasted meringue and candied peanuts. It was delicious, but I could only eat a few bites. Antoine had no such compunctions. He finished it off.

It would be good to get home, but I certainly had enjoyed the food in New Orleans. Antoine and I left the restaurant and strolled back through the French Quarter to my hotel. We said good-bye and I headed up to my room. Tomorrow I'd have one last foray to Café du Monde for *café au lait* and *beignets*. Then Antoine would take me to the airport.

I couldn't get past the unsettled feeling I had about Laurette, Slade and this case I considered unfinished. But George and Sabine Tedesco had been overjoyed to hear from Laurette, to know that she was alive and apparently just fine.

After I had my nightly check-in with Dan, I got ready for bed. Then Davina returned my call. "I'm sorry I sent you off on a fool's errand," she said. "I know how busy you are. And you had to stay extra days in New Orleans. I'll make it up to you, I promise."

"There's nothing wrong with extra days in the Big Easy," I told her. "We'll talk when I get home."

◿Chapter Fifteen

AS THE JET BROKE THROUGH the cloud cover, I looked out the window. My flight was due to land at Oakland International Airport at six-thirty Friday evening. Sunset reflected on the water transformed San Francisco Bay into a shimmering pool of copper and gold. Below me, I saw the flat white salt evaporation ponds at the southern end of the bay. Ahead were the bridges, the Dumbarton and then the San Mateo, alive with cars and trucks during the evening commute, head- and tail-lights twinkling as vehicles crossed the spans. In the distance was the Bay Bridge and the San Francisco skyline.

Home. And glad to be there. Or almost there. Home to my cats, home to my own comfortable house and familiar surroundings, my routine. As Dad always said, it's nice to get away, and it's even better to come home and sleep in one's own bed.

I shifted in my window seat as the flight attendant came by and asked the man on the aisle to put his seat upright. We were coming into Oakland, over the water now as we approached the runways that had been built on the land reclaimed from the bay. The plane touched down, a fairly smooth landing, and taxied to the gate at the end of Terminal Two. I turned on my phone and found a text message from Madison Brady, the tenant in my garage apartment, who was picking me up at the airport. Her message said she was waiting in the Park-and-Call lot. I responded, telling her we'd just landed. Once I'd collected my suitcase, I sent another text message to Madison, letting her know that I'd be waiting at the end of the passenger pick-up area.

Outside, mist was in the air, damp and cool, with the promise of rain. Indeed, to the northwest I saw clouds, high and dark blue in the sky. After the New Orleans heat, the chill felt good. A few minutes later, Madison's Subaru hatchback pulled up to the curb. I hefted my suitcase into the back cargo space and got in.

"Welcome back." Madison checked her side mirror, then pulled away from the curb, entering the flow of traffic. "Your fur babies will be so glad you're home."

"I'm glad I'm home. Can't wait to hug the kitties."

"Black Bart always acts like it's my fault that you're gone," she said. "Abigail, not so much. She sleeps a lot."

"I know. She's getting old." I'd had Abigail, my tabby cat, since she was a tiny kitten, just out of the litter and small enough to fit in the palm of my hand. She was elderly now, a geriatric cat, and I dreaded the thought of losing her. Black Bart had been a kitten, too, somewhat older when he showed up on the patio at my old apartment. I had put out food and water for the little guy and it had taken a while for him to trust me enough so that I could catch him.

"Everything's fine," Madison continued. "I watered your indoor plants and brought in the mail. The outside garden looks good. We had rain several times while you were gone. Did you solve whatever case it was that developed in New Orleans?"

I didn't normally talk about cases with civilians, but Madison wasn't exactly that. She was a graduate student, working on her master's degree in City Planning at the University of California in Berkeley. We'd met last fall when she came to me after the death of her father, a man I'd worked with at the Seville Agency. Madison was sure her father's demise wasn't an accident. She was right. Cal Brady had been murdered and I helped find his killers. At the time that case was winding down, the previous tenant of the studio apartment above my garage was moving out. I asked Madison if she wanted to take over the rental. At the time she had been sharing an apartment with several other grad students and had jumped at the chance to have a place of her own. That gave me a live-in caretaker and cat-sitter, whenever the need arose.

"Let's just say I got the answers to some questions, and I have still more questions," I said now. "Which will have to wait, though. Business was slow when Dad and I left for New Orleans, but I have a lot of catching up to do when I get to the office tomorrow."

We talked about New Orleans—the food, the music, the architecture and ambiance—the rest of the way home. The first thing I did when I came through my front door, from this and any other trip, was pick up Abigail and snuggle her close. She meowed indignantly, as she always did. Her vocalizations were easily translated. "Where were you? How dare you leave me alone?" She also gave me plenty of welcome-back head butts, using the scent glands that cats have on their heads to mark me as her own and eliminate any alien smells. Of course, Abigail hadn't been alone in the house. For company she'd had Black Bart. He was mostly black, but he had one white forepaw and an uneven white mask. That's why I had named him after the elusive California bandit who robbed stagecoaches. As was usually the case when I'd been away for a time, he hid in the bedroom closet until he was sure that it was me, then he sauntered out, his tail up, to greet me in his own way.

I unpacked and put away my suitcase. Most of the clothing went into the laundry basket, to be dealt with when I got around to it. Then I got ready for bed. It wasn't yet eight o'clock, but I was tired, and still on New Orleans time, two time zones ahead. I climbed into bed and made a couple of phone calls. The first was to Dad, letting him know that I was home. We made plans to meet for dinner on Saturday night. Then I called Dan. He was in the Jemez Mountains north of Santa Fe, at Los Alamos, site of the World War II–era Manhattan Project and still home to a Department of Energy lab. It was also near Bandelier National Monument and he was hiking trails there.

During my long conversation with Dan, both the cats had jumped on the bed to join me, wedging themselves against me on either side. I leaned over and turned off the bedside lamp. I was asleep almost as soon as my head hit the pillow.

When I woke the next morning, Black Bart was still tucked into my right side. Sometime during the night, Abigail had moved to the pillow, draping herself above my head. I propped myself up on my elbows and she meowed at me in protest. "I'm getting up," I told her. "You can have the whole pillow."

I headed for the kitchen and started a pot of coffee, then washed and refilled the cats' bowls. After a shower, breakfast was a piece of toast with jam. There wasn't much else to be had. I'd let the refrigerator empty out before leaving on my trip and I certainly needed to buy groceries. I scribbled a list while I finished the rest of the coffee, then tucked it into my bag and headed for my office.

Along with the law firm of Alwin, Taylor and Chao, I'd recently moved Howard Investigations into the one-story building near the corners of Twenty-seventh and Valdez streets, an area known as the Valdez Triangle. My friend Cassie Taylor was the law firm's middle principal. For years we'd all had offices in a building on Franklin Street near Oakland's Chinatown. Last fall the landlord had sent out notices of a rent increase, one large enough to make me consider a move. Cassie and her partners had the same reaction, spurred not only by the rising rent but the need to expand their firm. Their solution was to buy the new building, with the law firm taking up two-thirds of the office space and leasing the rest of the offices to tenants. I was their first tenant, and after we'd moved into the space in January, the other offices had filled with more tenants, including an accountant and an architect.

So now, instead of looking out my window to the roof of the building next door, as had been the case with my old building, I had a window that looked out on some landscaping, which included rhododendrons in bloom and some large succulents in pots. Though not as close to downtown, where I could walk to the Alameda County Courthouse in one direction and the Friday farmers' market in Old Oakland in the other, my new building had the advantage of a parking lot in the back, which meant I no longer had to pay for space at a lot. I parked in my designated spot and let myself in the back door.

A few of the law firm's associates were working, even though it was Saturday. I collected my mail and headed to my office, where I had my own coffeemaker. After I started a pot brewing, I turned on my computer and began sorting through the mail. I was midway through my second cup when someone knocked on my door, and then entered.

Cassie, wearing jeans and a T-shirt instead of her usual lawyer suit, strolled in and sat down in the chair in front of my desk. "You're back. I saw your car in the parking lot. How was New Orleans? You stayed longer. I thought you were going to be home a few days ago."

"Something came up. Hey, it's Saturday. I'm here because I have to catch up, but what are you doing here?"

"Just came in to pick up a file so I can work on it at home. Tell me about your trip."

"Dad and I had a great time." I told her about my adventures with Dad in the Big Easy, adding that I'd extended the trip as a favor to a friend. I didn't give her any details about the case and, as an attorney, she understood.

After we talked for a while, she got to her feet. "I'd better get that file and get home. My husband's looking after the baby and he has a date with some of his guy friends. Good to have you back."

When she had gone I poured myself another cup of coffee and got back to work. Having dealt with the regular mail, I turned my attention to the email. While in New Orleans, I'd used the computers in the hotel business center to keep up with the email, but that was no substitute for working in my own office, with access to my own files and resources. I worked a while on an ongoing investigation for a longtime client, an Oakland insurance company. Several times I stopped and called the phone number for Millicent Patchett that had appeared on Slade's rental application. I also looked up her address in Lafayette, finding a number for Millicent and Byron Patchett at that location. Both numbers netted me voice mail and an invitation to leave a message. I hung up instead. Then I went to my computer and initiated a background check on both Millicent and Byron.

My cell phone rang. It was Antoine, reporting in. He'd contacted a fellow investigator in Austin to see what he could find out about the car fire Luis Ortega had told us about.

"It happened a month before Slade left Austin for New Orleans," he said.

"Same pattern. A fire in Austin and he leaves town. Then the fire in New Orleans, the one that killed Brixton, and he leaves town again."

"Yeah. He was playing a gig with another guitarist named Dave Simmons. They got into some sort of disagreement. Nobody knows what it was about, but Slade was really mad at the guy from all reports. Told Simmons he'd be sorry. Simmons had just bought a new car—well, a newer used car. A few nights later, the car was parked in front of Simmons's apartment building and somebody lit it up. My buddy sent me the report. Looks like it was some sort of a device with a timer or a fuse."

Antoine had also received an email from Cam Gardner, the guitarist who had played with the Flames. Gardner was touring with a band, playing gigs all over the southeastern part of the country. "I'll forward it to you," Antoine said. "Cam says that Marsh is Slade's cousin, they grew up in the same town, he thinks, in Contra Costa County. He said he didn't see much of Slade once they were in Austin. He did say he got impatient with them. They had a cavalier attitude toward being in the band, which Cam started, and weren't always interested in practicing. It goes back to what I said a few days ago. If you're going to be a serious musician, you need to practice and work at it. Sounds like Slade and Marsh weren't interested in working."

"Thanks, I'll look forward to receiving that email. I started a background check on Millicent Patchett. It will take a few days to get the results."

When we ended the conversation, I went back to the report I was working on. After I finished it, I called Davina. "I'm back from New Orleans, got in last night. I'd like to talk. Are you available?"

She sounded subdued. "Yes, we do need to talk. I can be available as soon as I finish up something. I'm at the law school. Meet you at Caffè Strada in half an hour."

"I'm at my office. Let's call it forty-five minutes."

Caffè Strada was at the corner of College and Bancroft avenues on the southeast corner of the campus in Berkeley. It was a popular spot, where students and professors alike gathered. On this Saturday afternoon, there wasn't a table to be had, inside or out. I didn't want any more coffee, but cookies called to me. I selected a large chocolate chip and an oatmeal raisin. Davina ordered coffee and a brownie. We crossed Bancroft Avenue and sat on the low ledge circling the fountain on the other side. To our right was Kroeber Hall, site of the School of Anthropology. Behind us was Wurster Hall, site of the College of Environmental Design, where Madison was working on her degree. Up the hill to our left was the university's law school, Davina's home away from home.

I started in on the oatmeal cookie. "Have you heard from Laurette?"

"I did. Yesterday. She called and sent some pictures." Davina set her cappuccino on the ledge and pulled out her phone. She opened the app and showed me the pictures.

I scrolled through them and stopped at one. "Denver."

Davina looked bemused. "Yes. How did you know?"

I used my fingers to make the photo bigger, focusing my attention on a building in the photo's background. It looked like an angular, pointed spaceship that had come to rest on a cobbled plaza. "That's the Denver Art Museum, part of it, anyway. The newest building, designed by Daniel Libeskind. And in the background here—" I scrolled to another photo. "You can just see the Colorado state capitol, with the gold dome. The road trip continues. What's their ultimate destination? Are they heading for the Bay Area?"

She took a bite from her brownie. "Laurette didn't say. But yes, I'm guessing the Bay Area. They've been to Texas, New Mexico and now Colorado."

If they were headed to the Bay Area, it would take a few days to get here, depending how long they stayed in Colorado. It was a day's drive from Denver to Salt Lake City, Utah and another day to Reno, Nevada. From there, a good five or six hours to Oakland.

Neither of us said anything as I took another bite of my cookie. Then Davina sighed. "Laurette seems to be all right. When she called a few days ago, she sounded really upbeat. Maybe she just needed to get away for a while. I guess I was hasty in getting you involved in all of this. What worries me now is thinking I might be hasty in deciding it's all over and everything is fine."

I finished the cookie and dusted the crumbs from my hands. "Maybe it is fine, but Davina, I'm not sure that's the case. While I was in New Orleans, Antoine and I found out some things about Slade. I really need to bring you up to date on that."

I laid it out for her, everything that Antoine and I had learned about the fires that seemed to follow in Slade's wake. First there had been the car torched in Austin after he'd had a dispute with a fellow musician. Then there was the warehouse fire after Slade had been fired. And finally, the apartment fire after Slade's eviction, the most serious of them all, because Ray Brixton had died in that apartment.

"My God," Davina said, her coffee and brownie forgotten. "It sounds like he's a firebug."

"The operative phrase is 'sounds like,'" I cautioned. "It's all hearsay, thirdhand information. We have no way of proving Slade's involvement in any of these fires. Though I agree, I found out enough about him to be concerned. In the meantime, I'll continue looking into this. I've started a background check on the woman who is his emergency contact. Evidently she's his mother. I'll let you know if I find out anything. And you let me know if you hear from Laurette."

After leaving Davina, I got home at three-thirty and stretched out on the sofa, my feet up. I was immediately joined by Abigail and Black Bart. Abigail wanted to sit on my lap and Black Bart snuggled by my side. I had plenty of time before Dad arrived.

I'll just rest my eyes a bit, I told myself.

Rest my eyes indeed. I fell asleep.

When I woke up it was five-thirty. Dad was due at my house at six.

"You were supposed to wake me," I told the cats. Abigail, coiled into a tight ball on my stomach, grumbled at me as I struggled into a sitting position. She moved to a sofa pillow. Black Bart blinked, yawned, and took the other pillow.

I went down to my bedroom and bathroom, on the lower level of the house. After washing my face, I ran a comb through my hair and quickly changed clothes and put on shoes. I was at the front door when Dad knocked.

"What are you in the mood for?" I asked after greeting him with a hug.

"How about a big old juicy burger at Barney's?"

"Sounds good to me." I locked the door and we set out, walking down Chabot Road. I asked him about his friend who hadn't been able to go to New Orleans and was told that he was healing from his injuries. Dad and I crossed College Avenue and went into Barney's, a chain with outposts in the Bay Area and southern California. Seated at a table for two, we ordered drinks, a basket of fries to share and burgers, with bacon and cheddar for me. He opted for grilled onions and swiss cheese. The fries arrived and we helped ourselves.

He wanted to hear all about my last few days in New Orleans, of course. I told him as much as I could, that Laurette was on a road trip with Slade and that I thought they might show up here to visit Davina.

As the server delivered our burgers, we switched to other topics. He mentioned that my mother was planning to visit my brother, Brian, and his wife, Sheila. They lived in Petaluma with their two children and had been going through a bad patch in their marriage. They had been in counseling since last fall and Dad thought things were better between them.

I hoped so. I was divorced and so were my parents. It would be nice if one of the family marriages survived a bad patch. Dad and Mother were still friends despite their breakup. Dad had stayed in the Bay Area. Mother had returned to her hometown, Monterey, to pursue her dream of opening her own restaurant. The grown-up in me understood her making that choice. The little kid that lurked underneath resented Mother for doing it. I'd been upset about it for a long time and it had affected my relationship with my mother. We were on good terms now.

"When is Dan coming home?" Dad asked, setting his burger on the plate. He wiped his hands with a napkin and reached for his beer.

"He didn't say. I talked with him last night." I'd told Dad that Dan and I had agreed to consider the possibility of marriage. My marriage had been brief but Dan's had been of longer duration, and he had a couple of kids who lived with their mother and her second husband.

"Where is he now?" Dad asked. "I know he was in Santa Fe for a while."

"Yes. He's got a friend who lives there, so he had a place to stay. He told me he left and went up to Los Alamos. He's staying there while he hikes at Bandelier National Monument."

"Interesting place, Los Alamos." Dad segued into a discussion of the Manhattan Project, the development of the atomic bomb that took place at the remote and secretive community up at Los Alamos. He'd taught history for years, and he was interested in all aspects of the history of the west, both recent and farther back. That led him to the subject of historical novels. His sister Caroline, my aunt Caro, writes them. Her latest book was about the California Gold Rush. She'd finished it earlier this year and according to Dad, was laboring on the copyedited manuscript.

He, too, was planning to head up to Petaluma to see Brian, Sheila and the grandkids, probably while Mom was there. He figured he'd also see Caro and her husband, Neil, who was retired from the planning department in Santa Rosa.

"I'll try to get up there, too." I said. Then I waved to the server. The burger was delicious but it was too much. I'd take it home with me.

Chapter Sixteen

BACK AT WORK Monday morning, I sent a text message to Gary Manville, letting him know I was back in town. I worked at my desk until nine-thirty. I had a ten o'clock meeting with a new client in Berkeley and I wanted to give myself plenty of time to get to her office. I had just locked my door, heading for the back entrance and the parking lot, when my cell phone chimed. The text was a response from Gary. It read, "Lunch, 1 P.M., Zacky's?"

I responded, "See you there," sent the message and headed for my car. I returned to the office a couple of hours later and spent some time making notes on the meeting, determining how I would proceed with the new client's investigation. At a quarter to one, I locked my office again and left the building, this time to walk the few blocks to my lunch destination.

The pace of change in Oakland over the past few months was breathtaking. Despite the efforts of preservationists, the old round building on the corner of Twenty-seventh and Broadway that had for years housed Biff's Coffee Shop was gone. Now the whole block was a construction site, just like the surrounding area. Buildings were going up all over the Valdez Triangle, and there was more construction all along Broadway between downtown and the Oakland hills. Down on the waterfront, the Brooklyn Basin project on the Embarcadero was rapidly rising from what had once been abandoned industrial land.

The pattern of development was retail on the first floor, with apartments on the upper floors. We certainly needed more housing. Places to live were in short supply and rents, both commercial and residential, were skyrocketing. Before moving into my garage apartment, Madison, like many of the students at Cal, had been paying an enormous sum to rent a room in an apartment.

A couple of years ago there had been a huge fire at one of these sites, a building under construction at Twenty-fourth and Valdez. The fire had gutted the partially constructed building, known as the Alta Waverly project, destroyed nearly 200 apartment units and over 30,000 square feet of retail space. Residents of neighboring buildings, some 700 people, had been temporarily displaced. The fire had poured ugly black smoke, full of soot and ash, into the air. It took days to extinguish the hot spots. As far as I knew, it was still under investigation, by local police and fire departments as well as the ATF, the Bureau of Alcohol, Tobacco, Firearms and Explosives.

The prevailing opinion was that the fire had been arson. So had several other fires, here in Oakland and over in Emeryville. The fires had hit construction sites, destroying buildings in progress and causing grief not only for developers and investors, but residents of nearby apartment buildings who had to evacuate due to the danger of the fires, many faced with damage to their own buildings.

As far as I knew, investigators had not yet determined who had started the fires, or why. There was a theory, one I'd read many times, that the fires had been set by people who were upset about ongoing gentrification. If that was the case, it was an extreme tactic, one that endangered people and, as far as I could see, was ineffective. I wasn't convinced that was the reason.

Due to all the construction, I had to take a circuitous route. I walked over to Broadway, where I saw another sign of changing times. A young woman in a business suit, with a short skirt and sensible but stylish shoes, wearing a backpack and a helmet, zipped past me in the bike lane, riding one of the electric scooters that were taking over the city streets.

Zacky's Tavern was a new addition to the area, located on

Twenty-third Street, a block or so from the Oakland YMCA building. It was also just a few blocks from the Manville Security office on Telegraph Avenue. The place had good food, along with lots of beers on tap, many of them brewed locally.

I went inside and looked around, spotting Gary at the bar. He was a tall, broad-shouldered man in his mid-forties, with pale blue eyes in a square face and short blond hair. He was dressed in his usual uniform of gray slacks and a knit shirt, green today. The word uniform suited, since Gary still had what people call military bearing. He'd spent two decades in the Navy, retiring a few years ago to start his own business. We met last fall, when I was looking into the death of Cal Brady, Madison's father. Cal and Gary had served in the Navy together and when Cal, an alcoholic, had sobered up, Gary had given him a job as a security guard at his new firm. Gary didn't like me at first, but he'd thawed and now he called on my services from time to time.

Gary waved at me, then spoke to one of the servers as I walked over to join him. The server grabbed a couple of menus and led us to a booth near the back, somewhat secluded. Gary had something on his mind, I guessed, given his phone calls to me while I was in New Orleans.

I was tempted to get a beer to go with my grilled chicken on focaccia. But I had another client meeting later in the afternoon, so I decided against it. Gary opted for non-alcoholic as well. After the server brought us a round of iced tea, he asked where I'd been.

"New Orleans, with my father," I said. "I stayed a bit longer than I'd planned."

"It's a great town," Gary said. "I spent some of my Navy time in Pensacola, over in the Florida panhandle. Used to head over to the Big Easy on weekends. I love the music. And the food."

We chatted about New Orleans until the server brought our lunches. After a few bites of my sandwich, I wiped my hands on a napkin and said, "What's on your mind, Gary?"

He eyed me over his Reuben sandwich, then set it on the plate. "Arson."

Fire. It seemed to be an ongoing theme, this week and last.

"What happened?"

"Another fire at another construction site," Gary said. "One that Manville Security was guarding. A couple of my guards were injured and someone died. A homeless guy who'd put up a tent on the back side of the site."

"I hadn't heard about that," I said with a frown.

"No reason you would, you being out of town. There was a lot of news coverage, of course. You can look it up when you get back to the office." Gary paused and drank some tea. "The building was about halfway done. Four stories, with retail on the bottom, apartments on the other three floors. It was located on San Pablo Avenue near Forty-seventh, in that area near the Oakland–Emeryville border."

"Which is where some of the other fires have occurred," I said.

He nodded as he picked up his sandwich again. "Yeah. The fire happened eight days ago, late Sunday night. Fire department got the call around midnight. I had two security guards on the site at the time. One of them was Nathan Dupree. The other was a guy named Cisco Fernandez. Nathan called in the fire around midnight. Then he and Cisco tried to do what they could with the equipment they had. Then they had to let it go. They both wound up with some smoke inhalation and minor burns."

"I'm sorry to hear that. I like Nathan. He's a good guy."

"One of my best guards," Gary said. "They're both gonna be all right but they're off work for now. The homeless guy that died, last I heard he hadn't been identified. There have been a handful of suspicious fires in the past few years. Not the only fires, of course. There's the Ghost Ship, but that's in another category altogether."

Neither of us said anything for a moment. Memories were still raw concerning the Ghost Ship fire in the Fruitvale neighborhood a few years back. That conflagration broke out during a concert in a warehouse that had been illegally converted to a live-work artists' collective. Thirty-six people died at the Ghost Ship. It was Oakland's deadliest fire ever.

The construction site fires Gary was talking about were

troubling as well, especially now that they had claimed a life. All of them were arson, deliberately set. All of them had occurred in Oakland and Emeryville. The Alta Waverly project on Valdez, near my office. And before that, two fires in Emeryville, at the same location. That project, with 105 apartments and 21,000 square feet of retail space, had burned in midsummer and again ten months later. In one of the Emeryville fires, I recalled seeing grainy video footage of a man in a hoodie climbing over a fence.

All of these fires had been at partly constructed buildings, and at a time when construction was most vulnerable. Studs, joists and rafters—all wood—piled the sites, and fire protections, such as flame-resistant Sheetrock and sprinkler systems, were not yet installed. Empty stairwells became chimneys, funneling the hungry flames.

I brought up the theory that the fires were being set by people who were opposed to gentrification. "I'm not sure I buy into that one," I told Gary. "At least not all the way. It seems like such a drastic thing to do. Besides, there's also the theory that someone is benefiting financially from the fires."

"I could believe the gentrification thing, but not sure about the financial benefits," Gary argued. "This latest fire, for example. Bay Oak Development is the outfit that was bankrolling this project that just burned. They are upset, big time. Millions of dollars up in flames."

"Insurance," I countered. "Who gets the payout from the insurance company, and how much?"

"Early days on insurance. The fire was just last week and it's under investigation. I'll bet they don't see a penny for a long time."

I went into devil's advocate mode, taking the other side of the question. "On the other hand, I know a lot of people don't like all the changes happening in Oakland, on the waterfront and along the Broadway corridor. It's changing the character of the city. A lot of what's being constructed is housing, but it's not affordable housing. It's market rate. People who can afford an apartment in an older building aren't going to be able to rent a place is one of these new buildings. So yes, there's a lot of resentment. And we do have a lot of people in this area who I'd say are capable of torching a building because of gentrification."

Gary sighed as he finished off his sandwich. "Whether it's anti-gentrification radicals or guys out for insurance money, what I will say is that it feels methodical. I think there's a plan, some sort of agenda. It's sure as hell making people jumpy. Raising construction costs, making investors think twice about putting their money into developments. I hate to say it, but it's been good for my business. Developers are increasing their spending on security. They're outfitting construction sites with video cameras, fencing, alarms, lots of lighting and security guards, round the clock. But none of that helps if I've got two guards off the job because they've been injured in a fire."

"And the man who died."

"Believe me," he said, his expression grim, "I'm not forgetting that."

I had finished half my sandwich and decided to take the other half with me. I wiped my hands with a napkin and looked at Gary. "So why am I here?"

"I want you to take a look at the situation," he said.

"Surely the fire department and the cops are all over this one. And I'm sure they have information they aren't sharing with us civilians."

"I want another pair of eyes. And I want you to come to a meeting with me."

"What meeting is that?"

He reached into his pocket and pulled out a folded sheet of paper, a printout of an article from the *San Francisco Chronicle*. The headline read REWARD TARGETS EAST BAY CONSTRUCTION-SITE ARSONS. I read through the article. A group of developers and local business people had joined forces, announcing a reward leading to the conviction of the person responsible for the fires.

"This group is having a meeting on Wednesday. With a task force that includes law enforcement from Oakland and Emeryville.

I'd like you to come with me. Another pair of eyes, another set of ears."

I wasn't yet convinced that I could offer anything to the investigation that was already going on, but it might be worth attending the meeting. I pulled my phone from my bag. "Wednesday, where? And what time? I have another meeting that day, at one."

"This one's at three o'clock," Gary said. "It's in a conference room at Bay Oak Development. They're located in that office building at Broadway and Grand."

He rattled off the street address as I put the information on my calendar. "My one o'clock is in North Berkeley so if I'm a bit late, don't worry, I'll be there."

"Thanks. I really appreciate it. And to show my appreciation, I buy lunch."

I grinned at him. "Thanks, I'll let you."

◿Chapter Seventeen

ON TUESDAY AFTERNOON, I got the results of my background check on Millicent and Byron Patchett, I opened the file, gave it a quick once-over, then printed it out for a deeper read, jotting notes on a lined pad next to the papers spread out on my desk.

As I'd guessed, Millicent was Slade's mother. The surprising note was that Byron Patchett, Slade's stepfather, was a local developer. In fact, he was the chief executive officer of Bay Oak Development, the company whose latest project had burned last week in the fire Gary Manville told me about the day before. Bay Oak was a member of the coalition of developers and businesses offering a sizable reward for whoever was responsible for the spate of construction-site fires.

Another fire in the family, I thought. It was an interesting coincidence. Or was it? Was that just me being suspicious every time I heard about a fire? After all, Slade wasn't here when the fire happened. At least it didn't appear so.

I pushed the thought aside for now and focused my attention on the report, and the information it provided about Millicent and her son.

Eric Charles Slade, aka Slade, was twenty-seven, the only offspring of Millicent and Walter Slade. The Slades had divorced fifteen years ago, when Eric was twelve. Both had remarried after the divorce. Walter and wife number two, a woman named Linda, lived in one of the suburbs that had sprung up east of Sacramento, the state capital. Byron was Millicent's second husband.

The Patchetts jointly owned a house in Lafayette, a city of about 26,000 people located in Contra Costa County, on the other side of the hills that rose to the east of Berkeley and Oakland. That part of the East Bay was not as urban as my location, and it was full of grassy meadows, rolling hills and woodlands. Lafayette was one of the wealthier communities in that area and the population demographics skewed white. It was a place where even a bare-bones, mid-twentieth-century ranch-style house sold for well over a million dollars, and sometimes double or triple that.

Millicent also owned property in Walnut Creek, the large city that bordered Lafayette on the east. It was a condominium, and it looked like she'd bought it right after she and Walter had divorced. It appeared she'd lived there for a year or so, with her son. After she married Byron, she kept the condo, using it as a rental property. I did a search on the address and came up with a listing on a real estate site, showing the place in photos and on a map. The monthly rent on the two-bedroom unit made me glad I was out of the rental market. It was a good thing I'd bought my house a few years ago.

In addition to her rental property, Millicent owned a business. She and another woman named Rosalie Benson had filed a fictitious business name statement for a retail store called Bluebird, also with a Lafayette address. I couldn't tell from that name what the business entailed, so I plugged the name and address into my search engine. I came up with a website heavy on images of bluebirds, with text and photos that told me the shop sold vintage clothing and jewelry.

I had no more appointments today, so I closed my office and collected my Toyota from the lot in back of the building. It was the middle of the afternoon and the eastbound traffic on Highway 24 moved relatively well, far better than it would in an hour or so when the commuters began driving home. I drove through the Caldecott Tunnel, whose four bores pierced the steep slopes of the Oakland hills. On the east side of the tunnel, the highway curved as it went downhill to the town of Orinda. A few miles beyond were signs indicating that the next three exits led to Lafayette. I took an exit near the BART station and headed into town.

Hawthorne Drive was south of Moraga Boulevard, not far from the downtown business district. The street wound through a residential neighborhood, the street shaded by tall pines and mature oak trees. I drove slowly up the street, past one intersection with a blue postal service mailbox on the corner. Midway up the next block I found the Patchetts' address, a sprawling one-story house with a cream stucco exterior and brown trim. The front yard sloped upward, as did the driveway that led to a double garage. Rhododendrons—pink, white and purple—banked the front of the house, and planter boxes held red and orange tulips. It didn't look like anyone was home.

I parked at the curb and explored, hoping one of the neighbors didn't get curious and call the police. I walked up the driveway and down a walkway where the garbage and recycling bins were lined up. At the gate I peered into the backyard, seeing a covered patio with contemporary rattan furniture.

I retraced my steps and headed down the driveway to the street. Just as I reached the sidewalk I encountered a woman who appeared to be in her late fifties or early sixties, with short, silvery hair visible under her purple billed cap. She was dressed in cropped denim pants and a bright purple T-shirt that matched her cap. The small shaggy terrier with her bounded toward me, checked by the leash she held.

"That's Razzle," she told me. "He's really friendly."

"I can see that." I was hoping she was friendly, too, willing to share some information about her neighbors. The end of the leash was in one hand and the other held several envelopes. Evidently she was walking down to the mailbox I'd seen near the corner. I leaned down and let the little brown-and-white dog sniff my hand, and surreptitiously glanced at the label in the upper left corner of the top envelope. The name on the return address was Bonnie Redeker.

After giving me a friendly lick, the terrier concentrated his attention on my shoes and the hems of my slacks. "I have cats. He must smell them."

"We have cats, too," Ms. Redeker said. "He likes cats. I saw you at the Patchetts' house. I imagine they're at work. Millicent has a shop downtown and Byron has an office in Oakland."

"I'll try the shop next," I said. "Since I do want to talk with Millicent."

"Well, tell her Bonnie said hello. She works so much I hardly see her, and we just live three doors up the block."

I pointed at the Patchetts' house. "Have they lived here a long time?"

"Oh, yes. More than fifteen years," she said. "They moved in when they got married. It's a second marriage for both of them."

"Yes, I know. Blended families, right? That can sometimes be a problem."

"Oh, yes, it certainly can. Especially with her son." Bonnie Redeker's voice took on a gossipy tone, just dishing the dirt, the two of us. "Byron's son and daughter were just as nice as they could be. Of course, they never lived here. They were in Southern California with their mother. But they used to visit and they were so polite and well brought up. But Eric, Millicent's son, he was, well, troubled to say the least. My daughter Carrie was in the same class at Acalanes High School. She says he was always getting into trouble."

I nodded, encouraging her. "So I heard. Acting out. I guess that's what they call it."

"It seemed like he and that cousin of his were always getting up to something," she added. "That boy was a year or two older than Eric. He lived in Walnut Creek. His mother is the sister of Eric's father. What was his name?" She thought about it for a moment. "Marsh, I think."

Marsh Spencer, I thought. In his email, Cam Gardner, the bass guitarist for Slade's defunct group, the Flames, had told Antoine and me that the group's drummer, the one with all the restless energy, was Slade's cousin.

"Maybe Eric resented his parents getting a divorce. It happens."

She nodded in agreement. "It certainly does. Divorce is just hard on kids, that's all I can say about it."

"What kind of trouble did Eric get into when he and your daughter were in high school?"

"Well, I probably shouldn't be talking about this," she said.

Oh, please do, I thought.

"Carrie said..." Her voice trailed off, as though she was considering whether she'd revealed too much. "There's always the usual stupid stuff teenage boys get into. But Carrie always said it was more than that. I can't remember any specifics, but I do recall something Carrie said that stuck with me. She said the kids in school didn't want to get on Eric's bad side, because he's one of those who likes to get even. You know what I mean?"

I had a pretty good idea. "Was there a particular incident?"

"Oh, yes. There was a fire."

Another fire.

Somehow, I wasn't surprised. Slade had left a trail of ashes that extended from Texas to New Orleans. How long was the trail here in California?

"A fire? Really? I hadn't heard about that. Was it an accident? Or deliberate?"

"Oh, deliberate," Ms. Redeker said. "At least that's the story that was going around. Carrie said at the time it must have been Eric's fault. I heard other people say that, too. It was a school night, I remember that much. Late spring. In fact, it was just a few weeks before high school graduation. It was after dinner, later in the evening. Just getting dark, I think. We heard sirens and went outside. That house—" She gestured at a two-story stucco next door to the Patchetts' house. "That's the one. The garage was in flames and the fire trucks were heading up the street. Something like that is so dangerous, with all the trees around here. And who knows what they were storing in the garage, if my garage is any indication. My husband was one for keeping old cans of paint and varnish, that sort of thing."

"Why did your daughter say it must have been Eric's fault?"

She gestured at the house again. "Well, according to Carrie, Eric and the man who lived there got into some sort of a fight, a dispute. I don't remember what it was about, or if I ever knew. But it escalated. You know how these things happen. Carrie said that Eric threatened the man, said he would make him pay. I don't know when that happened, but then that man's garage went up in flames and the rumor going around was that Eric set the fire. I didn't believe it at first, but Carrie was sure it was true. That's when she told me about Eric getting even."

"Does the man still live in the house?"

She shook her head. "No. It's been years since it happened. He moved after that. He repaired the damage and put the house on the market. I think he just wanted to get out of the neighborhood. I don't know where he went."

With a little prompting, Bonnie Redeker recalled the name of the homeowner whose garage went up in flames, adding that he'd worked in nearby Walnut Creek. That, plus the address of the house he'd sold, would help me trace him. I wanted to hear what he had to say about the fire. A visit to the Lafayette Police Department should provide me with a copy of the report on the fire. Given the birth date I'd seen on Slade's rental application, he would have been eighteen at the time of the garage fire.

I'd already decided it would be a good idea to seek out Carrie Redeker. Was she still in the area? No, her mother told me. Carrie was in graduate school at the University of California in Los Angeles. I could track her down using the student locator on the UCLA website.

The terrier tugged on his leash, eager to get on with his walk. Ms. Redeker and I parted company, she and the dog heading down to the corner mailbox, me to my car.

I drove back to downtown Lafayette. The area was full of restaurants and shops, ranging from plain and budget to upscale, expensive and trendy. I turned off Mount Diablo Boulevard, the main thoroughfare, onto Lafayette Circle and made a left into the parking lot of a small shopping plaza. After feeding quarters into the parking meter, I walked up the sidewalk, past a coffee shop with tables, all of them full, arrayed in front of the plate glass window. Inside the shop, a barista worked the espresso machine while another took a pastry from a glass-fronted bakery case.

I moved through a small landscaped area with a couple of benches, then stopped. The sign near the front door said that Bluebird, the vintage clothing store, was open from 10 A.M. to 6 P.M. A blue canvas awning hung over the door and the display window. A set of wind chimes made of small metal birds hung from the awning. A large terra-cotta planter to one side of the door held an assortment of spring annuals, including velvety purple and yellow pansies and a mix of petunias ranging from pink to red to yellow. A decorative garden stake topped with a glass bird rose from the planter. On this pleasant spring day, the shop door was propped open and a breeze stirred the wind chimes into a tinkling musical sound. Near the door, a large stainless steel bowl held water for dogs who might be accompanying their people on a shopping expedition.

The display of clothing and jewelry in the shop window featured a spring palette of pink, yellow and green. An elaborately beaded dress from the 1920s draped a faceless white mannequin. The dress was gorgeous, with glittering green beads sewn in patterns on a rich peach chiffon. I strolled into the shop and saw a similar dress, this one pale blue with silver and gold beads. I leaned closer and peered at the price tag dangling discreetly from a shoulder strap. Ouch! I wouldn't be adding any beaded dresses to my wardrobe any time soon.

"Let me know if I can help you with something." The voice belonged to a woman who stood near the glass-fronted counter. She was about my height, and she looked cool and put-together in beige linen slacks with a lavender blouse. She was in her mid-fifties, I guessed. Her shoulder-length dark hair was threaded with gray. The angular planes of her face reminded me of the photos I'd seen of Slade. This must be Millicent Patchett.

"Thanks, I'm just looking for now." I hadn't yet decided how best to approach her. Better to observe and listen for the time being.

I moved on to a rack holding jackets and pulled out one at random. It was charcoal gray with pinstripes and shoulder pads, just the thing that Joan Crawford might have worn in *Mildred Pierce*. Definitely a style that didn't appeal to me.

A voice called, "Check this out." I looked up. A young woman with long blond hair emerged from a dressing room, which was cordoned off from the sales floor by a curtain made of fabric printed with flowers and bluebirds. Opposite this was a three-panel mirror. Now the young woman laughed and pirouetted in front of the mirror, showing off a wide skirt from the 1950s. The tan, calf-length skirt with a wide waistband looked good with her red tank top.

"I think it looks great," Millicent said, walking back to where the young woman stood. "It's a good fit."

"It's a start," the other woman said. "What I'm looking for is Audrey Hepburn in *Roman Holiday*." She reached up and pulled her long hair back from her face. "Of course, Audrey had that short Italian haircut. I'm not going to cut my hair, but I can tie it back. A ponytail. Or maybe a barrette."

"Got it." Millicent sorted through the blouses on a nearby rack and pulled out three of them, all in white. "Any of these would work. In the movie, she was wearing a white blouse with buttons up the front and the sleeves rolled up. And she wore a kerchief tied around her neck."

"Plus those open-toed shoes with the little straps around the ankles," the customer added. "Do you have anything like that?"

"Espadrilles. We got a pair in just a few days ago. Let me check." Millicent called, "Rosalie. The brown espadrilles that came in the other day. Where did we put those?"

Rosalie Benson, Millicent's business partner, appeared from the back of the shop. She was a good six inches shorter, and a few years older, than Millicent. She wore a pair of blue slacks and an oversized floral print blouse that hid her stocky frame.

"They're back in the stock room," Rosalie said. "I haven't priced them yet." She disappeared and came back a moment later, carrying the shoes. "Here they are. They're a size seven."

The customer took the shoes and examined them. "I do wear a seven, but those look a bit small. I hope they fit. They would be perfect with the clothes." She returned to the dressing room, carrying the shoes and several blouses.

I took a skirt from the rack. Here was the cinched waist and full skirt popular in the 1950s and what's more, this was the genuine article—a poodle skirt. It was hideous, a particularly nauseating shade of green decorated with yellow appliqués of poodles. I shook my head and put it back on the rack.

Millicent and Rosalie had walked to the counter where the cash register stood and were talking, heads bent toward one another. Then I heard the chirp of a cell phone. Millicent stepped away from the counter and pulled a phone from the pocket of her beige slacks. She looked at the readout. "Oh, it's Byron."

Millicent walked past me, heading out to the sidewalk. I made my way toward the front of the store, checking out some blouses on another rack as I eavesdropped on Millicent's end of the phone call. "Well, yes, I made a reservation for the four of us. Six-thirty, right." She paused, listening. "I know. But if their flight is on time, that shouldn't be a problem." Another pause. "Okay. I'll meet you at the restaurant. If there's any problem, call or send a text."

She ended the call and re-entered the shop, heading for the counter where Rosalie was sifting through the contents of a small cardboard box. "Are you getting caught up with the paperwork? You said something about coming in early to do that."

"Got put off again," Rosalie said. "I had to meet that guy about repairing my garage door. I'll come in early tomorrow or the next day."

"Oh, that reminds me," Millicent said. "I'll be in late day after tomorrow. I have a dental appointment at ten."

Rosalie nodded. "All right. Just so one of us is here to open up." She pointed at the box. "Take a look at the jewelry I picked up at that estate sale last weekend. This brooch is Bakelite and so are these bracelets."

The two women bent over the box, examining the jewelry. Millicent took out a silver necklace and dangled it from her fingers. "This one's Art Deco. Beautiful." She put the necklace back in the box and looked past Rosalie as the customer came out of the dressing room, wearing the whole *Roman Holiday*–inspired outfit. "That looks wonderful," she said as she walked back to the woman. "The blouse and shoes really pull it together."

I looked at my watch. I wasn't sure I could learn anything else by hanging out here. At some point I'd have to talk with Millicent. But now didn't seem like a good time.

I walked over to the coffee shop, where I got myself a latte for the road. As I stepped outside, car keys in hand, I saw a red Ford Escape pull into a vacant parking space just across from me. It was covered with dust and there were two people inside. The driver's-side door opened, and a man got out. He was about six feet tall, I guessed, with a medium build in his faded jeans and yellow T-shirt. His dark hair was on the long side, brushing his shoulders and falling into his face. He stretched his arms and rolled his shoulders, as though loosening the kinks after sitting in one position for a long time.

Speak of the devil. Slade.

Behind me, an annoyed voice said, "Excuse me, you're blocking the door."

"Oh, sorry." I moved away from the door and a woman bustled past me, coffee in hand.

I drifted down the sidewalk, watching as Laurette, wearing olive green slacks and a lighter green shirt, got out of the Ford's passenger seat. She put her hands in the small of her back, leaning backwards. Then she ran a hand through her brown hair and turned, looking around her as Slade fed coins into the parking meter.

Laurette had told her family that she and Slade were on a road trip and that they'd eventually return to New Orleans. But the Bay Area is over two thousand miles from NOLA. That was a long road trip.

Slade walked to the back of the Ford and I could see him full on. Heretofore I'd only seen photographs and videos. Now I saw that he had the same narrow, high-cheekboned face as his mother, notable for a discontented scowl. Attitude, he certainly had it. His frown smoothed a bit as Laurette joined him.

"So which one is your mom's shop?" she asked.

His voice was the same rough tenor I'd heard on the video. "That one over there, with the blue awning."

"Ooh, vintage clothes. I love to poke around in places like that. And look at that beaded dress in the window. It's scrumptious." She took a step in the direction of the shop.

His hand snaked out and caught her wrist, stopping her forward movement. "We don't have time for you to go shopping right now."

Laurette looked taken aback. She pulled her hand away from his and rubbed her wrist, as though it hurt. "Hey, lighten up. I'm not shopping. Just looking. And I'd love to meet your mother."

He backtracked. "Look, I'm sorry I snapped at you. It's just that things between me and my mother, well, sometimes it's a little— tense. You know what I mean?"

Laurette shrugged, ready to forgive him. "Sure. That's cool. I understand how it can be with mothers."

"I just need a little time with her, alone," he said. "I'll introduce you to her later. After all, we're going to be here for a while. Just let me talk with her. I won't be long. Then we can find a place to stay and chill."

"That would be good." Laurette stretched, then reached up and again ran a hand through her long hair. "After that drive from Reno, I could use a nice hot shower and a nap. I'll get some coffee and sit right here until you're ready."

As Laurette headed into the coffee shop, I strolled toward the vintage shop, a few steps behind Slade. I took a seat on one of the benches, set down my latte and took out my cell phone. It looked as though I was reading a text message or checking my email. In reality, I hit the camera button and started recording a video.

Slade stood for a moment in the open doorway, long enough for his mother to see him.

Millicent came outside, her voice low and urgent. It was clear she wasn't happy that her son had turned up. "What are you doing here?"

Sarcasm colored his words. "What, you're not glad to see me? Your only son, home again, to the bosom of his family."

"It's only been a year since you moved to Austin," she snapped. "You just had to leave the Bay Area, because the music scene was better in Austin and you really liked the place. Or so you said. But you were only there a few months. Then you went off to New Orleans. Again, you said the music scene was much better there and you loved the town. And again, you've been there just a few months. Now you're back here. Why? Please explain it to me. What are you doing back in the Bay Area?"

He shrugged. "I decided to come home for a while."

"And do what? Play music? There aren't as many opportunities here as there are in Austin or New Orleans. That's what you told me when you left." Millicent stopped, looking frazzled. "I can't continue to subsidize you, sending you money every time you move somewhere or lose another job. You're twenty-seven, Eric. You're a grown man. You need to settle into something."

Slade's face had taken on a look that I could read very well. It said he'd heard it all before and he didn't have much patience with his mother's views.

Millicent shook her head. "Why are you here? What else is going on? Eric, why do you keep running from place to place?"

I wondered about that, too.

Slade wiped the annoyed look from his face. His voice took on a placating tone. "Look, let's not argue about it. I have a friend with me. We're tired and we need a place to crash. I thought we could stay with you for a few days."

Interesting. Slade had already told Laurette they were going to find a place to stay. That implied a hotel. But if they could stay with his mother at no cost, I saw the attraction.

That wasn't happening, though. Millicent was shaking her head. "Oh, no, not with us. You can't stay there. Not after what happened the last time. Byron won't hear of it."

"Byron, Byron," he interrupted. "What happened last time was an accident."

I would have given anything to know what happened the last time Slade stayed at his mother's house.

I watched Millicent's face and body language, full of tension, as though she was a veteran of many battles with her son—and between her son and her husband. I had a feeling things had been rocky ever since she married Byron. Just what was her relationship with her son? I could see that they were at odds over her husband.

But did they clash on other things? She certainly didn't seem happy to see him.

"You can't stay with us," she said again. "Besides, Byron has friends coming into town and they'll be staying with us."

"Fine, fine. Whatever Byron wants is more important than what I want." Slade brought forth an elaborate, put-upon sigh. "Well, I can't afford to stay in a hotel. What about the condo?"

"I have a tenant moving in on Friday," Millicent countered.

"Okay, then give me some cash so I can get a room for the night. Or I guess I could sleep in my car. Park it in front of the house and come in to use the bathroom. Wouldn't that be fun? I'm sure the neighbors would talk."

He was good with the guilt trip. Now I understood. This whole exercise was designed to get money from Millicent. And his tactic was working. Evidently it usually did.

Millicent compressed her lips into a tight line. "All right," she said finally. She went back inside the shop and returned a moment later, carrying a wallet. She opened it and took out several bills, handing them to Slade. He gave her a perfunctory "Thanks." Then he turned away, a triumphant look on his face as he shoved the money into the pocket of his jeans.

Millicent stood in the shop doorway, watching him go with a troubled look on her face. Behind her, Rosalie's expression showed equal parts sympathy and irritation—sympathy for Millicent, no doubt, and irritation at Slade, who'd had a lot of practice manipulating his mother, from the looks of things. I had the feeling Rosalie had seen this scene played out before. She'd be a good one to talk to. I was sure she could give me an earful about Millicent and her relationship with her son.

I had noted the partners' earlier conversation. The day after tomorrow, Millicent had a 10 A.M. dental appointment, but Rosalie would be at the shop early. That would be a good time to approach her. But I'd better have a story ready. She'd be reluctant to talk about her business partner unless there was a good reason.

◿Chapter Eighteen

I STOPPED THE VIDEO recording as Slade walked past me. He joined Laurette at a table in front of the coffee shop, a couple yards or so from my bench, which made it good eavesdropping range. He pulled out a chair and helped himself to her coffee.

"Well? What did she say?" Laurette asked.

He shrugged and set the coffee cup on the table. "She was surprised to see me. She thought I was going to stay longer in New Orleans. I don't know that she's that thrilled."

"I'm sorry things are tense between you and your mother," Laurette said. "Why wouldn't she be happy that you're home? Besides, this is just a road trip. We're going back to New Orleans eventually. Right?"

Slade glided around the subject of returning to the Big Easy, his voice taking on an aggrieved tone. "It's that jerk she married, the guy who calls himself my stepfather. It was just the two of us after my father left, and we were fine. Then she met Byron." He spat out the name as though it tasted bad. "He took over her life and he turned her against me."

"I'm so sorry." She reached over and put her hand on his. "If there's anything I can do..."

"Thanks. You're good for me, you know that." He smiled at her and I could see how she had been taken in by him. At that moment he looked sweet and vulnerable, emitting charm like pheromones. I

146

might have bought that persona if I hadn't seen his interaction with his mother.

Laurette stifled a yawn. "I'm really tired. And I want a shower."

"Hey, I'm the one that did all the driving. Never mind. Let's head on down to Oakland and get settled."

"How long are we going to stay? I really want to do the things we talked about, like going down the coast to see Monterey and Carmel. And Big Sur and Hearst Castle. So much to see before we go back to New Orleans."

"We've got to see San Francisco first. How can you come all this way and not see San Francisco? We need to stick around Oakland for a little while, though. I gotta get some money first. For the trip, you know."

He'd just gotten money from his mother, I thought, wondering how much Millicent had handed over.

"My cousin Marsh is holding some cash for me," Slade continued, standing up. "He lives in Oakland. After we get a place to stay and settle in, I'll connect with him. Then we'll do the tourist thing."

"At some point we need to do laundry. And I need to call my sister. She'll definitely want to see us."

"Will she?" Slade's mouth twisted. "I don't think your sister likes me any better than your folks do."

Laurette's voice took on a placating tone as she got up from the table. "Now, I can't come all the way out to the West Coast without seeing my sister. Family's important, you know."

He gave a derisive laugh. "So they tell me. That's your family, not mine. Come on, let's go." He pulled the car keys from his pocket. Laurette tossed the coffee cup into a trash can. Then she and Slade walked to the Ford.

I got to my feet and disposed of my coffee cup. My Toyota was across from the Ford. Slade got into the driver's seat and Laurette the passenger seat. He backed out and headed for the exit. I followed. Slade got onto westbound Highway 24. Once through the Caldecott Tunnel, he headed for downtown Oakland, taking the exit for Telegraph Avenue. He turned left and drove south, turning left again, onto MacArthur Boulevard. There were several motels on this stretch of MacArthur. Slade turned into the parking lot of one of the motels. I followed suit, pulling into an empty parking space. I watched as Slade and Laurette went into the motel office. A few minutes later, they came out and got back into the Ford, moving it to the rear of the building. Slade backed the Ford into a parking spot. They both got out and Slade opened the rear hatch. He grabbed a guitar case and an amplifier, carrying them into the first-floor motel room they'd rented. I got out of my car and put on an A's ballcap, all in the name of camouflage, in case Laurette remembered me from the coffee shop in Lafayette.

I walked with my head down. The motel room door was open, and I took a sideways glance inside, where Laurette was checking out the room. "I'm so glad they have a coffeemaker *and* a fridge," she said. "I like having my first cup before I get dressed. But I like milk in my coffee, so we need to get some."

I was past the door now. When I reached the soda machine at the end of the walkway, I stood there, pretending to look at the offerings, while Laurette and Slade ferried their possessions into the motel room. I fed some quarters into the machine and pressed the button that got me a can of ginger ale. When I turned away from the soda machine, I saw Laurette outside the room, maneuvering a wheeled suitcase. "As soon as we're done," she said, "I'm going to take a long, hot shower. And a nap."

Slade, standing in the doorway, nodded. "That's cool. You grab your shower. I'll go get a few things. Milk, beer, some snacks. What else do you want?"

"I'll make a list," Laurette said, heading into the room.

Slade unloaded the last of the stuff from the Ford and headed inside. The door shut and I figured that Laurette was having that shower she'd talked about. I walked past the room to my car, got in and sat for a moment. Slade came outside. There were a few markets in the neighborhood, the kind that had a few staples as well as liquor. One of those was nearby, walking distance from the motel, near the corner of Telegraph and MacArthur.

But Slade wasn't walking. He got into the Ford, cell phone held at the side of his face as he made a call. He ended the call and tossed the phone on the passenger seat, then started the car, and drove out of the motel lot, onto MacArthur Boulevard. He headed downtown, winding up at Lake Merritt, where Grand Avenue curved around the edge of Lakeside Park. He parked near Euclid Avenue. I did the same. Carrying a tote bag with some items for camouflage, I followed him as he headed into the park. On the path that bordered Lake Merritt, Slade stopped, his back to me. He was meeting someone.

Cousin Marsh.

I recognized Marshall Spencer from the music videos of the Flames that Antoine and I had watched on the Internet. He was a few inches shorter than Slade, with a wiry build, dressed in faded jeans, torn at the knees, and a green Oakland A's T-shirt. His sandy brown hair curled at the nape of his neck and straggled untidily over his high forehead. Seeing him in person, this close, I could believe he was a drummer. He fidgeted, constantly in motion, moving his weight from one foot to the other and back again, as though dancing to his own internal rhythm. As I watched, his left hand went up and tugged at his earlobe, just as it had in the videos.

My steps slowed. I had my cell phone in my hand, the camera rolling, but my fingers playing on the screen as though I was typing a text message. Then I stopped a few feet from Slade and Marsh. I looked at my watch, then the path ahead, hoping that I looked like I was meeting someone who was late.

Marsh glanced at me, then dismissed me. I strained, listening to see if I could pick up part of the conversation and hoping the microphone on the phone was doing the same.

Slade's voice was heated. "That's not good enough, Marsh. I need that money, now."

Marsh raised both hands in a gesture of supplication. "I get that. But it's not like I got that much cash with me. It's in a safe deposit box. No way can I get to the bank and get the cash now."

A woman approached, pushing a stroller, a toddler at her side. The little boy emitted an excited cry and ran a few steps ahead and onto the grass, heading toward a pair of geese with a brace of fluffy yellow goslings. Mama and Papa Goose both hissed a warning, heads down as they moved to intercept the child. The goslings scuttled away. His mother caught up with him and grabbed him by the arm before the geese could go on the offensive.

Slade took a few steps, heading away from me. He was saying something that I couldn't quite make out. Marsh caught up with him, gesturing as he talked. But I couldn't hear. I risked a few steps in their direction, though I couldn't exactly hang over their shoulders and eavesdrop. I sidestepped a runner who was pelting along the path. The runner swerved to avoid Marsh and Slade, who were headed back this way. Now I could hear Marsh. He tugged on his earlobe again, his voice earnest. "Chill, man. I can get it tomorrow. Just tell me where to meet you."

Slade was coming toward me. "Chill? That's a laugh. Things are too hot in New Orleans, and I'm not talking about the weather. That's why I left. I had to get out of town."

"Why bring the girl with you?" Marsh asked. "She's baggage, man. She's slowing you down."

"It's complicated."

"So, what're you gonna do?"

As they passed, I stepped onto the grass, checking where I walked, because the geese that inhabited the park were notorious for their copious droppings. I had a paperback book in the tote bag and now I pulled it out, glancing at my watch again before opening to a random page.

Slade mumbled something, then I heard, "She wants to see the coast. I want to go north, to Canada. She wants to go south, you know, Monterey and Big Sur, down to LA and San Diego. Then head back to New Orleans."

"But you're not—" Marsh interrupted.

"Going back. Hell, no. She doesn't know that, though. I told you things are hot. I'm wondering if I should leave the country for a while. You know, get close to a border, whether it's Canada or Mexico, and just go over. Lay low for a while. She can do what she wants.

I've got the keys to the car. That's all I need. That, and money. If I'm going to disappear, I need money to do that. You owe me, Marsh."

Marsh sidestepped the issue of the money. Obligation or not, he didn't seem interested in parting with any cash. "What the hell did you do, man?"

He glanced up and saw me, frowning, as though I'd gotten too close. I had my nose in the book, then I raised my phone to my ear, answering an imaginary call. "Where are you? You're late. Ten minutes? Okay. I'll be here." I gave an exasperated sigh and walked a few feet down the path, away from Slade and Marsh. I'd heard enough.

As it happened, the conversation between the two cousins was over. They walked together toward Grand Avenue. Slade headed for the Ford. Marsh crossed Grand at the light, heading up Euclid Avenue. He turned to the left and entered a three-story apartment building, one of many that lined the street. When I looked back, Slade was still sitting in the Ford. I quickly got to my car and followed him as he checked oncoming traffic, then pulled away from the curb. He cut over to Lakeshore Avenue, went under the freeway and turned right into the Trader Joe's parking lot, ready to get those supplies on the list Laurette had given him.

Poor Laurette, I thought. It sounded like Slade was planning to ditch her as soon as he got the money. It appeared he had engineered this so-called road trip to get back to California to collect money from Marsh. Laurette's involvement had been the Ford, obviously. It had been purchased mostly with Laurette's money, and the trade-in of her Honda. I wondered if he'd ever cared for her at all. Moving into her apartment had been his way of dealing with getting evicted from his own. Laurette was a means to an end and she was about to get hurt. I had to tread carefully. How best to warn her? More evidence that Slade was an opportunistic creep—and criminal?

He was certainly trying to outrun his past, but I wasn't going to let him.

Further investigation of Cousin Marsh would help. I turned around and doubled back down Grand to Euclid. I was familiar with this neighborhood, called Adams Point, because I'd lived in an apartment here for many years before buying my house in another section of town. I checked out the apartment building I'd seen Marsh enter, finding the name SPENCER on the mailbox for a third-floor unit. Now that I had his address, I could do more research on Marshall Spencer when I got back to my office.

In the meantime, I had a phone call to make. I punched up Davina's number. When she answered, I said, "Laurette and Slade are in town."

◺Chapter Nineteen

DARREN LUO WAS A THIN, intense man in his late forties, with a few threads of gray in his black hair. He and his family had once lived next door to the Patchetts in Lafayette. After repairing the damage from the fire that consumed their garage, they'd put the house on the market, moving to nearby Walnut Creek, where Luo worked for an investment firm. I'd used property tax and real estate transaction records to trace him. When I called his office, which was on North California Boulevard near the Lesher Center for the Arts, Luo had agreed to meet me at a Starbucks just down the street. It was midmorning, a warm and sunny spring day, so we took our coffee outside and found a table. Luo unbent sufficiently to remove his suit jacket and loosen his tie.

I asked him about the fire. "I understand it was no accident."

He scowled at me over his cappuccino. "Of course not. It was set." He took a sip of the coffee, as though collecting his thoughts. "You know, my wife and I never felt welcome, living next door to the Patchetts."

I set my latte on the table. "Really? I haven't met Byron but I spoke briefly with Millicent. She seems nice enough."

"It wasn't them," he said. "They're all right, no better or worse than any of the other people on that street. It was Millicent's son, Eric. He was a mess. Probably still is. Him and that cousin of his. Marsh something or other. What a pair. I'm surprised the two of them aren't in jail. The things they said—"

I leaned forward in my chair. "Such as?"

He sighed. "Sometimes it felt like that particular neighborhood was a bit too white, if you know what I mean."

"I do, and I'm sorry to hear that." The Luos were Chinese American. Though the Bay Area is quite diverse, there are some areas where that layer is quite thin. Racially motivated incidents happen, even here.

"So what happened? Racial slurs?"

He nodded. "Yes. Both Eric and his cousin. Directed at me, my wife, my kids. I kept my distance, as much as you can when you live next door to someone. I did mention it to Byron at one point and he said Eric was Millicent's son and he'd certainly discuss it with her. It was like he was washing his hands of the whole thing. I got the impression there was no love lost between the two of them. There were other things, besides the nasty comments. Eric and his cousin were in some kind of band and they were always practicing, playing loud music. Then there was the issue of the pool. You see, our house had a swimming pool when we bought it. Later we put in a hot tub. Eric and his cousin would climb over the fence from the Patchetts' backyard and they'd use our pool and hot tub. Not only that, they'd leave trash. Once they even took a dump in the hot tub."

I made a face. "Oh, no."

The look on Luo's face mirrored my own. "Oh, yes, they did. I had to drain the tub and have it sanitized. I was sure it was them, but I didn't have any proof. So I set up one of those motion-sensor cameras and caught them at it. I had videotape. I threatened to press charges for trespassing. I mean, they were both eighteen or older. Eric was about to graduate from high school, and the cousin, Marsh, he was older by a year or two. After that last incident, I had a serious talk with Millicent and Byron. I said if I caught Eric trespassing again, I'd call the police and let them deal with it."

"How did the Patchetts react?"

"Millicent was very defensive," Luo said. "She didn't believe me at first. I showed them the video. Byron believed me from the start. He said they'd have a talk with Eric and that it wouldn't happen again." He gave a derisive snort. "Three days later, my garage goes up in flames. Eric and his cousin torched it, I'm sure of it, in retaliation for me catching them in my pool, and for talking to the Patchetts."

"What did the investigators say?"

"Oh, they'd made it look like an accident, of course," Luo said. "My wife and I had picked up a sideboard at an antique store. I was refinishing it in the garage. The whole neighborhood knew that. I had the garage door open, for ventilation. So yes, I had turpentine and linseed oil and all that stuff out there. But that fire did not start by accident, or my carelessness. Eric knew I was working on that piece of furniture. He'd seen me in the garage and he knew I had all these supplies."

"What time did the fire start?"

"I'm not sure exactly. We weren't home. My wife and I were at some school function for the children. The fire started while we were gone. One of the neighbors saw smoke and flames and called 911. Then he called me. It was after eight. I left my wife at the school and drove home immediately. By that time the fire department was there." He paused and downed the rest of his cappuccino. "It was a mess, as you can imagine. Dealing with the investigation and the cleanup and the insurance company. It took a while to get the payout, I can tell you that."

"So the official cause of the fire—up in the air?"

"They ruled it accidental," he said with another scowl. "But it was set, I'm sure of it. Eric and his cousin set that fire and made it look like an accident. The fact that I had all those refinishing supplies in the garage just made it easier for them to get away with it. The cops didn't seem inclined to believe me, even when I told them about the past incidents, with the trespassing. Eric and his cousin had alibis, of course. They were out eating pizza when the fire started, or so the story went. But they could have used some sort of timing device."

It was possible, I thought. They could have waited until Luo and his wife left for the evening, kids in tow, then entered the garage. But there was no proof. And Luo was still angry about it nine years later.

Luo checked his watch and pushed back his chair. "I've got to get back to work. If whatever you're investigating involves Eric and his cousin, I hope you nail those two. A pair of criminals. One of these days both of them are going to wind up in jail. Or dead."

Before meeting Luo, I'd done some research on Marshall Spencer, using various online tools available to private investigators. Marsh was eighteen months older than his cousin Eric. After graduating from high school he had taken some classes at Diablo Valley College. His employment history was spotty. He lived in Oakland and from what I could find out, he wasn't employed at the moment. He must be getting money from somewhere. I wondered if his mother was supporting him, the way Slade's mother had been subsidizing him. Or was he getting his money under the table, from some dubious source? He had some financial resources, that was clear. And Slade had said Marsh was holding some funds for him.

If Marsh had run afoul of the authorities as a juvenile, that would have been sealed. He had, however, been questioned by the police for several crimes, from breaking and entering to petty theft. In other words, he'd been caught a time or two. But he'd never wound up in jail. The worst thing I could find on his rap sheet was a fine and a spell of probation for a bar fight several years ago, when he was twenty-one. In other words, if he was walking on the criminal side of the street, he was slick.

The one that made me sit up and take notice was the fact that Marsh had been questioned by the police in Oakland four years ago. A former girlfriend had filed a complaint against him. She had broken up with him and in retaliation, she said, he'd torched her car.

Slade wasn't the only one who liked to set fires.

⁂

Carrie Redeker was in graduate school at the University of California, Los Angeles. The university had an online directory for faculty, staff and students. However, it came with a disclaimer stating that it only included those who chose to be listed. Further, the listings included only the information that people wished to make public. Hers was an unusual name, so when I typed in "Redeker, C," Carrie was the only Redeker who came up. She'd chosen to list an email address, nothing else. I sent an email, explaining why I wanted to talk with her, and added my contact information.

She responded quickly, asking me when it would be a good time to call. "How about now?" I wrote.

The phone rang a few minutes later. "You said in your email you wanted to ask me some questions about Eric Slade," Carrie said. "Is there something more specific I should know about? And this is strictly confidential, right?"

"Absolutely confidential. I'm just trying to get some background information on the guy. I spoke with your mother and she mentioned that you and Eric were in the same high school class. I thought you could give me some insights. As for anything specific, I'm interested in a fire that happened a few weeks before you graduated. A fire in the garage of a house belonging to a man named Darren Luo."

She was quiet for a moment. "I remember the fire," she said finally. "I told my mother at the time I would bet that Eric and Marsh had something to do with it."

"Why is that?"

"I knew what they were doing, climbing over the fence and using the Luos' swimming pool and hot tub late at night, after the Luos had gone to bed. Or times when they weren't home. Mr. Luo was touchy about it. Especially after Eric and Marsh caused some damage. Not that I blame him. At the time I thought he was overreacting. Now that I'm older, well, I get it. Anyway, next thing, I heard that he'd set up some cameras and caught them in the hot tub. He went over and read the riot act to Mr. and Mrs. Patchett, threatened to call the police, all that stuff. Eric's mom was always making excuses for him. But his stepfather—*whew!* He was livid. Very angry, that's what I heard. And I did hear part of it. They were out in the front yard arguing. Eric got into his car and just peeled away."

She paused, then went on. "It was a few days after that when the garage caught on fire. I think it was around eight o'clock in the evening, maybe later. Getting dark, anyway. I was outside with a friend of mine and we heard some sort of bang, like an explosion. I saw smoke coming from under the garage door. There was another neighbor, he ran across the street. He had his cell phone, he's the one who called it in. Then he grabbed the hose from the front of the Luos' house and started spraying water. The fire engines arrived not too long after that. Then Mr. Luo. He and his wife and kids were out that night and the neighbor with the hose called him. He was really upset. Who could blame him? It was a scary fire, lots of smoke and flames."

"Any idea how it started?"

"He had been refinishing this big piece of furniture. I heard that it was an accident but then Mr. Luo was telling everyone that Eric and Marsh started the fire. I told my mother I wouldn't be at all surprised if they had."

"Why is that?"

"They liked to get even," she said. "If something happened at school, with Eric, you had to watch your back. He might shove you or leave some nasty surprise in your locker. I know there was this guy, when we were juniors, he and Eric had some sort of disagreement. Eric booby-trapped his locker. With a firecracker."

Fire again, I thought.

"What about Marsh?"

"I didn't know Eric all that well," Carrie said. "Just enough to steer clear of him. And Marsh even less. They were together a lot. Eric didn't have any friends. Even the worst loners usually have someone, but he didn't. The only person he palled around with was Marsh. And get those two together, you just didn't want to mess with them. Eric getting even with anyone who crossed him was bad enough, but add Marsh to the mix, and it was worse. Marsh was, well, he's kind of a loose cannon."

She didn't have much more to say. I thanked her and ended the call.

◿ Chapter Twenty

BAY OAK DEVELOPMENT'S main office was located in the section of Oakland known as Uptown, on the fifth floor of a new office building on Grand Avenue at Valley Street, a block off Broadway. I'd taken to calling it the blue building, because of its facade, a dark blue-gray tile, and the plate glass windows that had a blue tint. In fact, I had a client here, on another floor.

Gary Manville was waiting for me in the lobby. We took the elevator to the fifth floor, where a set of double glass doors with the Bay Oak logo led into the development company's reception area, furnished with bland gray carpet and low chairs in a lighter shade of gray. The walls were covered with photos of the developer's projects. After checking in with the receptionist, a woman who was also bland and gray, we were directed to a large conference room with a wall of windows that looked out on Grand. In the center of the room was a huge oval conference table made of some highly polished and no doubt exotic wood. A table on one wall held large bowls filled with ice, with bottles of water and soft drinks inside, cooling.

Another set of tables held several large-scale models of Bay Oak's developments, showing the structures as they were supposed to look after they were finished, right down to the fake miniature landscaping. Gary pointed at one of the models. "This is the one that burned, at San Pablo and Forty-seventh. They have several other projects going up in the Valdez Triangle and along Broadway. And my firm is providing security guards for all three."

The area called the Valdez Triangle wasn't really triangular, according to the maps I'd seen. In fact, there was one such map framed and hanging on the wall near the table that held the models. The name came from Valdez Street, where my office was located.

The area that interested developers stretched from Grand Avenue, past the Interstate 580 overpass and the Kaiser medical complex, to West MacArthur Boulevard, encompassing city blocks on either side of Broadway. It was sometimes called Upper Broadway or the Broadway Corridor and in years past had been known as Auto Row, because of the car dealerships that lined both sides of the street. Many of the dealerships were gone but there were still car-related businesses, where one could get windows tinted, brakes tested, and collision damage repaired. Added to these were some corner markets and cafés as well as a couple of grocery stores. Interspersed with the existing businesses were the closed dealerships and other defunct businesses that were rapidly being torn down, replaced with construction sites.

While Gary talked with one of the other attendees, I turned my attention back to the models on the table. In addition to the construction site that had been hit by fire a week and a half ago, Bay Oak Development had three projects in the works, one on Twenty-sixth Street between Broadway and Telegraph, another on Webster Street near Thirtieth, and the third, farther up Broadway, where it intersected with Brook Street.

All of these were within the boundaries of what the City of Oakland called the Broadway–Valdez District Specific Plan. The plan, according to what I'd read, sought to transform the area into a busy retail core, full of apartments, restaurants and shops. The brochures and news articles I'd seen touted the plans, using words like "prosperous" and "vibrant" to describe what the developers hoped would happen.

The plan had been moving along in fits and starts. The city's goal, from what I'd heard was to create a shopping destination core in Oakland. People who lived here went elsewhere to shop. Walnut

Creek had its own busy Broadway Plaza, Emeryville bustled with shops, and if I wanted to do big-time shopping, I didn't go to a mall. I shopped in my neighborhood, Rockridge, which had plenty of restaurants and shops. Or I took BART to San Francisco's Union Square. And let's face it, these days, the Internet had changed the nature of shopping.

Of course, in years past, Oakland did have a vibrant downtown. People shopped at big department stores, such as Capwell's, Kahn Brothers and I. Magnin. But those days were long gone. Blocks of businesses, small and large, and grand old houses and stately apartment buildings had been ripped up in the name of urban renewal to create the City Center complex on Broadway between Twelfth and Fourteenth. That area was busy during the day, when workers were downtown, but at night it was fairly deserted and anything but lively.

From what I'd read, a lot of people would prefer that the Broadway Corridor grow organically rather than have a solution imposed upon them. But developers would be developers. There was money to be made and the construction went on. And on and on, from what I could see happening on the streets around me.

I really should read that book, I thought.

Madison, my tenant, was a budding city planner and she'd been after me to read a book by Jane Jacobs called *The Death and Life of Great American Cities*. It had a lot to say about urban renewal, gentrification and how cities evolve, according to Madison.

The fires that had destroyed some of the construction sites had readily been blamed on anti-gentrification activists, but as I'd told Gary, I wasn't sure I bought that story.

Money was always a motivator. But who would benefit if a construction site went up in flames?

And what if the perpetrator simply liked to set fires?

Gary and the other man parted, and he and I moved toward the table that held the drinks. Before this meeting started, I wanted something to sip. I snagged a bottle of water, then turned and came face to face with my ex-husband.

The last time I saw Sid Vernon was two months ago, at a retirement party for his former partner, Wayne Hobart. Sid and Wayne had worked the homicide detail together, transferring to other departments, then back to Homicide. Wayne had decided to pull the plug, but Sid was back to work after being sidelined last summer by a knee replacement. He had remarried, to a fellow officer named Graciela Portillo, and it looked as though this third marriage was agreeing with him. His hair, once a tawny blond, now had a lot of gray. He was now in his mid-fifties, and he looked to be in good shape, though he'd put on some weight in the middle. Still, he filled out his tan suit very well.

Sid greeted me with a gruff "What are you doing here?"

"Same thing you are, I suspect."

"I'm representing the department. Who do you represent?" Sid gave Gary a once-over.

"An interested party," I told him. "Gary, this is Detective Sid Vernon, Oakland Police Department. Sid, Gary Manville, of Manville Security."

"Manville," Sid said. "Your company was guarding the site at this last fire."

"That's right," Gary said. "And two of my guys were hurt."

"I hope they're doing better now," Sid said, inclining his head.

"I expect them back at work soon."

Someone else came over and drew Gary away. "So what's this about?" Sid asked.

"Gary wanted me to attend, another pair of eyes and ears. Between the two of us, how goes your investigation?"

Sid gave a humorless chuckle. "Not much progress. A lot of the people in this room are sure it's some radical, wild-eyed activist who hates gentrification and hopes to drive away the developers. But we haven't found any conclusive evidence to that effect. Then there's the follow-the-money motive. But I can't see that. The companies affected by the fires have gotten insurance payouts, sure, but it's not enough to offset the hassle of having to deal with their construction sites going up in smoke. All the time, all the planning, all the permits. Getting started takes a lot of time before they even start digging the foundation."

"Any theories?" I asked.

"Theories? From me? Or the people in this room?" He waved his arm, encompassing the attendees in his gesture. "Everyone here has their own theories. But there's not much evidence. All the trails are either too faint or leading nowhere. We just don't know who is setting these fires. And now someone is dead."

"The homeless man," I said. "What do you know about him?"

"He's been identified but we haven't released his name, pending notification of his next of kin. I can tell you he died of smoke inhalation. Before that, he sustained a blow to the head. So either he fell and hit his head, or someone hit him."

"Potential witness," I theorized. "The guy saw something and could have raised the alarm. Or identified the perpetrator."

"Either way, he's just as dead. Just between you and me, we're looking at more than one perp. The fires are in different locations in Emeryville and Oakland and they've targeted construction sites. But the fires have started in different ways. Some were cases of just lighting the match. There are lots of things on a construction site that will burn. In one case, it looks like someone threw a Molotov cocktail over a fence. A couple of the others were started with timing devices. That gave the arsonist time to plant the device and get off the site before it ignited. Of course, things like that are tricky. Sometimes they don't perform the way the perp wants them to."

"Copycats?"

"Possibly," he said. "People with different agendas, different reasons for burning developments. That's why it's so hard to get a handle on this thing."

I took a sip from my water bottle. "What if there is no agenda? What if it's just a firebug, someone who likes to start fires?"

He nodded. "Lighting matches for the sake of watching things burn. Yeah, they're out there. We've considered that."

"What do the Feds say? I know ATF has been involved in the investigation."

Sid smiled. "The Feds are, as usual, playing it close to the chest. They don't as a rule like to share information."

"What's the deal with this meeting?"

Now Sid rolled his eyes. "You know how I feel about meetings."

"That they accomplish little and give everyone a chance to pontificate. Yeah, I hear you and most of the time I agree."

"I think all the developers would just like to vent and find out what we're doing. After that, they'll tell us it's not enough. That guy over there—" He pointed. "He's from the fire department. And there are people here from the Emeryville Fire and Police Departments." Sid looked at his watch. "I hope they get started soon. I've got things to do back at the office."

"Do you know which one is Byron Patchett?"

Sid looked around the room, then pointed. "That's him over there, in the gray suit."

"Thanks. It's good to talk with you. Say hi to Gracie from me."

"Will do." Sid moved off to talk with his counterpart from the Oakland Fire Department. I stood to one side, examining Slade's stepfather. He was short, with close-cropped gray hair, dressed in a lightweight gray suit with a pinstriped tie and a white shirt. Right now he had a pleasant manner as he talked with another man in a suit. Then he became aware of my scrutiny. His face took on a speculative look, as though he was sure he'd seen me, or my photograph, at one time. He may have. Some of my investigations had resulted in news coverage. Now he walked over and introduced himself.

"Good afternoon, I'm Byron Patchett, Bay Oak Development."

"Jeri Howard. I'm a private investigator."

His smile dimmed a bit. "I know who you are. Stephen Cardoza is a friend of mine. Their company is now on the ropes because of what you did."

"A man is dead because of what they did," I countered, keeping my face pleasant and my voice even.

The man who'd died was Cal Brady, Madison's father, who'd been a friend of mine, and Gary's. Because of some shady dealings by the Cardoza development company, Stephen and his brother Brice were facing jail time, and an Oakland City Council member might not get reelected—at least I hoped not. The case, last year, had also revealed information on another suspicious fire at a site on the Oakland waterfront, a fire instigated by the Cardozas.

Patchett had no answer to my comment. Instead he gave me a withering look and stalked off.

Slade had a point, I thought as I watched him go. I didn't much like his stepfather either.

One of the Bay Oak Development people called the meeting to order and the people around the table introduced themselves. I wasn't at the table. I elected to stand at the back of the room, listening and examining faces as Sid and the representatives from the Oakland Fire Department and their Emeryville counterparts talked about the investigations that were ongoing and the leads that had come in since the news went out about the reward. As Sid had indicated in our own conversation, even with all the investigating and the tips, the authorities were no closer to figuring out who was responsible for the fires and why they were being set.

Sid brought up the man who had died, telling the attendees what he'd told me, that he'd been struck in the head and the death was being treated as a homicide. A man in an expensive suit, one of the developers I'd seen talking with Patchett, made a flippant remark. "It was only a homeless guy. Who cares about him?"

I fixed him with an icy stare and he dropped his gaze. Only a homeless guy, I thought. And the more market-rate apartments you developers build, the fewer people in this town will be able to afford a home.

The guy from the fire department segued past that rough spot and talked about how hard it was to fight fires at construction sites. Such sites had a huge load of flammable materials. Added to that was the lack of water supply and the likelihood of the structure collapsing.

I'd heard enough. I signaled to Gary that I was going to leave. He joined me at the conference room door.

"I'm not getting any insights here," I told him. "Looks like they're stumped. If they have any clues as to who is doing this, they're not saying."

"Agreed," Gary said. "I wondered if this meeting would be a waste of time."

Not a complete waste, I thought as I went through the Bay Oak office and headed out to the elevator. At least I met Byron Patchett.

◿Chapter Twenty-one

I HAD WALKED TO THE MEETING. Now I left the office building and headed up Broadway. I crossed the busy thoroughfare at Twenty-seventh Street. When I reached my building I didn't go inside. Instead, I headed for the parking lot. By now it was past four. I figured I'd just go home.

Then my cell phone pinged. I reached for it. A text message from Davina, a short one that read, "Call me asap."

I had her number stored in my favorites, so I pressed her name and listened to the phone ring on the other end. She answered right away.

Before I had a chance to speak, she began talking. "Hey, thanks for getting back to me. I'm home from class now. I did go to that meeting we talked about and I got some handouts for you. But you'll have to come by and pick them up soon. I'm going to dinner with my sister and her friend. They're here right now, visiting from New Orleans."

"On my way." I ended the call and started my car.

I drove up Broadway. As I approached Brook Street, the traffic light changed to red. I braked and waited. Glancing to the right, I saw a construction site enclosed by a chain-link fence which bore a large sign with the Bay Oak Development logo. This was the project I'd seen as a scale model at the developer's office. The foundation was in and the walls were going up, a superstructure rising from ground level.

The light changed to green and I turned my attention back to the road, driving through Oakland city streets to Berkeley. Davina rented a one-bedroom cottage at the back of a larger house on Grant Street near Channing, west of downtown Berkeley and walking distance to the campus. I spotted the Ford Escape that Slade and Laurette were driving parked at the end of the block. Parking spaces are always in short supply in Berkeley, but I angled my Toyota into a tight space on the side street. I doubled back and headed for Davina's place, walking up the driveway that led to the wood-framed cottage at the back of the lot.

Davina had lived here for several years and she'd made the place a quiet and cozy refuge. Painted a cheery yellow, the cottage had a porch that spanned the front. The porch and the area surrounding the cottage held plants in ceramic and terra-cotta pots. The resulting profusion of color included bright red geraniums, deep purple lavender, and an assortment of tulips and daffodils. At one end of the porch she'd planted a lemon tree in a container and at the other end, a rose bush was covered with pale pink blooms.

Just outside the front door was a small round patio table with matching chairs. Three of the chairs were occupied. Davina sat in one, with a tall glass of iced tea in front of her. She was trying to look relaxed and not quite succeeding. Her flyaway red hair contrasted with the bright blue blouse she was wearing over a pair of khaki slacks. As I walked toward the cottage, she got up from her chair to greet me.

"Jeri, there you are. I'm glad you could drop by and pick up those handouts. This is my sister, Laurette Mason, from New Orleans. And this is her friend, Eric Slade."

Finally, my first meeting with the mercurial Slade. All my eavesdropping and observing yesterday didn't count as being formally introduced.

Both Laurette and Slade looked more rested than they had when I'd seen them yesterday afternoon. Laurette smiled and sipped tea from her glass. She was wearing denim slacks and a red shirt printed with tropical flowers. Her brown hair was swept back from her face and held with a pair of white barrettes. Slade, on the other hand, looked wary, as though he wasn't particularly glad to see another person, especially one he didn't know. Dressed in faded jeans and a gray T-shirt, his unsmiling face looked closed. He seemed on edge. He was polite enough, going along with the niceties to please Laurette. Everyone was on their best behavior, I thought, trying really hard to be polite. But there was an awkward feeling swirling around us. It felt as though Slade knew damn well that Davina didn't care for him. And Laurette was being bright and cheery, bending over backwards to make everything nice and make everyone get along.

I flashed a big smile that encompassed everyone and stuck out my hand. "So you're Laurette. Davina has told me about you. And Eric." I paused. "It's nice to meet both of you."

Laurette smiled and took my hand. "It's great to meet you, too. Davina has mentioned you." She tilted her head to one side. "You know, you do look familiar. Have we met before?"

Had Laurette registered my presence outside the vintage shop in Lafayette, or at the motel in Oakland? I shrugged. "I guess I just have one of those faces. People say that to me all the time. No, I don't think we've ever met."

"I've only been here once before. It was after—" She stopped. I knew what it was after, the death of her daughter in the car accident.

"You must have seen a picture of me at some time or another," I said. "Davina and I have been friends for a long time."

Laurette nodded. "I know you used to work together."

"Oh, that was the distant past." I dismissed our coworker phase with a wave of my hand. Did Laurette know that Davina and I had worked together for a private investigator? I didn't want the mention of my profession to put Slade on his guard—any more than he already was. "Mostly now we get together socially. Lunch dates and so forth."

"And that meeting. The handouts are inside," Davina said, waving me toward the front door. "Have you got a minute? How about a glass of tea?"

"That would be great. I'm parched." I followed her into the

cottage. There was a tiny kitchen, separated from the living room by a counter. On the near side of the counter, Davina had set up her dining table as an office, the shelves along that wall crowded with books and papers.

Davina picked up a file folder, the supposed handouts, and gave it to me. "Here. These are actually from a seminar on environmental justice. Fake it."

"I'm good at that."

"Yes, you are." She went into the kitchen, pulling a glass from a cupboard and filling it with ice. She had a pitcher of tea in the refrigerator and she poured it into the glass, handing it across the counter.

"When did they show up?"

"About forty minutes ago," she said. "Just as I was getting home from class. Obviously, I wasn't expecting them. Laurette wants to go to dinner and tell me all about their road trip. That's why I texted you. And cooked up that spur-of-the-moment story about you coming over to get handouts. This would be a good opportunity to find out if they're planning to stay or if they're eventually going back to New Orleans. And I figured those questions might be better coming from you."

"Since I'm supposedly a disinterested party." I took a sip of tea. "Well, let's see what I can find out."

We went back outside and I settled into one of the chairs around the small table. "So, Laurette and Eric, are you in town long?"

"We're not sure," Slade said.

Almost at the same time, Laurette added, "We're going to do some sightseeing and then head back to New Orleans on the southern route. Road trip, you know. We've been to Santa Fe and Denver and Salt Lake City. Drove in from Reno yesterday. Next, I really want to see the coast, go down to Monterey, though Eric suggests Mendocino."

"Mendocino is beautiful," I said. "It's one of my favorite places."

I glanced at Slade. He was being a man of few words and he looked a bit dismayed at Laurette. Did he think she was talking too much? I recalled what he'd said to Marsh yesterday. It sounded like Slade was planning to ditch Laurette, now that he was in California, about to retrieve the money he was after. But Laurette thought they were going back to New Orleans—together.

Slade also looked like he was waiting for something, or someone. Sure enough, his face changed as he looked toward the driveway. I followed the direction of his gaze. It was Cousin Marsh, brash and edgy, walking briskly toward the cottage.

"Who's that?" Laurette asked, glancing at Davina.

"I have no idea," Davina said.

Slade's words were terse. "It's my cousin. I asked him to meet us here."

"Is he going to dinner with us?" Laurette asked.

"No." Slade shook his head. "He's got something for me."

Payday, I thought. The money Slade was so anxious to get.

"Hey, hey, hey." Marsh stopped a few feet short of the porch, moving restlessly, as he had when I saw him and Slade yesterday in the park. "How are all you fine ladies this afternoon? I'm Marsh."

Slade got to his feet and mumbled his way through the introductions. "This is Laurette, the lady I told you about. And her sister, Davina. And—" He stopped and gave me a "what was your name again" look.

I smiled at Marsh. "I'm Jeri, a friend of Davina's."

Marsh turned on the rakish charm, complimenting all us fine ladies on how lovely we were. He was certainly more outgoing than his moody cousin.

Slade was getting impatient. He stepped off the porch and took Marsh by the arm, his voice low. "You've got it?"

Marsh shook off Slade's arm. Then he reached up and pulled his earlobe, the same gesture he'd made the day before. Now that I was this close to him, I could see that he had earrings in both ears, tiny gold studs. I hadn't noticed that yesterday, or on the music videos.

"Yeah, I've got it," Marsh said. "Told you I would. But we need to talk."

The two men walked up the driveway a few feet, stopping in the shade of a sycamore tree. Marsh pulled a thick envelope from his back pocket and handed it to Slade. The money that Slade had come to California to collect, I assumed. Slade opened the flap and examined the contents. Head down and fingers working, he counted the cash. Then he looked up at his cousin. Even at this distance, I could see anger on his face.

"This isn't right," Slade hissed, his voice loud enough to be heard. "You said—"

"Listen, man." Marsh took Slade's arm and steered him further away. I could no longer hear what they were saying, but I could read the body language loud and clear. The amount of money in the envelope wasn't the amount Slade was expecting. Marsh was trying to stiff his cousin on the cash.

Slade wasn't having any of that. He was so angry his voice was audible now, though I was hearing the conversation in fragments. "What am I supposed to do with— My mother won't— That asshole Byron put the brakes—"

I could translate that easily enough. From what I'd seen yesterday, Millicent was in the habit of giving her wandering son money. I would bet that her husband had found out, and told her to turn off the money spigot. And Slade was upset about it.

Laurette and Davina looked increasingly uncomfortable as the conversation between Slade and Marsh got louder. Finally Laurette got to her feet and approached Slade, attempting to cut through the palpable tension.

"Let's go to dinner," she said, her voice taking on that placating tone. "I'm really hungry."

Slade backed away from Marsh, smoothing the anger from his face with effort. He tucked the envelope of cash into his pocket.

Davina stepped off the porch and walked toward them. "Marsh, you're welcome to join us. We're heading over to Angeline's Louisiana Kitchen. It's not home cooking, at least as far as this New Orleans girl is concerned. But it's the next best thing."

"I love Angeline's," I said. "They've got great jambalaya. And red beans and rice and gumbo. Oh, just anything on the menu. You'll be glad to know they also have Abita beer."

Laurette laughed. "It'll have to go a long way to beat the food in New Orleans."

"Sounds good," Marsh said, "but I'll pass. Another time, maybe."

"Well, let's go then," Laurette said. She turned to Slade. "You want to drive? Or should I?"

"I'd suggest walking," Davina said. "Parking in downtown Berkeley can be difficult. It's not far, just a few blocks over on Shattuck Avenue."

"Why don't I drop you off at the restaurant?" Marsh said, going back to his charmer role. "Then you can walk back here."

Slade didn't say anything, having difficulty wiping the disgruntled expression off his face. But Laurette and Davina thought it was an excellent idea. I declined their invitation to join them for dinner. Much as I loved the food at Angeline's, I knew I wouldn't enjoy my jambalaya with all the tension bouncing between the others, and off the walls.

Davina went inside to grab her purse. She locked the cottage and led the way out to the street. I wanted to see what kind of car Marsh was driving, since I hadn't gotten a look at it yesterday. We strolled down the sidewalk and he pressed the button in his key ring fob, unlocking a dark green Nissan Pathfinder with a coating of dust. It looked like it was a few years old and well used. He opened the rear doors and cleaned off the backseat, tossing a jacket, a gray backpack and a fast-food sack into the rear cargo hatch.

I hugged Davina. She turned her head and whispered in my ear. "Get me some answers, please. And soon."

"I will." I released her and stepped away from the group. Then I pulled out my phone and looked at it. "Oh, I need to return this call." I raised the phone and clicked into the camera, then moved the phone to my ear. When they were inside the Pathfinder and Marsh started the car, I stood on the sidewalk and watched as he pulled away from the curb, still pretending to talk on the phone. Then I lowered the phone and managed to snap a photo of Marsh's license plate. There was a dent on the left side of the rear bumper and right above it, a V-shaped scratch, a slash of gray against the dark green finish. I snapped another photo, making sure I caught the scratch.

◹ Chapter Twenty-two

"I DON'T KNOW if I should be talking with you,"

Rosalie Benson's face mirrored the reluctance I heard in her voice.

But she was talking with me, at least for the time being.

I had waylaid her outside the vintage clothing store, shortly after nine o'clock Thursday morning. After parking in the lot, I bought coffee at the nearby java joint, then staked out a spot on the bench near the store, watching the street and lot. I'd been sitting there for about ten minutes when I saw Rosalie.

She walked briskly along the sidewalk, wearing gray slacks and a floral blouse, a gray bag slung over one shoulder. She crossed the parking lot, then detoured into the coffee shop, joining a queue at the counter as she removed a wallet from her bag. A few minutes later, she stepped outside and headed for the store. In her left hand was a cup of her morning brew, a pastry bag balanced on top. A set of keys dangled from her right hand.

I stood up and intercepted her. Up close, I saw lines around her mouth and her wide blue eyes. I put her age as mid-sixties, older than Millicent. She frowned at me, wondering why I was between her and the front door of her shop. When I explained, her frown deepened.

"A private investigator? And it's about Eric? I saw you in the store the other day," she added. "Is that why you were here? Casing the joint? Or casing Millie?"

"I overheard you say that you'd be here early this morning," I said. "And I heard Millicent say she'd be late. I'd like to talk with you and get some insights into Millicent and her son—and their relationship. Before I talk with Millicent. So, what can you tell me about Eric?"

Rosalie hesitated. She didn't have much of a poker face. It reflected her internal struggle. She weighed the store keys in her hand as though weighing whether to talk with me. Talk finally won out.

I held her coffee and pastry while she unlocked the door of the vintage store. Opening it, she waved me inside, locking the door after me. Then she stuck the keys into a pocket and relieved me of her coffee and pastry. "Let's go back to the office. I'll try to answer your questions. Within reason. And if they get too personal, no dice."

"I understand."

I walked with her past the racks of clothing and the glass-fronted counter with its display of vintage jewelry. We passed the fitting room and mirror. A door led back to the office, where clothing hung on racks and shoes and other accessories lined shelves. A desk with a computer sat to one side. Rosalie sat down at her desk chair and waved me toward a chair that held a hatbox. I moved the box to a shelf and sat down.

Rosalie sipped her coffee and opened the sack, revealing a blueberry Danish. She tore off a piece and nibbled at it. "Millie and I have been friends a long time," she said. "I'm feeling disloyal, even agreeing to talk with you."

"Why did you?" I asked.

She wiped her hands on a napkin, leaving a blue smear from the Danish. "I worry about Millie's well-being. Things were fine. She'd been doing well since Eric left the area. And then he shows up."

"Has she got some health problems?"

Rosalie nodded. "High blood pressure. You wouldn't think it to look at her. She's tall and slim. She looks like the picture of health. But—" She paused and reached for another piece of the Danish. "She takes medication. The doctor told her to watch her stress level."

"What is it about her son that affects her stress level?"

She frowned again. "Eric's a problem child. Has been most of his life. I've known Millie for ages, back when she was married to Walt Slade. That kid was always acting out."

"Any particular reason? The divorce, maybe?"

"I'm sure that was part of it. But Eric's behavior problems started before Millie and Walt broke up. Millie was always inclined to blame things on that cousin of his."

"Marshall Spencer," I said.

Rosalie nodded. "Yes, that's him. Marsh, they call him. His mother is Walt's sister. Her name's Debra Spencer and she lives in Walnut Creek. At least as far as I know. Debra's a piece of work herself, to hear Millie tell it."

I filed that information for further investigation. "Why blame Marsh?"

"He's a year older than Eric," Rosalie said. "And always in trouble, Millie says. From the time he was a kid. But I'm only getting her perspective, of course. Truth be told, there was never any love lost between Millie and her sister-in-law. Debra divorced her husband early on and she relied on Walt for help, constantly. Financial help as well as other stuff. Millie felt she was taking advantage of Walt. Sucked up all his attention, was the way she put it. Walt was fooling around on Millie, for a couple of years before she found out. When she did, Walt moved out and eventually they got a divorce. As soon as it was final, he married his girlfriend and they moved up to Sacramento. He has a consulting business. At least that's what he calls it."

She paused and took another bite of her Danish, washing it down with a swallow of coffee.

"So Eric's father wasn't around," I said.

Rosalie shook her head. "He never was, even when he was there physically. According to Millie, Walt was just never much interested in Eric. One of those remote, detached fathers. Raising Eric was Millie's problem, as far as he was concerned. After Millie and Walt got divorced, he pretty much washed his hands of the situation. I often wonder how the two of them ever got together, much less had a child. Byron is a far better choice for a husband. And from what I can see, he really tried to be a dad to Eric. At first. But I guess it was too late. Eric was twelve when his parents split up. That's a tough age for kids. I went through it with both my son and daughter."

"What do you mean when you say Byron tried to be a dad to Eric, at first? They don't get along?" Having overheard what Slade had said about his stepfather, on Tuesday as well as Wednesday, I was sure they didn't. But I wanted to hear Rosalie's take on the relationship.

Rosalie was shaking her head. "Oh, no. They don't. When Eric was a teenager they would just go at it hammer-and-tongs. Byron wanted Eric to behave, do well in school, have some manners. And Eric just wasn't having any of it. If Byron said something, Eric would push back and do the opposite. It was an awful tug-of-war between the two of them, with Millie caught in the middle."

"What happened the last time Eric stayed with them?" She looked startled at my question. "When I was here on Tuesday, I overheard the conversation between Millicent and Eric."

"Eavesdropped, you mean," she countered.

"Yes. That's what I do. Anyway, Eric said something about staying with her and she said no, not after what happened the last time. So, what happened?"

Rosalie sighed. "It was about two years ago. Eric had been living over in Marin County, playing music over there, or so he said. Then he didn't have a place to stay. Got kicked out of his apartment is my guess. He moved in with Millie and Byron. They went away for a long weekend, Eric had some friends over, including Marsh, of course. Things got out of hand. They trashed the den, the kitchen, the guest room. Millie had to replace some flooring and drapes, along with glassware that got broken. Byron put his foot down. He told Eric to get out and said he was no longer welcome to stay at the house. It was hard on Millie. She gave Eric money, of course. She's always giving him money. Even when he left to move to Texas. It's a real sore point between Millie and Byron."

"It sounds like Millicent was hoping Eric would stay in Texas."

"She was." Rosalie tore off another bite of her Danish. "She was relieved when he told her he was moving to Austin. And a lot calmer this past year when he was gone. She hoped that he would find his footing and stay away. Now he's back. Watching her on Tuesday, the same old pattern, giving him money. It was like I could see her stress level and blood pressure going through the roof."

I steered the conversation back to the cousins. "Tell me more about Eric and Marsh."

"They were always running around together when they were growing up. I think Millie viewed that in a favorable light at first, since they were so close in age. I guess she figured it was good for Eric to have his cousin as a friend. She changed her mind when those boys were a little older. Because Marsh, I swear, that kid's a bad seed. He really is. As soon as Marsh was able to drive, he'd pick Eric up and they'd go off and do stuff together."

"Sounds like what most teenaged boys do," I said.

"It was more than that." Rosalie shook her head. "They would get caught shoplifting. Or speeding. Get traffic tickets, things like that. Trying to get someone to buy liquor for them. And I know Marsh got caught with drugs a time or two, as a juvenile. God knows what kind of record he has as an adult. I know—" She stopped again, her face taking on a wary look, as though she felt she was saying too much. Then she took a deep breath and went on. "Millie says that Marsh liked to set fires."

I sat back in my chair. "Did he?"

Had Slade acquired his propensity for setting fires from hanging around with his cousin? Was Marsh still lighting matches?

"I'm afraid he had a really bad influence on Eric," Rosalie said. "There was an incident, right before he graduated from high school—" She stopped again, reluctant to go on.

"If it's about the neighbor's garage," I said, "I've already heard about it."

"There's more." Rosalie sighed. "The man whose garage got burned up, he wanted to press charges against Eric. That would have been serious, because Eric had just turned eighteen. But Millicent told me there wasn't enough evidence to connect him with the fire. Besides, she was sure Marsh was involved, too. But Eric is the one who got blamed, because he'd had some sort of run-in with the neighbor. The police came to the house and interviewed him."

I made note of this new information. I'd have to get a copy of the police report concerning the incident.

"By that time, Byron had had it with Eric," Rosalie continued. "It's a good thing he was graduating from high school. He went off to college and I think that was good for Millie, to have him out of the house. Of course, he moved in with Marsh. The two of them shared an apartment in Oakland while Eric went to school at Cal State down in Hayward."

"Getting back to the fires," I said. "Have you heard of any other instances where Eric might have been involved in setting fires? I mean, if Marsh was setting fires, stands to reason that Eric could have picked up the habit."

She thought about it for a moment, frowning. "Yes, there was another fire. At a club where Eric used to play. I think it was in Oakland. I have no idea whether he was involved. Or Marsh, for that matter. But it happened right before Eric decided to move to Austin. His decision to leave was so out-of-the-blue that I've always wondered if that's the reason he left. To get away from something, I mean."

She broke off and looked up and past me, shock on her face. I turned and saw Millicent standing in the doorway. Her eyebrows were drawn together and she looked upset. Upset enough to make me think she'd overheard a good bit of my conversation with Rosalie.

"Millie! I thought you were going to be late today," Rosalie exclaimed.

"My dental appointment got canceled," Millicent said, staring at me. "What in the world are you doing? Talking about Eric behind my back? And to a stranger? How dare you? I thought you were my friend."

"I am your friend." Rosalie scrambled to her feet and went to Millicent, putting a hand on the taller woman's arm. Millicent shook her off. "I've been your friend for ages, and always will be. But Millie,

I'm worried about you. I saw you when Eric was here yesterday. I saw you give him money, as you have so many times before. After he left, you looked awful. But you wouldn't tell me anything."

"So you're talking to this person?" Millicent gave me a withering look. Then she narrowed her eyes. "You were in the store on Tuesday, hanging around. What were you doing, spying on me? And what are you doing here now?"

I stood up and took out one of my business cards, deciding the truth was the best approach. "I'm a private investigator based in Oakland. I'm working on a case that involves your son."

She took the card and looked at it, turning it over in her hands. When she spoke, there was resignation in her voice, and the expression on her face was tinged with fear. "What has he done now?"

"I don't have proof that he's done anything." Which was true enough. My suspicions weren't absolute facts. "I can't talk about the details of the case. But it involves a young woman he's traveling with."

She frowned, her words coming slowly. "He said he had a friend with him. Is that the young woman?"

I nodded. "It is. Her family is concerned about her. And her relationship with your son. I haven't talked with either of them yet."

Millicent walked over and sat down heavily in the chair I'd vacated. "Do you know why Eric left New Orleans?"

"I'm not sure," I said. "It's possible he and the young woman are on a road trip and that they will return to New Orleans." At least I thought it possible that Laurette would go back, eventually. I wasn't sure about Slade.

"I understand that your son has been in some trouble in the past," I said.

Millicent didn't say anything at first. Then tears slid from her eyes. She put her hands up to her face and cried.

Rosalie was on her feet, alarmed. She tore a tissue from the box on her desk and held it out. "Millie, I'm so sorry. I didn't mean to speak out of turn. But I'm so worried about you, ever since I saw Eric on Tuesday."

Millicent took the tissue and used it to blot the tears on her face. "I had a fight with Byron. A big one."

"What happened?" I asked, though I suspected I knew the answer.

"Eric called last night. He was asking for money. Byron overheard. He put his foot down, told me I can't continue giving money to my—as he put it—deadbeat son. We argued about it. And Eric's upset with me. He's my son. I love him. And I worry about him. If he could just settle on something."

I doubted that he would. Slade had gotten used to his mother's financial subsidies. He wasn't about to step away from that. It made me wonder what he'd do next. The money he'd been counting on from Marsh wasn't enough, according to him. Though I had no idea what constituted enough.

"Getting back to my earlier comment," I said, "I understand that Eric has been in trouble in the past."

Millicent's lips thinned. She blotted her face again and squared her shoulders. "He has. But I blame Marsh. His cousin has been a bad influence on him for years."

Millicent was in deep denial when it came to her son. That much was clear.

It couldn't all be Marsh's fault. My theory was that Eric and Marsh fed off each other's unhealthy energy, the way a fire tornado feeds off the heat generated by the blaze. Were they still at it? Was Slade aware of this energy? Was his move to Austin and then New Orleans an attempt to get away from his cousin?

I pressed her for more information. "What sort of trouble?"

She shook her head. "I'd rather not talk about that. It's all in the past."

Yet when I'd introduced myself as a private investigator, she'd asked what her son had done now. I tried another tack.

"As Eric was leaving, I overheard him say something about collecting some money that Marsh is holding for him. Do you know anything about that?"

Alarm, quickly suppressed, spasmed across Millicent's face.

"No, I don't. That's news to me. Look, Eric left the Bay Area a year ago. He hasn't had any contact with Marsh. Not as far as I know," she added. "Besides, if Marsh has money for Eric, why is Eric asking me for money?"

Because you can't say no, I thought.

Time for a change of subject. "Has Eric always wanted to be a musician?"

Her expression softened. "Yes. He loves music. He took piano lessons when he was younger. And then he got into playing the guitar. After he graduated from high school he went to Cal State down in Hayward. He wasn't sure what he wanted to study. His grades weren't very good, so after a while he dropped out. He worked then, and played music. He had gigs all over the East Bay. Then he came to me and said he wanted to try his luck in Austin, because of the music scene there. He said it was much better for musicians down there."

I had been looking at Rosalie's face while Millicent talked. She'd heard it all before, her face said, listening to her friend make excuses for her son.

"It's ten o'clock," Rosalie said, getting to her feet. "Time to open the shop. I'll walk you out."

She placed a hand on my arm and steered me out of the office, through the shop. She unlocked the front door and turned the sign from CLOSED to OPEN.

Then she turned to me. "Herkimer's. That was the name of the club in Oakland, the one that had a fire before Eric left for Austin last year. Look, Millie has been in denial about Eric his whole life. I hate for her to get hurt over things her son has done. I don't know what it is you're investigating but I have a feeling there's more to it than this girl he's traveling with. Is he in serious trouble?"

I thought about Cindy Brixton back in New Orleans, accusing Eric of murdering her brother. No proof of that as yet, but—

I nodded. "He could be."

⊲ Chapter Twenty-three

HERKIMER'S HAD BEEN an Oakland fixture for years, a venue for all sorts of music—blues, jazz, bluegrass, rock. I'd been to the club several times, though not recently. The nightspot was located in Oakland's increasingly trendy Uptown district, on Telegraph Avenue at the corner of Twenty-third Street. And it had been closed for a year, after a fire that had seriously damaged the building.

Back in my office, I turned to the Internet and began clicking my way through the links that popped up on my search. I located a few online images of the club's calendars and looked at the lineup of musicians for the weeks just before the fire. Among them was a popular Bay Area act, Lavay Smith and her Red Hot Skillet Lickers, that played jazz, blues and swing, fronted by the sultry Lavay. That same week, a bluegrass group had been featured, along with a blues singer and an R&B duo. On Sunday nights, the club had what they called Open Mike Nights, where anyone who had a yen to get up on stage with a microphone was given the chance to perform.

The blaze happened on a Monday night in April. The club had been closed that night. That was fortunate. No one had been killed or injured.

The fire at Herkimer's was on a much smaller scale than the blazes at the construction sites, or the Ghost Ship debacle. The club was primarily a bar and performance venue, but it had served food. So there was a kitchen, and it appeared that the fire had started there. Initial news coverage said the fire's cause was unknown, but under investigation. Later reports said it was arson.

Rory Davis, who owned Herkimer's as well as another bar and two local restaurants, vowed that Herkimer's would reopen. But thus far, the club was still closed. A couple of news articles outlined Davis's plans for a bigger and better club, but talked about delays due to the fire investigation, insurance woes, design reviews, and the permitting process.

I searched for contact information on the owner. I found a phone number and made the call, expecting to get voice mail. Instead I got Rory Davis.

"My name is Jeri Howard," I said. "I'm a local private investigator and I'd like to ask some questions about last year's fire at Herkimer's."

"Why is that?"

"There's a possibility the club fire could relate to a case I'm working on."

A few seconds of silence as Davis thought about it. "Sure. I'll be at one of my restaurants within the next hour. It's Temescal, on Telegraph at Forty-fifth Street. Come on over, we'll talk."

I locked up my office and went out to the parking lot, getting into my Toyota. Before going to the restaurant, I drove over to Herkimer's. I found a parking space on Twenty-third Street, next to a fenced-off area where the BART tracks came out of a tunnel that led back to the underground stations at Twelfth and Nineteenth streets. To the northeast, paralleling the elevated section of the Interstate 980 freeway, was the above-ground MacArthur BART station. As I glanced down into the right-of-way, with its twin tracks, I heard the rumble of an approaching train. Then a moment later, the first of several silvery cars emerged from the tunnel, heading toward the station.

I turned and walked in the direction of Telegraph. This block had a funky urban vibe, partly residential, partly business. To my left were several apartment buildings and on the other side of the street, a parking lot. I reached the corner. The one-story building that

housed Herkimer's had a stucco exterior that had once been pale
green, with darker green trim on the windows. Now the walls were
blackened with soot that had withstood a season of winter rains, the
grime ingrained with the stucco. The windows were boarded up and
covered with graffiti. So were the display cases that had held posters.
The marquee above the front entrance was wrapped in duct tape
and a layer of protective plastic that had come loose at one corner.

Standing at the front of the building, I noticed the location
of two security cameras affixed high on the building, both angled
toward the entrance. When I retraced my steps to the side of the
building, I saw another camera pointing at another door which led
into the building, presumably the kitchen.

I turned and looked across Twenty-third Street. On the opposite
corner was a Mexican restaurant, an order-at-the-counter burrito
joint that was doing a brisk lunchtime business. It, too, had a security camera.

Where there were cameras, I thought, there had to be some
video footage. I headed back to my car.

Temescal, the restaurant where I was meeting Rory Davis, was
named after the neighborhood where it was located. The eatery had
opened within the past year and I'd been meaning to try it, since the
reviews were good. The dining room and bar had a trendy industrial
look, with concrete floors and a high open ceiling that bounced with
noise, shiny stainless steel fixtures and lots of varnished pine. The
counter fronted on an open kitchen. It was after one o'clock and
the lunch crowd was thinning out. A man and woman at a nearby
table had just been served—a fried chicken sandwich with sweet
potato fries for him and for her, a generous salad of mixed greens,
scattered with cranberries, blue cheese, walnuts and slivers of roast
chicken. At another table, two men were working their way through
enormous burgers.

A young woman stood at a small front counter that held menus
and a reservation book. Like the servers, she was attired in black
jeans and a black T-shirt.

"Table for one?" she asked.

"I have an appointment with Rory Davis."

She nodded and picked up a phone, making a call. Then she said, "This way, please."

I followed as she led the way past the bar to a hallway that led back to the restrooms. Beyond this we went through a swinging door and the woman pointed me toward a small square office off the kitchen. Seated at a desk with a computer and the usual peripherals was a short, compact woman in her fifties, with a sun-browned complexion and brown hair, silvered at the temples. She wore it short, showing off a pair of dangling silver earrings that went with several silver chains around her neck. She had a habit of twining her fingers in the chains as she talked. She was casually dressed in blue slacks and a bright pink pullover.

"Ms. Davis, I'm Jeri Howard." I handed her my business card.

"Call me Rory," she said. "Have a seat. What will you have to drink?"

I pointed at her desk, at a tall glass of tea with ice cubes and slices of lemon. "That looks good."

"Sure." She picked up a phone and punched a button. "Gina, will you please bring another lemon iced tea? Thanks."

A moment later one of the servers appeared at the door, carrying a frosty glass. I thanked her. When she'd left, I took a sip, then I said, "Tell me about Herkimer's. I know it's been around a long time. I've been there several times. And I used to wonder about the name."

She smiled. "I used to go there myself, when I was in college, and after that. I love music. I was always hanging out at Yoshi's here in Oakland, Freight and Salvage or Ashkenaz in Berkeley, or any of the clubs over in San Francisco. And Herkimer's, of course. I grew up here in Oakland and it was an institution, really. As for the name, it was the guy that started the club. His name was George Herkimer. He opened way back in the sixties, and he ran it for years. When he retired, his son took over. Then the son decided to retire. By that time, I'd gotten into the restaurant and bar business. When I heard that Herkimer's was up for sale, I jumped on it. I liked the club, so I made an offer and there I was, in the club business. I had a good run."

"But the fire," I said.

"Yeah, the fire." Rory sighed and shook her head. "It's been a major headache ever since. Thank God it happened on a Monday, when the place was dark. The hassles of dealing with the fire have been bad enough, God knows. But I'd just be devastated if anyone had been hurt—or killed." She shuddered. "Like the Ghost Ship. God, that was awful."

"It was. Walk me through what happened the night of the fire."

She took another sip of her iced tea. "I was at another place I own, a bar on Eighteenth Street near the Fox Theater. That's just a few blocks from the club. The manager and I were talking, and we heard the sirens. Didn't think anything about it at the time. You hear sirens every night in Oakland. Then my cell phone rang. It was the guy who owns the Mexican restaurant across the street from the club. They're open late and he was there. He tells me, Get over here, Herkimer's is on fire."

Rory threw up her hands. "When I got there, I nearly cried. It was bad. Seeing flames coming out the windows in front, and all that black smoke. I'm surprised the whole building didn't go up. But the fire department got it under control. The whole inside was gutted, a mess. All that equipment, the furnishings." She shook her head. "People were wondering if it was the wiring or the electrical stuff, but no way. It was up to code. In fact, I'd just had an inspector out there a month before. Then the fire department came to me and said it was arson. Who the hell would do a thing like that? I had employees out of work. Not to mention losing the income. And musicians losing a venue."

"I stopped by the club before I came over here. It looks rather forlorn, all boarded up like that. Are you going to reopen?"

"Forlorn. Yes, it does look abandoned. The taggers have graffiti'd the walls like crazy. As for reopening, yes, I certainly plan to do that. Making it happen has already taken longer than I would like. Over a year dealing with the insurance company, the investigation and all that stuff. A major hassle. Complicated and convoluted. But things are falling into place. Knock wood."

She did just that, on the wooden surface of the desk. "I finally got a payout from the insurance and I finally jumped through all the hoops provided by the city of Oakland. That was a chore, let me tell you. I've hired a contractor. So Herkimer's will indeed reopen, with a complete remodel inside and out and new, state-of-the-art equipment. It's April now. I'm hoping for fall or at least before the end of the year. I'm going to line up some big acts and throw the damnedest party you ever saw." She laughed. "I've got your card. I'll invite you to the grand reopening."

I smiled. "Send me an invitation, I'll put it on my calendar." I paused and then went on. "Going back to what you said. Who would do a thing like that?"

She shook her head. "Don't have a clue. The arson investigators asked the same question, over and over again. I wondered if it was just some idiot who liked to set fires and the club was an easy target. But I don't think so. The building was locked up, like it usually was. And the investigation bore that out. Since you've been to the building, you know it's on the corner, facing Telegraph Avenue. Whoever set the fire broke in through the door on the Twenty-third Street side. That door led to the kitchen and a big storage area. The fire started in the kitchen, according to the arson investigators. Some sort of accelerant. Cooking oil, probably. Since it was a kitchen, there were all sorts of things that would burn."

"May I have copies of the reports?"

"If it will help find out who did this, sure thing. I've got your card. Tell you what, I'll scan the reports and email them to you."

"Thanks, I appreciate that. When I stopped by Herkimer's on the way over here, I noticed the security cameras. Three on your building and at least one on the Mexican restaurant on the other side of the street. Were you able to get any useful video from those?"

Rory nodded. "Some, mostly from mine, but also a short film clip from the Mexican restaurant. Let me call those up and you can take a look at both of them. I've got them stored on the cloud so I can access them from here." She turned to the computer and her fingers played over the keyboard. "The first video is from the security cameras at the club. It cycles around, front to back to front, and so forth." She clicked on the icon that started the video and beckoned me to move closer.

I stood up and leaned toward the monitor. Here was a silent nighttime view of Herkimer's, so different from the nights I'd been there when a band was playing, music spilling out of the club, when the marquee was lit up and club patrons, talking over one another as they crowded the sidewalk in front of the building. On this Monday night, the club was dark, the only illumination the spill of light from a nearby street lamp. At first there wasn't much to see. Three young men, laughing and talking, walked by the front entrance of the club, then disappeared from view. Several cars drove by. Then another view, from Twenty-third Street, the back door of the club visible. Just past the door were several large waste and recycling bins and a scraggly-looking street tree. A dog with pit bull antecedents trotted by and stopped to sniff the tree. It raised a leg and urinated, then resumed its journey.

Another view of the Telegraph Avenue side of the building showed a man and a woman walking past. Back to the side street, where a homeless man approached the back door, wheeling a shopping cart. He stopped at the recycling bin behind Herkimer's and raised the lid, removing several bottles and cans. He put them in his cart and pushed on toward Telegraph. The video switched views again, in time to catch the man with the shopping cart turning onto Telegraph. When the footage switched back to a view on Twenty-third, there was a car parked at the curb, farther down the street. It was dark, looking gray or black in the dim light, indistinguishable from any of the other vehicles in the shadows. The camera panned on the street and then back, in time to show two figures slipping through the side door, heading into the club. One of them was tall, the other a few inches shorter, and both were dressed in black, with hoodies over their heads, pulled down to obscure their faces.

"The firebugs," I said. "Men, I'm guessing, from their height and build."

Rory nodded, running a hand through her hair. "None of the people who worked for me would have had any reason to be entering the building at—" She pointed at the time stamp on the video. "At nine fifty-seven on a Monday night. Unfortunately, they're both wearing hoodies and none of the video shows the slightest glimpse of their faces."

The two men were inside the building less than three minutes. When they came outside they moved quickly down Twenty-third Street, disappearing into the shadows. The video switched back to the front of the building, in time to show a car stopped at the corner of Twenty-third and Telegraph. It was the same dark generic car, at least I thought so. The vehicle stopped longer than I would have thought necessary at that time of night. The driver seemed to be looking to his left, as though checking oncoming traffic. Or was he looking at the building that housed Herkimer's? The hoodie was still pulled over his head and I couldn't get a good look at his face.

Then the driver made a movement. He reached up and his left hand brushed the side of the hood that covered his head. Was he tugging at it, pulling it down further? The hand moved back to the steering wheel, turning it. The car made a right onto Telegraph, heading past the Mexican restaurant. I couldn't see the vehicle's license plate. In fact, it looked as though it had been covered with something, mud or dirt, perhaps. The fire happened in April, which meant it could have rained recently. It was possible the mud on the license plate had happened in the course of driving the local roads. But I wondered if it was in fact deliberate.

A moment after the car turned and disappeared, the camera cycled back to the front of the building. Through the building's windows I saw a faint glow that got bigger, then expanded dramatically as the interior of Herkimer's burst into flames.

"I'd give anything for a better picture of that car," I said when the video ended.

"Wouldn't we all," Rory said. "Here's the footage from the Mexican restaurant."

She pulled up another video. This was one was grainy, quite short. It showed a view across Twenty-third Street, looking toward Herkimer's, and it had captured the vehicle just as it pulled up to the stop sign. Bathed in light from the street lamp, I still couldn't tell what color the finish was, though it looked gray or black.

"Someone in the passenger seat, still wearing the hoodie over his head. Those must be the guys. But it's frustrating. I can't see enough of them."

"I had a guy I know work on it," Rory said. "He zoomed and enhanced several of these shots. This is what he came up with." She worked the keyboard again, pulling up a series of images that had been blown up. Despite the enhancements, each picture looked blurry.

I pointed at one of them. "This one, the picture of the driver. I noticed it in the video. It looks like he's pulling at the edge of the hoodie." Something stirred in my memory, then disappeared as quickly as it had appeared. "Could you share the videos and photos with me?"

"Absolutely."

"I'll study them again, along with the reports when you send them. Maybe something will jump out at me." I paused for a sip of iced tea. "So the fire at Herkimer's was no accident. And I doubt that it was random. That leaves us with deliberate. Who did you piss off?"

She shrugged. "Beats the hell out of me. I like to think I get along with everyone."

I pulled out my phone and clicked into the photos I'd taken when Slade and Marsh met at Lakeside Park. One shot showed Slade, his face full on. His cousin was in the second photo, a three-quarter shot. "Have you ever seen these guys before?"

Rory shook her head. "I don't think so. But I'm in the restaurant and bar business. I see hundreds of people. The thing is, if anyone got pissed off at Herkimer's, it wouldn't have been with me. I was at the club a lot, mind you. But not every night. I'm betting that person would have interacted with the manager, the bartender, the bouncers."

"Good point. I'd like to talk with the Herkimer's manager, then. Is he still in the area? Working somewhere else?"

"You're in luck. He works here. And he's working today."

She got up from the desk and left the office. A few minutes later she returned with a slender man in his thirties, dressed in black like the other employees I'd seen. His hair was also black, slicked back into a short ponytail at the nape of his neck. Rory introduced him as Tomás Calderón.

"Jeri Howard. I'm a local private investigator. I'm working on a case that might involve the Herkimer's fire."

"I'd sure like it if somebody caught up with those *cabrones*," Tomás said. "Herkimer's was a great place. I loved working there."

I showed Tomás the same photo I'd shown Rory.

"Oh, yeah. I remember those guys," he said. "I had a run-in with them. Twice."

Things were looking up. "What happened?"

Tomás thought for a moment. "The first time was when they played at the club on Open Mike Night. We always did those on Sunday nights. The whole idea was to give local people the opportunity to perform at a venue with an audience. The Open Mike Nights were really popular. We had singers, guitar pickers, you name it. We had a set procedure, though. You couldn't just walk in and get a spot. The way it worked was, the doors opened at seven o'clock and people who wanted to perform put their names in the hat, right away."

"It was a lottery," Rory added. "And we literally drew names out of a hat, a beat-up old fedora that had belonged to Mr. Herkimer."

Tomás nodded. "Yeah. Lost that hat in the fire. Anyway, we kept to a strict schedule. I drew names out of the hat about twenty minutes after seven, so if you didn't get your name in the hat by a quarter after, you were out of luck. And we usually had more people wanting to play than we had slots available. Once I drew the names, the show started at seven-thirty, sharp. The solo performers, they got to play one song, and if it was a group, they got to play two songs. Some-times if I felt a performer deserved an extra song, I got to make that call. And we limited introductions to about thirty seconds. I was the sheriff, cutting people off if they went over their time. Or I could give them the hook, if necessary. My privilege, and responsibility, as the club manager."

"So these two played at the club on Open Mike Night. Do you recall when?"

Tomás shook his head. I don't remember when, but I remember those two. Because that one—" He pointed at Slade. "He was an argumentative son of a bitch. Everything had to be his way and he was always right, that kind of guy. I've got no use for prima donnas and there are a lot of them in the music business. I'll put up with more from a headliner than I will from a guy on the margins, and he was definitely on the margins. He wasn't as good as he thought he was."

"What about the second time?" I asked.

"Second time, I threw them out." Tomás shrugged. "Well, the bouncer did. On my say-so. Goes with the territory, managing a club. And I do remember when that happened. It was a week or two before the fire."

"You had a confrontation with them?"

"It was verbal," Tomás said, his expression sour as though he'd bit into a pickle. "Not physical, no fists flying, nothing like that. But words. And they got nasty." He pointed at the picture of Marsh and Slade. "The shorter guy, the one with lighter hair, he was making racist remarks, because I'm Chicano." Rory started to say something, but he put up his hand. "Hey, that kind of stuff happens. It goes with the territory. I don't let it get to me. But that is why I remember those guys."

"What led to this altercation?" I asked.

"They wanted to perform that night, but they didn't get their name in the hat in time. That one—" He pointed at Marsh Spencer's face. "He'd been drinking and he was a nasty drunk. He was pissed because they didn't make the cut. They stayed. I remember they were sitting at a table at the back, both of them throwing back beers, getting loud. They started heckling the performers. I told them to put a lid on it and I got attitude. Finally I said, you guys are out of here. That's when this guy started throwing out the racist bullshit. I had a couple of big guys acting as bouncers and they escorted these two bozos and their gear out the door."

And Slade liked to get even, or so I'd heard. It wasn't too much of a stretch to imagine that Slade and his cousin Marsh came back to the club a week later and set the fire that ultimately destroyed Herkimer's, putting the venue out of business.

◢ Chapter Twenty-four

BACK IN MY OFFICE, I checked my email to see if I'd received the reports and videos that Rory promised to send. Not yet. Either she hadn't sent them, or they were floating around the Internet and hadn't found my in-box. If I hadn't received them by tomorrow, I'd contact her again.

In the meantime, I answered emails and returned a couple of phone calls, then finalized a report for a client I was meeting later in the afternoon. The client, who had requested several background checks, was located in the same building where I'd attended the developers' meeting the day before. I walked to my destination, the report in an envelope tucked into my shoulder bag, and entered the building with its blue-gray exterior walls and blue-tinted glass. My client was on the fourth floor, at the back of the building. I spent the better part of an hour going over the results of my investigation.

I left the building, walked up Grand Avenue and turned left, heading up Broadway. I dodged a guy on a scooter who was barreling down the sidewalk, weaving in and out of groups of pedestrians. I watched him zoom across the street against the light, marveling that he didn't get nailed by a car.

It was midafternoon, and I could use coffee and a treat. And just a couple of blocks away was Sweet Bar, the café and bakery on the corner of Broadway and Twenty-fourth Street. Chocolate, I thought. Maybe a chocolate cupcake, though the carrot cake was worthy of consideration. I quickened my step, taste buds at the ready.

I had almost reached Twenty-third when I spotted Slade walking toward me.

I turned and stepped into the doorway of a restaurant that had closed. I faced the plate glass window as I peered inside, hand up and shading my face. In the reflection from the glass, I saw Slade pass me. I turned from the doorway and followed him. He was moving at a brisk pace, heading toward Grand Avenue.

Where was he going? To Byron's office? He sidestepped a group of women and took a right onto Grand. I quickened my pace and when I reached the corner, I saw him half a block ahead of me. He stopped at the corner of Grand and Valley and took a cell phone from his pocket. Then he made a call, moving in a restless circle, one hand holding the phone to his ear, the other hand punctuating the air as he talked.

I moved a bit closer, filtering out street noise as I strained to hear.

"—come up to your damn office," Slade said. "You'd like that, wouldn't you." He paused, as though listening to the person on the other end of the line. "Not good enough. Either you come down here or I'll—"

His threat had the desired effect. Slade ended the call with an aggressive punch to the screen of his phone.

A few minutes later, Byron Patchett came out the double glass doors of the building. He didn't look happy. "What do you want?"

Slade, who was a few inches taller than his stepfather, leaned forward, getting into Byron's face. "I want you to stop interfering. What goes on between me and Mom is our business, not yours."

"It's my business if you're bleeding her of money," Byron snapped. Slade tried to interrupt, but Bryon wasn't having any of it. "The same damn story, over and over. You can't make a go of whatever you're doing so you come to her. You've been bleeding her for years. Well, the bank is closed."

I edged closer, wanting to hear more, wary of being seen. Their voices were loud enough to be heard over the cacophony of traffic at this busy intersection—and loud enough to attract the attention of passersby.

The argument went on in the same vein, with Slade making threats and Byron standing his ground, insisting that the time had come for Slade to stand on his own two feet financially. Finally Byron threw up his hands in disgust. "This conversation is over." He turned and went back into the building.

Slade sputtered with anger, yelling an expletive loud enough to earn him a nasty look from an older woman who'd just come out of the building. He turned quickly, heading back in the direction he'd come from, stalking past me with his head down. He was furiously typing onto the screen of his phone, a text message, no doubt.

So Byron had put his foot down. Millicent had said as much when I spoke with her and Rosalie this morning at the shop. The question now was, what would Slade do about it?

Slade made a left off Grand onto Broadway, heading back in the direction from which he'd come. As he neared Twenty-fourth, he detoured into the very bakery I'd been planning to visit. I stopped outside and looked in as he walked past the counter to a vacant table. He sat down, back to the wall, glancing at the door. He was waiting for someone. Marsh, I would guess.

I went inside the bakery and lingered in front of the glass case, taking in the display of cookies, cakes and other delectables. I always had difficulty deciding which of them to purchase, and today, that would be my cover.

Slade looked up and past me, at the front door. In my peripheral vision, I saw Marsh walk to the table where his cousin sat.

The server behind the counter turned his attention to me, waiting for my order. I smiled and stepped back from the counter. "Give me a couple of minutes. I'm having trouble making up my mind."

"Take your time." Another customer moved up to take my place and the server leaned forward as he took the order.

I moved to my right, edging closer to the table where Slade sat with Marsh. As I examined the contents of the bakery case, I tuned out most of the voices around me, honing in on the conversation between the two cousins. Their voices were low and indistinct, and a woman at a nearby table was talking on her cell phone loudly. Still, I managed to hear a few words.

"—fix that son of a bitch," Slade said.

Marsh laughed. Just then the woman ended her conversation and I heard Marsh say, "—get even. Be like old times. Got an idea."

Just then, Marsh looked up from the table and saw me. He recognized me from yesterday.

As he leaned toward Slade, I waved at the server, who'd come my way again. "I'll have a latte to go. And I'm going to get some cupcakes."

Slade and Marsh got up from the table, stepping over to where I stood at the counter. "You're Davina's friend, right?" Slade's eyes looked suspicious.

I glanced at him as though I didn't recognize him, then said, "Davina? Oh, yes, I met you yesterday afternoon. You were with Davina's sister. Your name is—" I stopped. "I'm sorry, I don't remember."

"Eric," he said.

"You work around here?" Marsh asked, putting his charm to work on me.

"Yeah, just down the street. Taking a break. I need a caffeine jolt to get me through the afternoon." Close enough to the truth. I did like my coffee. But I preferred asking questions, not answering them, at least in this situation. I glanced at Slade. "You went to dinner last night at Angeline's. Did you enjoy it?"

"It was okay," Slade said, scowling.

The server had put my latte on top of the counter and was hovering, waiting for me to decide. "I'll have, let's see—" I smiled again, "Everything is so good here, I have trouble making up my mind. So I might as well get all three. One chocolate, one carrot and one of the lemon." I took a sip of the latte as the server boxed up my cupcakes, then pulled out my wallet.

Another server looked over the counter at Slade and Marsh. "May I help you?"

Slade shook his head, turning to Marsh. "Let's get out of here."

The two of them headed for the door. I saw them exit onto Broadway. Then they turned and walked up Twenty-fourth Street.

They'd seen me. And they recognized me. That was cause for concern. But I didn't think they'd realized I was eavesdropping. At least I hoped not. Perhaps my ruse had worked.

I left the bakery, carrying my purchases. At the intersection, I looked up Twenty-fourth. No sign of them on the two blocks between Broadway and Telegraph. Then a vehicle pulled away from the curb, heading toward Telegraph. I couldn't tell what color it was, but it was dark, and the shape looked a lot like the Nissan Pathfinder Marsh had been driving last night.

⁂

When I reached my building, I headed for Cassie's office. Her eyes lit up at the sight of the bakery box. I opened it and waved the cupcakes under her nose. "Help yourself. Of course, the chocolate is mine."

"Somehow I knew that." She reached into the bakery box and liberated the lemon cupcake. "Thanks, I could use a break from working on this brief."

We talked for a few minutes, polishing off our midafternoon noshes. That should hold me till dinner. Of course, I hadn't really had lunch, just an apple and a hunk of cheddar from my little refrigerator, while I worked on the client report.

After that, I went down the hall to my own office. I deposited the bakery box on my credenza and switched on the computer. This time, my in-box contained the reports and videos that Rory had sent. I opened the reports concerning the fire at Herkimer's and sent them to my printer.

My computer setup, new since I'd moved into my new digs, featured a laptop hooked up to a big monitor, with two wireless peripherals, a keyboard and mouse, both ergonomic. This gave me the option of viewing two screens at once. I loaded the videos from the security cameras, one on each screen. My large monitor was bigger than the one on Rory's computer, where I'd watched the videos earlier. As I viewed them again, I hoped I would see something I'd missed earlier.

I clicked to start the video on the large screen, the footage the security cameras had taken outside the club. Then my phone rang.

I paused the video and checked the caller ID. My mother, Marie Doyle, who had used her family's name since her divorce from my father. I reached for the receiver.

Mother was something of a workaholic. She owned a restaurant, Café Marie, that was quite good. It consistently made the lists of the best restaurants on the Monterey Peninsula. When Dad and I had dinner the other night, he told me that Mother was heading this way, planning to spend a few days with my brother, Brian, and his family in Petaluma.

Now, Mother confirmed that she was driving up on Tuesday of the following week. Was I free for lunch?

Meals out with Mother, the chef and restaurant owner, were always interesting since she was predisposed to critique the establishment. I was forever looking for new places to take her. Well, what about the restaurant I'd just been to?

I consulted my calendar. I had a client meeting at ten o'clock that morning, but it was here in Oakland, so I should be available by noon. My next appointment wasn't until three that afternoon. That was the good thing about being self-employed, with a schedule that had some flexibility in it.

"Yes, I am free for lunch, if we do it around one. There's this restaurant I've been meaning to try, called Temescal. Why don't you come to my new office first? You haven't seen it yet."

I gave Mother directions and told her there was parking available at the rear of the building. Parking had always been a problem in my previous location, in Oakland's Chinatown. After hanging up the phone, I noted the appointment on my calendar.

Then I turned back to the computer and started the video again, watching the footage from the Herkimer's security cameras. Once again, I saw two men in hooded sweatshirts entering the club through the side door. They left the club a few minutes later. Then two men in a car, presumably the same two men. It was reasonable to assume that these same two men had set the fire that broke out a short time later. But could I be sure based on these scraps of movement?

I reversed the video and replayed the segment that showed the car driving away. The night was dark and so was the vehicle. It could have been black, gray, dark blue. Or dark green, like the Nissan that Marsh Spencer drove.

I thought about what Tomás Calderón had told me. He'd thrown Slade and Marsh out of Herkimer's on Open Mike Night, a week or two before the fire. They were my first choices as suspects. But I needed evidence, not feelings.

I watched the video again, this time looking at the grainy footage that showed the driver and the passenger. I stopped the action on the shot where the driver made a gesture with his left hand, coming in contact with the edge of the hood. Earlier I'd thought he was pulling at it. But the more I peered at the image, I thought he was reaching past the edge. Touching his face? Scratching his chin?

Tugging on his ear? The way Marsh did, when I'd seen him in person and on the music video of the Flames, the group he'd been in with Slade and Cam Gardner.

I switched my attention to the laptop, looking for the video I'd shot Tuesday afternoon when Slade met Marsh near Lake Merritt. As I watched it, I made note of the gesture. Marsh Spencer was definitely tugging on his earlobe, a nervous habit that was again visible on the next video I watched, which was the Flames, with Slade on lead guitar, Cam on bass and Marsh on drums. At the end of the song, Marsh reached up and tugged his ear. He'd made the same gesture when he showed up at Davina's cottage on Wednesday.

Was it Marsh at the wheel of the car at the scene of the Herkimer's fire, tugging on his ear as he drove away from the scene? Or was I reading too much into a simple gesture? Seeing things because I wanted to see them?

It was evidence, somewhat tenuous. Not enough, though. I needed something more.

I looked at the photos I'd snapped on Wednesday, of Marsh's car. The license plate on the car at the fire scene had been covered up, obscured with mud or some other substance. But— I looked at the photo of the V-shaped scratch on Marsh's bumper. The thin line on the dark green finish didn't look new. It had been there a while.

What if it had been there last year?

I put the photo on the laptop screen and looked at its location in relation to the blurred license plate. Then I looked at the video again, pausing the action and increasing the size. Was there something on the bumper? Or was it my imagination?

Yes, there was a scratch on the car's bumper. And it was V-shaped.

Marsh was driving the car. And I'd bet money the man in the passenger seat was Slade.

I was convinced. Would anyone else be?

✍ Chapter Twenty-five

"IT'S NOT MUCH," Gary Manville told me when I called him Thursday afternoon.

He'd walked over to my office to look at the videos and photos, and he'd read through the reports concerning the fire at Herkimer's. Then we headed for Z Café, which was located in an old auto show-room at Broadway and Twenty-seventh.

"I agree, it's not." I scooped up another forkful of grilled salmon and basmati rice. "But from what I overheard earlier today, Slade is angry with his stepfather, angry enough to 'fix that son of a bitch,' as he said. And Marsh suggested getting even. My investigation sug-gests that Slade likes to get even by setting fires. Those two are going to start a fire. I'd like to prevent that from happening."

Gary was tucking into a homey-looking plate of meatloaf, replete with garlic mashed potatoes and gravy. "How are you going to do that?"

"I can talk with Sid Vernon."

"The guy from the Oakland PD? You know him?"

"We have some history." I didn't add that Sid and I had once been married. Gary didn't need to know that. "If you were going to start a fire tonight, which site would you pick?"

"Tonight?" Gary grimaced and looked out the window. It was twilight, getting dark, and neither of us wanted to think about what could happen when the sun went down. He gestured in the direc-tion of Twenty-seventh Street, where the First Presbyterian Church had stood for decades. "That site on Twenty-sixth is too close to the church. A lot of businesses there, and also a lot of apartment buildings. Too many people around."

"That didn't stop whoever torched that site on San Pablo. That's a very busy street."

"You've got a point," Gary said. "The site at Webster and Thirtieth is a possibility. So is the one at Brook Street. A few houses and apartment buildings farther down, but where the building is going up, there are a bunch of auto businesses, and they're closed at night."

"So, how do we deal with this?"

"I've already got guards on those sites twenty-four hours a day," he said. "I'll add people. Better to be safe than sorry."

I did call Sid. He had the same skeptical reaction that Gary had. My conclusions, drawn from the Herkimer's tapes and my observations of Slade and Marsh, weren't concrete evidence. More proof, he said.

I hoped we would get some. I also hoped we'd prevent a fire.

Nothing happened Thursday night on any of the three Bay Oak Development sites. That was fine by me. I wanted my theory about a revenge fire to be wrong. But I still had the feeling that something was going to happen—and soon.

Gary had put extra employees on each of the Bay Oak construction sites, the numbers of guards depending on the size of the site. This was stretching his available staff to the limit. The extra workers included Nathan Dupree, who was back on the job after recuperating from his minor injuries in the fire a couple of weeks earlier. In addition, Gary and I had decided that he and I would rotate between sites again tonight, moving from Twenty-sixth, to Webster and then up to Brook Street, keeping an eye out for anything unusual.

Gary and I crossed paths about eleven-thirty, at the site on Twenty-sixth Street. Gary's guards worked in three shifts, and the night watch had just started, scheduled from eleven till seven the next morning. We stood together on the sidewalk, near his silver SUV.

"I was just over at Brook Street," he said. "All quiet, nothing happening."

"Same at Webster and Thirtieth." Both of us carried coffee in insulated mugs. I took a sip from mine, listening to the late-night traffic noise from Broadway, a block away. "Maybe I'm wrong. Maybe I'm misreading the signs."

"And maybe you're not." Gary raised his mug and swallowed more coffee. "I'd rather spend a few nights out here patrolling than run the risk of another fire."

"Okay. If nothing happens tonight, we can reassess the situation in the morning."

We talked for a while longer, as we walked the perimeter of the construction site. Then I headed for my car. I drove up Broadway and made a right turn onto Brook Street. It was a short, hidden street, like many that one encounters in Oakland, slanting at a sharp right-hand angle where it intersected Broadway, then turning right again, so that it almost paralleled Broadway as it ran one long block past the auto repair businesses, houses and apartment buildings. Brook ended at Thirtieth Street.

When I arrived, everything looked quiet. The street was dark at the residential end, but the construction site was illuminated by powerful lights. I drove past a closed-for-the-night transmission repair shop and a shop that sold brake pads and linings, then past the construction site itself. It was long and narrow, backing up to a wooded area that separated Brook from another residential street, Richmond Avenue. The site faced the back sides of the businesses that fronted on Broadway, red brick walls, stucco surfaces and metal doors covered with colorful graffiti, sidewalks with weeds poking through the cracks.

I found a parking space farther down the block, in front of an apartment building, got out of my car and walked up the street, along the perimeter. When I reached the gate leading into the site, I saw Nathan Dupree and two other guards, standing just inside the partly constructed building. One of the men turned and disappeared inside the structure, while the other man strode purposefully along the inside of the chain-link fence, heading toward the Broadway end of the site.

Nathan walked toward me. "Hey, Jeri. All quiet here. I sure hope it stays that way."

"You and me both. It's almost midnight. That other fire, the one where you got hurt, that started just after midnight."

Nathan nodded. "Yeah. Maybe twenty minutes after."

And the fire at Herkimer's had started just before ten o'clock. It didn't seem the arsonist—or arsonists, assuming that I was right and they were Slade and Marsh—were sticking to any pattern.

I'd left my coffee mug in my car. It was just as well. I was overloaded on caffeine, which meant getting any rest would be difficult when I got home. Nathan and I talked for a moment, then he began another walk around the building. I decided to walk around the outside of the site before heading to my next stop, the project that was going up at Webster and Thirtieth. I had a flashlight stuck in my pocket, but there was enough light from the overhead fixtures for me to pick my way along the fence. An area about three feet wide, scraped clean down to the dirt, extended beyond the fence that encompassed the construction site. Beyond this bare perimeter was a thicket of what looked like blackberry brambles. On the other side of the dense vegetation was the back of a stucco apartment building that faced Richmond Avenue, with a house on either side, one a two-story wood-frame and the other stucco.

As I made my way along the back of the construction site, I heard a noise coming from the darkness beyond the spill of light. My nerves went on alert. I pulled the flashlight from my pocket and shined it toward the brambles. A pair of eyes stared back at me from a black mask on a gray-and-white face. I saw pointed ears and snout, large canines visible as the raccoon opened its mouth and hissed, warning me not to get any closer. It gave me a once-over and turned, disappearing into the bushes. Looking for a trash can to raid, I thought.

I stuck the flashlight into my pocket and continued walking

along the back fence, turning the corner and heading back toward Brook Street, with the security fence to my right and a small apartment building to my left. Here the path was narrow, with the building's driveway and Dumpster separated from the construction site by a low fence and a couple of feet. I saw movement inside the construction site and made out a uniform jacket. It was one of the security guards. Then I heard a crash, coming from the street, followed by loud voices. The security guard inside the site started running toward the gate. I rounded the corner onto Brook Street and headed the same way.

There was some sort of altercation taking place in front of the gate leading into the construction site. A man wearing layers of ragged clothing was reeling against the fence. He appeared to be drunk, and belligerent. He was cursing loudly as he reached into a bag and took out a glass bottle. Then he threw it at the fence. The glass broke. It wasn't the first bottle he'd lobbed. The sidewalk was littered with shards.

All three of the security guards had gathered just inside the fence and Nathan was talking, his voice steady.

"What's going on?" I asked.

"This homeless guy just showed up a few minutes ago," Nathan said. "He's drunk, throwing bottles and cussing a blue streak. Hey, man. Give it a rest. Move along."

The man with the sack of bottles lurched toward me and I backed away. He was muttering curses. Then I caught a glimpse of the man's face. He didn't look drunk, I though suddenly. In fact, he looked as though things were going just the way he'd planned.

Why would he—? I was already moving as I shouted, "Nathan! It's a diversion."

Nathan let loose with an expletive and began running along the inside of the fence, between the chain-link and the structure. I headed down Brook Street on the outside of the security fence, reaching the corner I had turned a few minutes ago. I turned and ran up the path between the security fence and the driveway of the apartment building. I spotted two men, in dark clothes and hoodies. They'd shoved the apartment building's Dumpster close to the fence and now they were using it to climb over the top. They jumped down, inside the construction site, illuminated by the overhead lights. As I pulled out my cell phone they ran into the partially constructed building.

After I dialed 911 and reported the incident, I called Gary. "Brook Street," I yelled.

"On my way!"

So was the fire department. Already I could hear sirens in the distance.

Nathan came running up on the inside of the fence. "You were right. The homeless guy took off running as soon as you hollered. My guys have seen him around before, though. We can find him. You see anything?"

"Two men. They ran into the building. Over that way." As I pointed, flames flickered to life, deep inside the structure.

Then came an explosion, loud, deafening. A flash lit up the shadows inside the structure. It caught me by surprise. I'd expected a slow burn, similar to the other arson fires, especially since Sid had told me some of them had been started with timing devices.

But this had the force of a bomb. Nathan backed away from the blaze as the other security guards came running. Then I saw a figure wearing a hoodie streak out of the burning building. Nathan and the other guards moved to intercept him, but he dodged past them with agility born of fear, or panic. He sprang at the fence and was up and over it, falling onto the Dumpster with a thud. He seemed momentarily stunned. As I ran toward the Dumpster he scrambled to his feet and jumped down onto the apartment building driveway, shoving me aside. I stumbled, then regained my feet, running after him as he pounded down the street.

He had almost reached the end of Brook Street, where it met Thirtieth, when he changed direction to dodge a car. I recognized the vehicle. Gary Manville's SUV screeched to a halt and he got out, joining me in pursuit, trying to cut off the running figure. The man in the hoodie sidestepped Gary, got away from me, and cut away from the street, heading up the driveway between two houses. He put on a burst of speed. So did I.

I overtook him and tackled him in the driveway. A couple of dogs in the house's fenced backyard rushed and jumped against the chain-link barrier, providing a counterpoint of serious, intruder-alert barking. Gary appeared beside me, adding his own weight as we held down the struggling figure in the black hoodie. A light went on above the back porch and the homeowner, a middle-aged man swathed in a bathrobe, opened his back door, yelling, "What the hell is going on out there?"

I reached up and tugged the hood from the head of the man we'd caught. "Hello, Slade."

⚓Chapter Twenty-six

GARY AND I STOOD at the end of Brook Street and watched the Oakland Fire Department pour water on the construction site. We were too far away to feel the heat from the flames, but watching the blaze was sobering.

"That building's going to be a loss," Gary said. "This is the second Bay Oak Development project to burn in less than a month. Those folks are going to be pissed."

"Byron Patchett will be beyond pissed when he finds out his stepson set that fire." I looked past Gary at the Oakland Police Department cruiser parked at the intersection of Brook and Thirtieth. Slade was in the backseat, handcuffed. Gary and I had turned him over to the officers who'd first arrived on the scene, saying he was a suspect in the arson blaze.

Slade had been defiant at first. While he was fighting to get away from Gary and me, I said, "Marsh didn't make it out."

He stilled. That took some of the bravado out of his eyes.

"You're going to have to live with that," I said. "Just like Ray Brixton in New Orleans."

Now he was still, almost motionless. "You know about that?"

"Yeah, I know about it." Though I wondered if I'd ever find out the full story. "I know about that, the fire at the warehouse in NOLA, the car fire in Austin. And Herkimer's. You see, Slade, I've had my eye on you for a while."

After the police tucked Slade into the cruiser, Gary and I turned and saw Nathan and one of the other security guards walking toward us. Between them was the homeless man who'd been throwing bottles earlier. "We found him around the corner, on Broadway," Nathan said. "Grabbed him and hauled him back here."

I leaned toward the man, saying in a conversational tone, "You better talk, man. You're in a world of trouble, helping those guys set this fire."

The guy drew himself up and glared back at me. "I didn't help anybody set no damn fire. You can't put that on me."

"Then why were you throwing bottles at the gate? And cussing at the guards? You were pretending to be drunk, but you're not."

"Okay, okay." The homeless man shook himself and shifted, trying to pull away from Nathan and the other guard as he tried to explain his way out of the situation. "I didn't have nothing to do with that fire. It was like you said when you ran off. A diversion. Those two guys, the ones wearing hoodies, they gave me money. They said, Just go up there to that gate. Make noise and yell, throw bottles. Make a lot of noise, make it look good, make it look like you're drunk and wanting a fight." His voice took on a pleading tone. "Honest to God, I thought it was a joke. I didn't know they were going to torch the place."

"Fine," I said. "We're going to go right over to that police officer and you're going to tell him what you just told us."

At a signal from Gary, Nathan and the other guard propelled the man over to the cruiser. He repeated his story. He, too, earned a ride downtown.

Sid showed up just then, wearing jeans and a jacket, showing his ID to the cops who'd cordoned off the street. "I heard you caught the bad guy."

"One of them, anyway." I briefed Sid, telling him about the possibility Slade was responsible for Brixton's death in the New Orleans apartment fire, as well as the fire that destroyed Herkimer's. "I'll send you a more detailed summary of what I found out in NOLA."

"Thanks. In the meantime, you and Manville will need to go downtown and give statements."

"Will do. Slade and his cousin set this fire," I added, "but there's no evidence that I've uncovered that ties them to the other construction site fires."

Sid nodded. "I wonder if we'll ever find out who's torching those."

⁂

"I can't believe you were spying on me!"

Laurette was angry. She was taking it out on Davina—and me. Her dark hair was in disarray as she ran her hands through it, and her eyes flashed as she railed at us. "How dare you sic one of your private eye friends on me? Invading my privacy, butting into my life."

It was Saturday morning. The utilitarian motel room that Laurette had shared with Slade since their arrival in the Bay Area was furnished in shades of orange and brown, the queen-sized bed unmade, the coverings tossed here and there. Laurette hadn't slept well. She was red-eyed from crying and there were dark circles under her eyes. Worry had etched shadows on her face.

Slade hadn't returned to the motel Friday night. He was in jail, having been arrested on suspicion of arson. But if he'd made his one phone call, it wasn't to Laurette. She didn't know what had happened until Davina and I told her. Emotions bounced all over the room, most of them coming from Laurette. Her worries about Slade turned into anger, the room barely large enough to contain her as she paced the worn carpet in front of the bed.

"We were concerned about you," Davina argued, giving as good as she got. She was sitting on one of the chairs grouped around a small round table, leaning forward, hands gesturing. "What the hell were we supposed to do? You quit your job, gave up your apartment and just disappeared, without a word. Mom and Dad were frantic. You weren't communicating—"

"Because I'd lost my phone," Laurette interrupted. "As for leaving without a word, I did that because I figured you'd all do exactly what you did. I'm a grown woman. You all think I can't be trusted to take a little break from my boring, routine life."

I'd been hanging back, leaning against the long dresser which was scattered with Laurette's bag and toiletries. Now I stepped forward, hoping to act as peacemaker, although it was my investigative activities that had Laurette fuming, holding both her sister and me responsible.

"Let's get some perspective," I said. "Your family was worried. I was in New Orleans, on vacation. Since I was already in town, Davina asked me to get involved, to see if I could find out what happened to you. So I started looking. I thought that finding information about who Slade is would help me find out where the two of you had gone. You got in touch with your family before I figured out where you were. However, I did uncover a few things about him that concerned me."

Now Laurette transferred her animosity to me. "What sort of things? That he's a musician and he moves from job to job? Musicians do that." She shook her head. "I knew Mom and Dad would hold that against him. I knew they didn't like him moving in with me."

I glanced at Davina, then back to Laurette. I hadn't yet told Laurette about Slade and the fires. I was waiting, choosing my moment. Better to let her anger burn itself out before hitting her with that.

"There's more to it than that," Davina said. "More than being a musician and more—" She broke off and looked at me for support, then back at her sister. "Laurette, he just wasn't the right guy for you."

"Who are you to decide if he's the right guy for me?" Laurette shot back. "Okay, he wasn't the ideal man. He had his faults. I will concede that. But I enjoyed being with him. It was exciting. I felt like I was finally coming out of my cocoon. And whether he was the right guy or not, I have the right to make my own mistakes. Lord knows you've made plenty of them." With this last remark, she skewered her older sister with a look.

"Yes, I have." Davina's voice was subdued. "But you're my baby sister. You've been through a hard time with losing Chris and the baby. I just don't want you to get hurt."

Laurette stopped pacing and sat down on the bed, as though

her sleepless night was catching up with her. "I'm so tired of everyone wrapping me in tissue paper, like I'm going to break. I'm not as fragile as you think."

No, I didn't think she was. There was a hint of steel in her eyes. And I could understand what she was saying. She had a point, I thought, looking back on my own part in this situation. There was a fine line between being concerned and overreacting, one that had perhaps been crossed. But sometimes it depends on who you're with when you're making those mistakes. Slade was more than the wrong guy. In my opinion, he was dangerous. And Laurette had been in danger while she was with him. I was convinced of that.

"Do you know where he is?" Laurette asked now. That question had gotten pushed to one side while she vented about being the subject of an investigation.

"I do." Earlier she'd asked what sort of things I'd found out about Slade. It was time to tell her some of the seamier facts of Slade's life. "Slade is in jail. And it's possible his cousin Marsh is dead."

The color drained from her face. I continued. "He was arrested last night. He and Marsh are suspected of causing an arson fire here in Oakland. Slade got out of the building. Marsh didn't."

Laurette raised her hands to her face, horrified. "He told me Marsh was kind of crazy. Likely to do anything. But Slade? I don't understand. Why would they do that?"

"It's not the first time Slade has been suspected of setting a fire," I said. "When I was in New Orleans, and back here, looking for information about him, I discovered a few things that I think are disturbing."

"What did you find out?" Laurette took a deep breath and straightened, preparing herself for the worst. "What is it? Tell me what you found out that's so disturbing."

I laid it out for her, as unemotionally as I could, in chronological order, starting with the fire in the neighbor's garage in Lafayette, then the Herkimer's fire, the car fire in Austin, and the fire at the New Orleans warehouse where Slade had worked, then the apartment fire that had killed Ray Brixton.

I watched the expressions on Laurette's face change as she took it all in. As it turned out, she had witnessed the confrontation between Cindy Brixton and Slade on that afternoon when Brixton waylaid him outside Laurette's apartment building. "I wondered what that was about," she said now, looking subdued. "I thought maybe she was an old girlfriend."

When I stopped talking, Laurette slumped on the bed, looking stunned, as though my words had sucked out all her energy. Davina propelled herself from the chair where she'd been sitting. "You can't stay here in this motel room. Come home with me. I know my place is small, but you can stay as long as you like. While you sort things out."

Laurette shook her head. "I have to be here in case he comes back." She waved a hand at Slade's guitar, propped up in one corner of the room. "What about his guitar? The rest of his stuff?"

"We take it with us," Davina argued. "We can stash it at my house, until—" She broke off and looked at me.

I didn't think Slade was coming back any time soon, but I said, "I think that's a good idea. I'll relay the information that Slade's things are at Davina's." Besides, I thought, it was likely the police would want to take a look at his belongings. And I was sure they'd want to talk with Laurette.

In the end, Davina and I prevailed on Laurette and she agreed to move. We packed up the contents of the room, loaded everything into the Ford and Laurette checked out of the motel. She left, following Davina's car out of the parking lot as they headed for Berkeley.

Eventually Laurette would figure out what she wanted to do. My guess was that she'd head back to New Orleans. Maybe. It would take some time for her to sort it all out.

I had silenced my cell phone earlier and now I took it out. I had a couple of text messages, as well as a voice mail from Sid, asking me to call him. We'd had two conversations already, one last night and another early this morning. Last night I'd shared with Sid the information that I'd uncovered in New Orleans, that Slade may have set the fire that caused Ray Brixton's death. I didn't know what would come of it, but this morning, Sid told me he'd gotten in touch with the New Orleans Police Department. Maybe Cindy Brixton would find some closure concerning her brother's death. Sid had also looked at the videos tying Slade and Marsh to the fire at Herkimer's and he was following up on that, along with the summary of all the information Antoine and I had discovered in New Orleans.

As for Marsh Spencer, he added, he never came out of the partially constructed building that he and Slade had set on fire. The assumption was that his burned body was still in the ashes. Slade, shaken by the incident, was talking, though not much.

I returned Sid's call. "Just wanted to let you know," he said. "Slade's parents showed up at headquarters this morning, along with Marsh Spencer's mother. The mother was weepy, not surprising. The stepfather's all for letting Slade rot in jail. As for Marsh's mother, she blames Slade. Her boy could do no wrong, according to her. She and Millicent Patchett got into a screaming fight."

I shook my head. "I'm sorry for Millicent. I really liked her. Look, if you need to talk with Laurette Mason, she's checked out of the motel where she and Slade were staying. I was over there a while ago, with Davina. She's staying with Davina for the time being. We packed up Slade's stuff, too, if you want it. I doubt there will be anything in his belongings that ties him to the fires, though. He did a pretty good job of concealing that side of himself from Laurette."

"Thanks, I'll pass that information along."

When I ended the call, I made another, to Antoine in New Orleans. I gave him a detailed update. "Congratulations," he said. "You cleared the case. Did he cop to Ray Brixton's death?"

"Sort of. Not that it would stand up in court. Sid's going to follow up with the NOLA PD."

"Maybe that will help Cindy Brixton. I'll pass the info to her. Keep safe, Jeri. And let me know the next time you're coming to the Big Easy. There's a bunch of restaurants we gotta try."

"I will. Thanks for everything, Antoine." I hung up.

Then I saw that I'd had another voice mail while I was talking. This one was from Dan. I pressed the buttons and listened.

"Hey, I'm done with research for a while. I'm on a nonstop heading home, leaving in a few minutes." He told me what time the flight was due to land in Oakland, adding, "If you're available to pick me up, fine. If not, I'll take a cab home."

Now I looked at my watch. Dan's plane would be landing in about an hour. I called him back and left a message saying I'd be at the airport, waiting for his call. Then I got into my car and headed for my office. It was fairly quiet this Saturday morning. I saw a few cars in the parking lot at the back of the building, and a few people at desks in the law firm.

At my desk, I leaned back in my chair and thought about the case. Slade and Marsh and the fires. Was Marsh, alone or with Slade, the arsonist who'd been burning construction sites in the East Bay? Some, perhaps, but not all. I remembered what Sid had told me a few days earlier, at the developers' meeting. The fires didn't fit a single pattern. That made me think there was more than one arsonist.

Running, I thought. Slade had been running, from job to job, from town to town. He was trying to outrun his past, that was my theory. But because of his behavior patterns, the past kept catching up with him. I thought about Millicent, who loved her son, no matter how bad he was. I felt sorry for her. But there was little I could do. Her son was in jail and likely to be there a long, long time.

I turned to my computer and wrote a report of the case, one I'd share with Gary, my client. As I read through it, a wave of fatigue swept over me. My own late night and early morning were catching up with me. I glanced at the clock on the wall. It was time to leave for the airport.

Some twenty minutes later, I pulled into the Park-and-Call lot at Oakland Airport, waiting there with several other cars. When my phone rang, I answered, saying, "Welcome home!"

"Glad to be here," Dan said. "We were a bit late getting in and I'm headed down to baggage claim."

"I'm at the Park-and-Call. I'll circle around and pick you up at the end of the sidewalk."

I started my car and navigated my way out of the lot and onto the main road that circled through the airport. Baggage claim was at the far end of Terminal Two and the sidewalk extended past the cab stand. The curb was busy with other cars, jockeying for space to pick up arriving passengers, some getting evicted by sheriff's deputies if they lingered too long.

Dan waited at the very end of the sidewalk, easy to spot with his burnt-orange rolling duffel bag. He was tall and rangy, with dark hair curling around his face. Today he was dressed in his usual casual attire, a pair of khaki slacks and a blue T-shirt, both looking good on his lean frame. He had a jacket tucked under his arm and a small blue nylon case that carried his laptop computer.

I pulled into a recently vacated spot at the curb, popped the trunk and got out as he hoisted the duffel and the laptop case into the cargo space. We managed a quick hug and a kiss, his arms enveloping me and pulling me close. I kept my eye on the deputy, who had an implacable look on her face as she told a guy in an SUV to get moving.

"We'd better go." I headed around to the driver's side as Dan got into the passenger seat. "I've missed you," I said as I glanced over my shoulder and pulled into the flow of traffic. "I'll have you home soon." Dan had an apartment in Berkeley, I had a house in Oakland, and we hadn't yet reached the stage of moving in together.

He stretched, adjusting the strap of his shoulder harness. "Do you want to get some lunch?"

"I've had quite a night, and morning," I said. "What I'd really like is a nap."

He grinned. "I'll join you."

AUTHOR'S NOTE

As of late fall 2018, there have been at least nine arson fires at construction sites in Oakland and Emeryville, California. In all cases, the fires destroyed sites where multi-unit housing was being built. There has been a number of theories regarding who is responsible for the fires and the motivations behind them, but there is little evidence to prove any of these theories. In late November 2018, one person was arrested and charged with causing one fire, though the case has yet to move forward. The other fires and their causes and perpetrators remain mysteries.

ABOUT THE AUTHOR

In fall 2016, Janet Dawson joined a thousand or so mystery writers and fans in New Orleans to attend Bouchercon, the World Mystery Convention. While enjoying a week in NOLA and its environs, sampling the city's food and music, Dawson began thinking of a way to send her fictional Oakland private eye, Jeri Howard, to the Big Easy. *The Devil Close Behind* is the result.

The novel is the 13th in the series, which began with *Kindred Crimes*, winner of the St. Martin's Press/Private Eye Writers of America contest for Best Private Eye Novel, and a nominee for several best first awards. Her Jeri Howard book *Bit Player* was nominated for a Golden Nugget award for best California mystery. Her most recent Jeri Howard novel, *Water Signs*, was published in April 2017.

Dawson also writes historical mysteries. The California Zephyr series features protagonist Jill McLeod, who is a Zephyrette aboard the sleek streamliner train. The books are set in the early 1950s and the titles are *Death Rides the Zephyr*, *Death Deals a Hand* and *The Ghost in Roomette Four*.

In addition, Dawson has written a suspense novel, *What You Wish For*, and a novella, *But Not Forgotten*, as well as numerous short stories, including "Voice Mail," which won a Macavity award. She welcomes visitors and email at www.janetdawson.com and on Facebook.

More Traditional Mysteries from Perseverance Press
For the New Golden Age

Wendy Hornsby
MAGGIE MACGOWEN SERIES
In the Guise of Mercy
ISBN 978-1-56474-482-1

The Paramour's Daughter
ISBN 978-1-56474-496-8

The Hanging
ISBN 978-1-56474-526-2

The Color of Light
ISBN 978-1-56474-542-2

Disturbing the Dark
ISBN 978-1-56474-576-7

Number 7, Rue Jacob
ISBN 978-1-56474-599-6

A Bouquet of Rue
ISBN 978-1-56474-607-8

Janet LaPierre
PORT SILVA SERIES
Baby Mine
ISBN 978-1-880284-32-2

Keepers
Shamus Award nominee, Best Paperback Original
ISBN 978-1-880284-44-5

Death Duties
ISBN 978-1-880284-74-2

Family Business
ISBN 978-1-880284-85-8

Run a Crooked Mile
ISBN 978-1-880284-88-9

Lev Raphael
NICK HOFFMAN SERIES
Tropic of Murder
ISBN 978-1-880284-68-1

Hot Rocks
ISBN 978-1-880284-83-4

State University of Murder
ISBN 978-1-56474-609-2

Lora Roberts
BRIDGET MONTROSE SERIES
Another Fine Mess
ISBN 978-1-880284-54-4

SHERLOCK HOLMES SERIES
The Affair of the Incognito Tenant
ISBN 978-1-880284-67-4

Rebecca Rothenberg
BOTANICAL SERIES
The Tumbleweed Murders
(completed by Taffy Cannon)
ISBN 978-1-880284-43-8

Sheila Simonson
LATOUCHE COUNTY SERIES
Buffalo Bill's Defunct
WILLA Award, Best Softcover Fiction
ISBN 978-1-880284-96-4

An Old Chaos
ISBN 978-1-880284-99-5

Beyond Confusion
ISBN 978-1-56474-519-4

Call Down the Hawk
ISBN 978-1-56474-597-2

Lea Wait
SHADOWS ANTIQUES SERIES
Shadows of a Down East Summer
ISBN 978-1-56474-497-5

Shadows on a Cape Cod Wedding
ISBN 1-978-56474-531-6

Shadows on a Maine Christmas
ISBN 978-1-56474-531-6

Shadows on a Morning in Maine
ISBN 978-1-56474-577-4

Eric Wright
JOE BARLEY SERIES
The Kidnapping of Rosie Dawn
Barry Award, Best Paperback Original. Edgar,
Ellis, and Anthony awards nominee
ISBN 978-1-880284-40-7

Nancy Means Wright
MARY WOLLSTONECRAFT SERIES
Midnight Fires
ISBN 978-1-56474-488-3

The Nightmare
ISBN 978-1-56474-509-5

REFERENCE/MYSTERY WRITING

Kathy Lynn Emerson
How To Write Killer Historical Mysteries: The Art and Adventure of Sleuthing Through the Past
Agatha Award, Best Nonfiction. Anthony and
Macavity awards nominee
ISBN 978-1-880284-92-6

Carolyn Wheat
How To Write Killer Fiction: The Funhouse of Mystery & the Roller Coaster of Suspense
ISBN 978-1-880284-62-9

**Available from your local bookstore
or from Perseverance Press/John Daniel & Company
(800) 662–8351 or www.danielpublishing.com/perseverance**